MW01298324

13 HILLCREST DRIVE

ALSO BY AUTHOR

Money Men

One-Shot Deal

To Die in Beverly Hills

To Live and Die in L.A.

The Quality of the Informant

Shakedown

Earth Angels

Paramour

The Sentinel

GERALD
PETIEVICH

13 HILLCREST DRIVE

RARE BIRD
LOS ANGELES, CALIF.

THIS IS A GENUINE RARE BIRD BOOK

Rare Bird Books
6044 North Figueroa Street
Los Angeles, California 90042
rarebirdbooks.com

FIRST HARDCOVER EDITION

For more information, address:
Rare Bird Books Subsidiary Rights Department
6044 North Figueroa Street
Los Angeles, California 90042

Set in Adobe Garamond
Printed in the United States

10 9 8 7 6 5 4 3 2 1

Library of Congress Cataloging-in-Publication Data available upon request

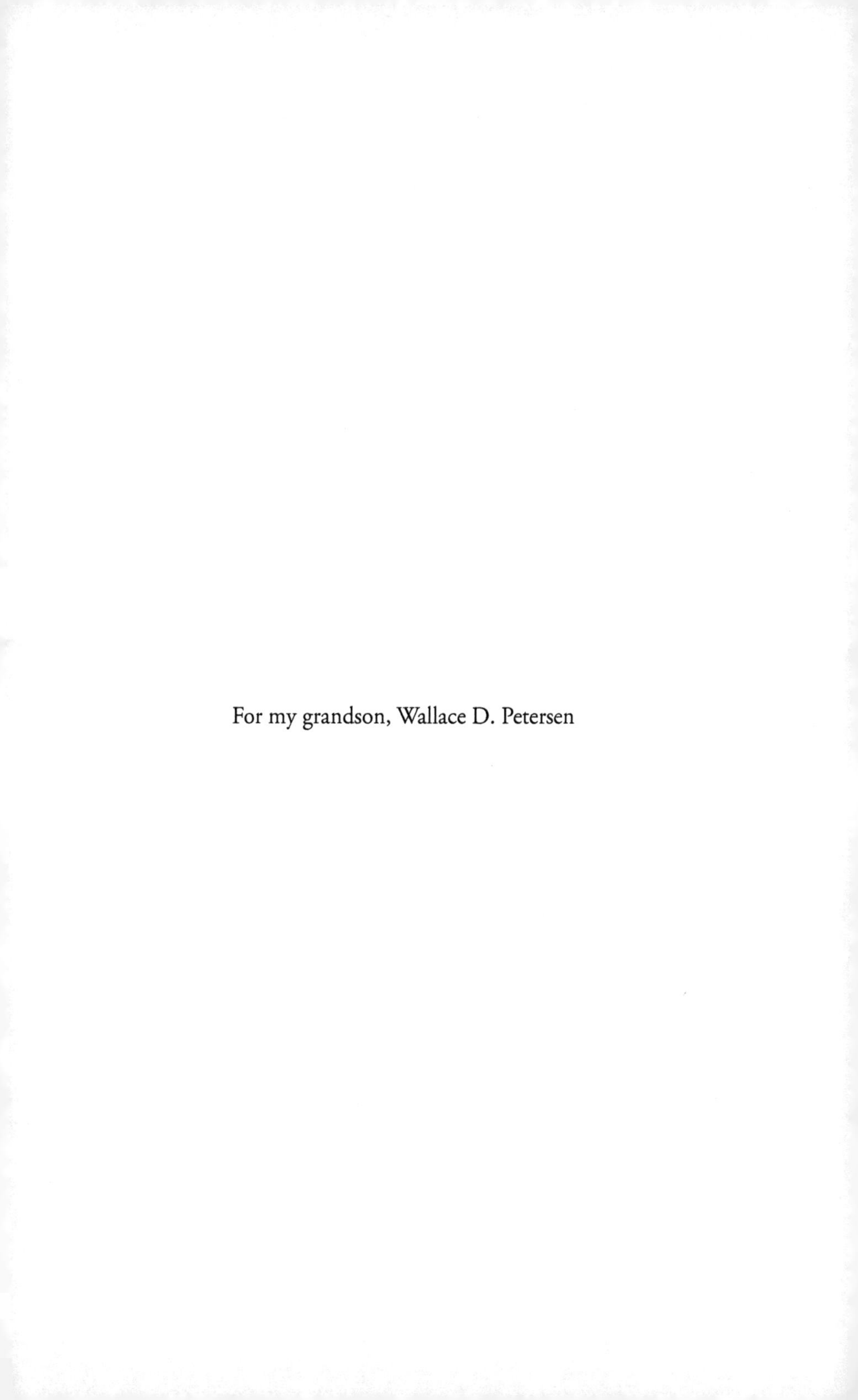
For my grandson, Wallace D. Petersen

CHAPTER ONE

Meredith Fox awoke to light streaming in through the tall windows of her Wilshire Boulevard penthouse condo and quietly got out of bed to avoid waking Anthony. She put on black Vuori joggers, a tank top, and a hooded zip-up with the emblem of the Beverly Hills Health and Fitness Club.

"Where are you going?" Anthony mumbled sleepily.

"A meeting."

"Where?"

"Warner Brothers."

It was none of his business that she was on her way to pick up a briefcase filled with hundred-dollar bills.

"Later," he said, rolling over.

Anthony, thirteen years younger and manager of the Greenroom, a Sunset Boulevard celebrity hangout, had a tanned, Mr. Universe physique. To her relentless competitors in the Hollywood marketing trade, he was a prize escort to Roget's, Soho House, or the Palm and living proof she was still in the publicity biz. Years of psychoanalysis had washed away the emptiness she felt at UCLA twenty-four years ago when the boys ignored her. Hollywood agent Meredith Fox saw men as inconsequential and replaceable. She wrapped her Rolex Pearlmaster onto her left wrist. It was 9:37 a.m.

She heard the sound of the living room television. Anthony must have left it on when he went to bed. Turning it off, she walked by the five-by-five color blowup of a photograph taken at a Hollywood movie premiere: Meredith Fox posing with two big-name actors whose careers she boosted from minor TV roles to high-budget flicks. She opened the closet in the front entryway and turned off the night alarm. Grabbing her .32-caliber Beretta automatic pistol, she put it in a monogrammed athletic bag she used to carry cash.

She took the elevator six stories down to the spacious underground garage. Using the remote key to unlock her new Mercedes-Benz AMG sports car, she got in, fastened the seat belt, and turned on the ignition. Backing out of the parking space, she changed gears, sped to the exit, and raced out the driveway to enter the stream of morning traffic, aggressively cutting in front of a Chevy. She reached Santa Monica Boulevard and swerved across two lanes to turn right. Two blocks later, she slowed at the driveway entrance at the Beverly Mandarin Hotel. Breezing by the valet station, she stopped at the automatic parking machine at the entrance of the five-story parking garage, slapped a green plastic button, and grabbed the ticket that came out of the dispenser. The gate lifted.

As expected, there were no other cars on the rooftop parking level. In Beverly Hills, nothing happened before 10:30 a.m. Parking the Benz near the guest elevator, she turned off the engine and got out. A four-foot fence surrounded the parking level. She stretched in the sunlight. The cloudless, azure sky reminded her of the gigantic movie backdrop at Paramount Studios. Below was the Beverly Hills golden triangle—a mecca of exclusive stores where tourists shopped for accessories they didn't need. Only recently had she come to consider it her town.

Anxiously glancing at the Rolex, she took out her cellphone and keyed numbers. She heard three rings.

"Hello."

"Where are you?" she asked.

"Fighting traffic."

"You have everything?"

"Of course."

"I don't like waiting."

"I'll be there shortly."

She turned off the phone. Feeling the rising sun on her face and neck, she got back in the car, reached into the athletic bag for the Beretta. She'd be leaving the garage with a lot of cash and didn't intend to get robbed before reaching her safety-deposit box in the Beverly Hills Community Bank. With street crime on the rise for years, she'd bought the gun for protection and took a two-hour class on how to fire it. She slipped the gun into her jacket pocket and leaned back in the seat. Closing her eyes, she practiced rhythmic breathing.

She mused about her early years before she began working as a freelance Hollywood publicity agent. Following her own logic, she'd changed her name from Maxine Eels to Meredith Fox to make others assume she was a member of the Fox family who owned Fox, an exclusive Beverly Hills restaurant that for more than ten years had been the watering hole of Hollywood's biggest celebrities. Pleasantly surprised when a few potential customers approached her for representation, she spent her first years in show business representing a few talentless drones whom no amount of publicity could help: a mousy acting school graduate who wangled a role in a low-budget vampire movie, a dopey vocalist, and a TV news producer's son whose father paid her to publicize sonny boy's crappy, ghostwritten mystery novels. For Meredith Fox, nothing came easy. But after years of bribing photographers, wheedling magazine editors for puff pieces, cultivating the right connections, and taking as much time to publicize herself as she spent on her clients, she'd managed to raise a small stable of mid-level show business clients.

Her big break came when she managed to talk a gossip magazine editor into penning a favorable article about how Meredith Fox's Hollywood connections had created big stars out of actors whose careers had been failing. Movie actors began calling her the next day.

She began working sixty-hour weeks. Soon, she was within reach of the top rung on the Hollywood publicity agent career ladder and raised her fees.

Then, like a bolt of lightning in a desert thunderstorm, the ghostly hand of her cocaine addiction caught up with her. As she spiraled quickly downward, not only her ambitious competitors but her publicity clients and her valuable contacts at 20th Century Fox, Musk Studios, and *People* magazine began referring to her as a has-been. Her working capital dried up. She lost her twelve-bedroom Hollywood Hills home to bankruptcy and ended up living with her sister in North Las Vegas.

For a while she contemplated suicide, but after borrowing money to pay for six months in a smelly drug rehab center in Orange County, she was finally sober and drug free. The dope days were behind her, and the entertainment business was working better than she'd ever thought possible. Her secret was that she'd taken the advice of friends she'd made while in rehab and then embarked on a new tack. While early in her career she believed the secret to gaining a stable of big-time celebrity clients was making a hundred phone calls to wrangle a daytime talk show gig, begging some stupid magazine editor for a puff piece, or creating false news to trick a newspaper reporter into mentioning one of her clients, now she knew the truth: that arranging for glossy photographs and crafting TV appearances had nothing to do with success. The key was neither perseverance nor publicity but rather learning and then utilizing the secrets celebrities knew could destroy their public image. For the first time in her life, she was raking in the heavy gold.

The Hollywood mentors who'd advised her years earlier that "cash was king" and "gold was better than any piece of ass" were right. If she'd have followed their advice, her luck might've never cooled. Now she was back, and her Hollywood business connections were calling her with the same speed they'd shown when they dumped her after hearing that she'd been driven to rehab in a straitjacket. While keeping her new career twist secret, she'd taken to teasing them with false hints about new celebrity contacts.

She heard the elevator and opened her eyes. The doors opened.

Rolling down the driver's window, she said, "What took you so long?" at the moment she saw the gun aimed at her. She reached for the Beretta but it was too late. Everything had gone wrong. The loud pop she heard was a bullet blasting through her cranium.

CHAPTER TWO

At 10:00 a.m., Beverly Hills Police Detective Michael Casey sipped cognac in the elegant bar of Roget's restaurant, the kitchen sounds mixed with Edith Piaf coming from hidden speakers installed throughout the dining area, which was hung with original oils of the French countryside. Fresh flowers had been delivered and were stacked on a cart waiting to be put in vases. The retractable roof was open above strung lights and a large, garish fountain surrounded by tables set with fine linen. Roget's didn't open till 5:00 p.m. and reservations were impossible. Movie celebrities came there as much to be photographed by the paparazzi as to eat what *Los Angeles Magazine* described as "the finest French cuisine on the West Coast."

Casey said, "The cognac is great." He meant it.

Roget picked up the bottle and refilled the two snifters. He was a fiftyish, lanky former Legionnaire with a pencil-thin moustache. He wore a white T-shirt, Bermuda shorts, and rubber-soled kitchen shoes.

"Bring your girlfriends in for a cognac tasting."

Casey smiled. "I don't want you to run out of cognac."

"I bought ten cases yesterday."

Casey smiled. "That should be enough."

"I'm serious. You used to come in for dinner...now you probably take your women to some steak house where they serve baked potatoes wrapped in aluminum foil."

Casey shrugged. "American cuisine."

"*Cuisine Americaine* is eating incinerated beef...and corn...and dollops of ketchup."

Roget's phone rang. He touched the screen and said hello. "Yes… because the meat was gray! That's why! Go sell it to a hamburger stand! I'm running a restaurant, not a dog kennel."

While Roget was shouting into his phone, Casey sipped the cognac and felt its warmth. He ordinarily didn't drink during the day, but for the past six weeks, while assigned to handling stolen car reports, a punishment Beverly Hills police detectives referred to as the "barrel," Roget's had been his hideout. Rather than remain in the office like a bad boy in kindergarten, in the morning he completed a few phone calls regarding stolen cars before driving to Roget's to drink cognac and eat a leisurely lunch before returning to the squad room in the afternoon to sign out on the police duty roster. So far, no one had detected his scam.

Casey's cellphone vibrated. The phone screen displayed the Beverly Hills Police Department number. The vibration stopped. He checked for messages. There was only one.

"This is Chief of Police Slade," she said. "Meet me at 13 Hillcrest Drive, ASAP."

13 Hillcrest Drive was movie star Gloria Channing's place. Like all Beverly Hills cops, Casey knew the city's celebrity addresses. He assumed Channing's car had been stolen and she'd called Donna Slade, the chief of police, for help. Slade would have Casey take Channing's stolen car report while Slade would schmooze with Channing or pitch her for a donation to her rumored upcoming campaign for Los Angeles County sheriff.

Casey got up from the barstool, mouthed "thanks" to Roget, and hurried outside to his unmarked police sedan. He drove north on Camden to Sunset Boulevard. Turning right, he made a left onto Hillcrest Drive, lined with stately, extravagant homes perched on terraced lots owned by people who controlled motion picture studios, hospitals, museums, nation-states, and politicians. Near Robert Lane, three police black and whites and the chief's unmarked Chevrolet sedan lined the curb in front of Gloria Channing's neocolonial estate surrounded by a tall wrought-iron fence. He realized the crime involved something more than a stolen car.

Casey parked behind Chief Slade's car, reached into the large bag of breath mints he kept in the glove compartment, refilled his shirt pocket, and shoved some into his mouth. Getting out of the sedan, he walked to the Chevrolet. Slade was behind the wheel. She motioned him inside. He opened the passenger door and got in. She was forty-six and wore a black sheath dress and matching jacket, a chunky gold bobble necklace, and red Manolo pumps. Two years ago, when sworn in on the city hall steps, she was the first Beverly Hills chief not to wear a police uniform.

She spoke coolly. "This is your lucky day, Legs. I have something for you more interesting than filing stolen car reports."

The nickname came from his first year on the job, when he captured a fugitive after a long foot chase.

"Thanks, Chief."

"Don't thank me too soon. Captain Dollinger will be nitpicking the investigation."

"Is Gloria Channing the victim?"

She shook her head. "Dollinger will fill you in."

"No problem."

"Where were you?"

"Just now?"

"Yes," she said, "just now."

"Uh, taking a stolen car report."

"I can tell by the liquor on your breath."

Casey said nothing. She'd gone to bat for him once and he respected her.

"Wait here. I'm going inside to talk to Dollinger."

"Sure."

She got out of the car and walked to a uniformed officer posted at the driveway entrance. She opened the iron gate. A crème-colored Ford SUV was parked in the driveway. She walked to the front porch where another officer opened the door and she disappeared inside. Assuming someone had been killed, Casey sat back. As a patrol officer he'd made a lot of solid felony arrests and had been promoted to the rank of detective and gotten a raise. Rather than spend time handling traffic accidents, writing misdemeanor reports, and working midnight shifts patrolling the same palm-lined streets, as a detective he was allowed to take off his uniform, wear plain clothes, and investigate armed robberies. He received a commendation for solving all his cases. His career had been on the rise until a series of events landed him "on the shelf." He'd never expected that at thirty-five he'd be waiting in the chief's car for a reprieve from the barrel.

His first setback was being wounded in a jewelry store shootout with three robbers. After four agonizing months recovering in Cedars-Sinai Medical Center, he returned to duty recovered but for insomnia stemming from flashbacks of the shooting. A week later, while investigating a robbery, he met the gorgeous professional dancer Antoinette Van Patten, a bank customer who'd witnessed a robbery. She was soft-spoken, graceful, and shadowy, but neither remote nor affected. He considered her unique, unclassifiable. He was so taken with her he hesitated before making the first move.

At dinner, Antoinette impressed Roget and his staff with her fluency in French and her easygoing charm. Casey learned that she read little but loved music. Unable to resist her, he let their relationship quickly become passionate and thrilling. The next month was a whirlwind of flowers, gifts, expensive dinners, and flying back and forth to Las Vegas every weekend while she was performing in a swanky casino stage show. Seeing no reason to slow things down, he continued, and the relationship culminated in a Las Vegas wedding chapel marriage—the biggest mistake of his life.

Any pragmatist could have told him what came next. As if his years of dating hadn't taught him women occasionally turned out to be different than first perceived, the moment Antoinette Van Patten moved into his Westwood apartment, her spiteful, narcissistic temperament bounded to life like a monster jumping out of a dark closet. For a while, he tried to adjust. But after catching her in an affair with a choreographer she'd known for years, Casey gave up and filed for divorce.

Completing his trifecta of personal stumbling blocks, Casey celebrated the divorce with some pals at the Nightwatch, a cop bar in nearby Culver City. Departing drunk at 2:00 a.m., he fell asleep on the front seat of his city car, parked across the street from the bar. A dutiful private security officer found him at 4:00 a.m. and called the department. Charged with conduct unbecoming of an officer, Casey was assigned to handling stolen car reports. Now Slade was helping him get out from under the storm cloud.

Slade and Captain Dollinger walked out of the mansion's front door onto the porch. It was obvious to Casey that they were in conversation. He guessed Slade was telling Dollinger what she wanted done....

—

On the porch, Slade said, "Dollinger, what would you think of assigning this investigation to Casey?"

"Frankly, not much."

"Why?"

"He's a rule breaker."

Irritated at the remark, she said, "But Casey solves his cases."

Dollinger grimaced. "Often the hard way."

"What does that mean?"

"He can be a thorn in the saddle."

"That doesn't sound like too much to bear, particularly for a celebrity case that the press will be following."

"He's a problem drinker."

Dollinger wore a well-cut business suit that gave him the look of a stockbroker or funeral director. To him, crimes were something to be catalogued and scribbled onto a whiteboard list. After twenty-five years, he knew the operations manual of the cliquish Beverly Hills Police Department by heart. This knowledge was his strength.

She said, "If he locks up bad guys, so what?"

"In Beverly Hills, when celebrity investigations go wrong, the long knives come out at city hall."

"I'm not afraid of politicians."

Dollinger spoke with a condescending smirk. "I've known Casey longer than you."

Consciously moderating her tone, Slade said, "Your attitude is getting on my nerves."

"I meant nothing personal—"

"Yes, you did. Get over it."

"Ma'am?"

"You're not the first captain to get passed over for chief," she said. "Rise above it."

"Just trying to help."

"So, what's your plan for solving these murders?"

"I'd assign Kristina Sutherland to investigate."

"Why?"

"Because she'll solve the case without causing a lot of unnecessary problems."

"Like she has the Meredith Fox murder?"

"It's not like there are any clues."

"Casey and Sutherland will be partners on this investigation," Slade said.

"Whatever you say."

She stepped closer to him. A look of concern crossed his face.

She said, "When it comes to inquiries regarding this investigation, I will deal with the media. No one else."

"I'll put out a memo."

"Good idea. Any questions?"

"Not at the moment, Chief."

"I have some advice for you. Supervising detective is one of the best jobs in the department. Be happy in your work."

"Yes, ma'am."

—

Casey, watching from the car, saw Slade walking toward him from the porch. He got out of the car.

Slade said, "Dollinger will fill you in on this investigation. Kristina Sutherland will be your partner. I expect to see you digging into the case with both hands."

"No problem. Thanks, Chief."

"A word to the wise: if you get in any personal trouble, I'm not going to step in and round off the edges for you again. That's over. You'll be on your own."

"I understand."

"I hope so. Good luck, Legs."

Slade got in her car and departed.

Casey walked to the house elated at getting back to real investigative work. He had no mental picture of what the multimillion-dollar house would look like inside but was aware that movie stars lived extravagantly. He went in. On the living room's cathedral ceiling was an enormous hand-painted mural: a triple-sized advertising poster for the motion picture *Mystery Girl* depicting Gloria Channing in a afari outfit, emerging from dark-green jungle flora and fauna holding a long-barreled pistol. Each of the high-backed upholstered chairs around a thirty-foot dining room table had a gold crown painted on the back. The walls were hung with paintings, including a cartoon mouse in front of a white house with a neon minaret atop its portico, headless nudes running toward a crimson river, and a narrow path between dark trees. The contemporary art junk reminded Casey of other celebrity mansions whose living rooms looked like they'd been designed as backdrops for television interviews.

The kitchen door was open. Two bodies were on a checkerboard-tiled floor: a man near the stove and a woman next to the door leading outside to the pool. Near the sinks, Dollinger was talking to a uniformed officer and a woman Casey recognized as a coroner's investigator. The police photographer was aiming an audio-video camera at the male victim; Casey guessed that the deceased was thirty years old. He was of medium height and weight. His head wounds had oozed a lot of blood. His eyes were closed; his hair was neatly parted and combed. He wore boxer-style swimming trunks, gladiator sandals, and a thick gold bracelet on his right wrist, and on the left, a wristwatch with a gold-weave band. His fingernails were manicured. He had no defensive wounds on his arms or hands. An ejected bullet casing was on the floor next to him.

Casey said, "Who is he?"

"Gloria Channing's ex-husband, Bobby Lanza," Dollinger said.

"The woman is Rosa Hernandez, Channing's full-time housekeeper."

She was on her right side, her feet near the door. A metal ring with keys was in her hand. Her hair was pulled back in a tight bun. She wore sturdy SAS work shoes with thick soles and a simple cotton dress. The strap of a straw purse was over her arm. The two blood spots on her back looked like entry wounds. Her only jewelry was a thin, inexpensive necklace with petite yellow gold script that spelled ESPERANZA. She looked to him like others from El Salvador and Guatemala and Mexico and Bakersfield who worked in the big houses on the quiet streets of Beverly Hills—employees who tiptoed through the mansions, cooking, cleaning, and dusting off bottles of rare vintage reds before trudging to a bus stop on Sunset Boulevard for the trip home.

Casey said, "Looks to me like she was walking in the door when she got it."

Dollinger nodded. "The bullet casing next to Lanza is .22-caliber Wolf Match target ammo, the same kind used in the Meredith Fox murder. If forensics tells us the rounds came from the same gun, it'll be something to go on."

Staring at Rosa Hernandez, Casey said, "The shooter must have hidden behind the door…where's Gloria Channing?"

"In France, at a film festival."

"Who made the first call?"

"Channing's personal assistant. She came here because she needed a telephone number that was in the house. The assistant couldn't reach the housekeeper or Lanza, who was staying here with Channing's permission while she was out of town. She drove here, didn't recognize the car parked in the driveway, and called 911. Patrol Officer Mark Fukunaga arrived here five minutes later. The assistant gave him the house key. He goes inside and finds the scene. The body temperatures indicate both victims were killed last night. The glass sliding door to Channing's first-floor bedroom was jimmied and the room was ransacked. It looks like the burglar killed Lanza and then, when the housekeeper arrived for work, he had to kill her. Any more questions?"

"Not at the moment."

"Legs, I'm going to be completely above board. If you get into any avoidable trouble on this case, I'll see to it that you are finished as a detective in this department."

"Okay."

"You'll work this case with Kristina Sutherland. She's on her way here."

Casey nodded. He considered Dollinger a competent captain—a "process" man who defended his detectives when they were trying to do their job but unapologetically punished them for on-duty drinking or romantic entanglements. Three years ago, when the last chief of police retired, Dollinger scored highest on the written test given to candidates eligible to replace him. But when the Beverly Hills city council gave the job to former Los Angeles Police Department Commander Donna Slade, Dollinger made it known that he'd taken his last promotion test.

Casey knew the role politics played in the upper echelons of the department. During the three years he spent in the US Army, Casey had gotten used to the ambition, treachery, and bureaucratic plots required to become a command officer. As a cop, he was able to avoid the political backbiting by simply not taking promotion tests. He figured if his reports were on time and he avoided too much drinking, there was little even dedicated pencil pushers like Captain Dollinger could do to him.

"In case you're wondering," Dollinger said, "I'll be the one reporting any case developments to the chief. No one else."

"I understand."

Dollinger returned to speaking with the coroner's deputy. Casey exited the kitchen to a backyard centered by an enormous, black-bottomed swimming pool, the surface of which rippled with arching streams of water from two slate fountains. Next to the pool, lounge chairs, outdoor sofas, and umbrellas surrounded a twenty-stool, thatched-roof cocktail bar. Mark Fukunaga, a young and muscle-bound uniformed officer, was sitting on a barstool writing on a Report of Investigation form attached to a metal clipboard.

"Hey, Legs."

“Dollinger told me you found the body.”

“The call came out as *see the woman, possible burglary*. When I got here, Gloria Channing’s personal assistant, Courtney Wellstone, was waiting in the driveway.”

He told him Wellstone’s story as Dollinger had related it earlier to Casey.

“What was her reaction to seeing the bodies?”

“She went weak at the knees, like she was going to faint.”

“And now?”

“She’s flustered but cooperative. I asked her to wait in my car until a detective arrived.”

“Thanks, Mark.”

Walking along the driveway, Casey slipped breath mints into his mouth. Fukunaga’s black and white was parked at the curb. A fortyish, well-tanned blonde was sitting in the front passenger seat. Her eyes were slightly red, as if she might’ve been crying. He showed her his badge.

“I’m Detective Casey, Miss Wellstone. Thanks for your patience. I have a few questions.”

“Of course.”

CHAPTER THREE

Casey got in on the driver's side. Courtney Wellstone wore designer eyeglasses and a tropical-print halter dress he guessed was unique and expensive. He guessed her age as late forties.

"I'm sorry about Mr. Lanza and Ms. Hernandez."

She shook her head. "I still can't believe it."

"You're employed by Gloria Channing?"

"I'm her personal assistant. I handle her schedule, everything for her. She called me yesterday and asked me to come here and get a phone number she forgot to take with her. When I arrived, I didn't recognize the car in the driveway." Wiping her eyes with a handkerchief, she said, "This is a huge nightmare."

"Have you informed Ms. Channing?"

"I just got off the phone with her."

"What was her reaction?"

"Stunned, upset...Bobby Lanza was her ex-husband...she asked me whether there was any press coverage. She told me she's leaving the film festival and flying home tonight."

"How did she get along with Mr. Lanza?"

"I don't know."

"She doesn't tell you that kind of thing?"

"Not really."

"How long have you known her?"

"Almost thirty years. We were both twenty-one and in acting school when we met. I got her a part-time waitressing job where I was working in Studio City. After signing her first movie contract, the next thing Gloria did was hire me as her assistant. The first time I'd been on an airplane was the flight I took with her to Nairobi to shoot *Mystery Girl.* The movie became the biggest grossing motion picture of the year and was nominated for the Golden Globes and won three Academy Awards."

"Is she dating anyone now?"

"I don't know."

"She gives you the key to her house, but doesn't mention anything about her social life?"

"All movie celebrities are cautious about sharing their personal business."

"Who do you think broke into the house?"

She stared at him with an expression of incredulity. "I have absolutely no idea."

"Who knew she was overseas?"

"There wasn't anything released to the press about her trip, if that's what you're asking."

"Would it be safe to say she and Lanza got divorced because they didn't get along?"

"Like a million other couples. Everyone told her marrying him wouldn't work. He was fifteen years younger. She married him because he was handsome, sexy. It lasted for two years. Their divorce was final about a year ago. Gloria realized she made a mistake."

"Had either of them threatened one another?"

"Recently?"

"Whenever."

"Gloria never mentioned anything like that."

"What kind of person was Bobby Lanza?"

"Complicated—a dreamer with big ideas and the ability to sell them—but hobbled by his inability to play by the rules. He was articulate and had a cool and confident manner. He attracted women by his good looks and his way with words. I've never met a better conversationalist. After attending a cocktail party with forty strangers, he would leave remembering everyone's name."

She was avoiding eye contact. He knew it may not mean anything, that with some people it was a habit, but her reticence to talk about the Channing/Lanza relationship might indicate something more. Women usually talked to one another about the men in their lives, particularly their ex-husbands.

"Who were Mr. Lanza's friends?"

Wringing her hands, Courtney Wellstone stared blankly at the windshield. "I don't know."

"Do you know anything about whether there are security cameras on this property?"

"Yes. Now, none of them are operational."

"Since when?"

"They haven't worked for more than a year."

"What's the problem?"

"Gloria told me she didn't want to spend the money to have them repaired."

"Did she say why?"

"I don't feel comfortable sharing information about Gloria's personal finances."

"I'm asking because a double murder occurred here. Two people are dead."

"Gloria is a movie actor. Actors have financial ups and downs in their careers. The ups and downs relate to whether they are offered movie roles and the size of the budget of the motion picture. She…she hasn't been offered any roles recently."

"Who do you think broke in?"

Wellstone furrowed her brow. "Again, I have no earthly idea."

Casey asked for her address and phone number. She gave them. He noted the information.

"Thanks for being patient," he said. "I don't have anything further. Do you need a ride somewhere?"

"No, I have my car."

They got out of the cruiser. He walked with her to a new, four-door Cadillac parked at the curb.

"If you think of anything," he said, handing her his police business card, "I'd appreciate a call."

"Surely."

She got in the Cadillac. Casey glanced at the license plate number. She drove away. He keyed the number into his cellphone and walked back to the house.

In the kitchen, Detective Kristina Sutherland was staring at Lanza's corpse. She was sixteen years older than Casey, nearly six feet tall and broad shouldered. Her skin was Sudanese black. She wore dark plum lipstick. Her gray hair, tapered closely on the sides and longer on top, gave her an offbeat appearance.

"Hey, Legs," she said. "It sounds like you and I will be working this together."

"Looking forward to it."

Smiling, she whispered, "A step up from being stuck on the stolen car desk?"

"You bet."

"I've been working the Meredith Fox murder, and so far I've come up with nothing but some expended cartridges of the same kind of ammo used here. Fox died of shots to her head while seated in the driver's seat of her car. It may or may not have been a random street robbery or a carjacking gone bad."

Sutherland began as a motorcycle officer and had been promoted to detective early in her career. Now, with more than twenty-seven years' service, was at the top of the seniority list. Because of her reputation for diligence and attention to detail, Sutherland was often assigned to handle high-profile investigations. Casey and the other Beverly Hills detectives embraced her as "solid," an officer who could maintain secrecy. As far as Casey knew, she'd never been married. She lived with her mother, who'd helped her raise her two daughters, both of whom were now Naval officers. Sutherland taught self-defense in her spare time and served as an official in judo competitions. Having worked a few cases with her, Casey respected her abilities. She was a computer whiz, and during complex investigations she created spreadsheets to connect clues.

"A carjacking?"

"Maybe. Her wallet and credit cards were missing."

"Witnesses?"

"None. And a handgun registered to her was on the front seat. The press jumped on the case because she used to be a publicity agent for some movie stars. With Lanza being Gloria Channing's ex-husband, you can be sure the reporters will be sticking their noses into this investigation."

He and Sutherland spent the next few hours searching the house and cataloging what they thought might be evidence. All that was left was interviewing Rosa Hernandez's relatives and searching Lanza's car in the driveway. Sutherland offered to search the car.

—

Casey drove away from Hillcrest Drive with the windows of his car rolled down. Pleased at his transfer from the punishment desk to a big case, he couldn't get the maudlin image of Rosa Hernandez lying dead out of his mind: an innocent gunned down wearing work shoes, the horrific collateral damage left by a killer.

He got on the 405 freeway and drove south, transitioning to the eastbound Santa Monica Freeway. He made good time, reaching Interstate 5 about eighteen minutes later. At First Street, he took the off-ramp east to a neighborhood where most of the streets had Spanish names. Extended Mexican-American families and their near relatives once encompassed entire blocks, but now with the incursion of millions of border crossers, impelled by poverty and Central American civil wars, a lot of the Mexican-Americans had moved east to San Bernardino, Chino, and Riverside.

Rosa Hernandez's mother lived on a street with cracked sidewalks and one tall, shaggy palm tree. Her small, stucco house was like the others on the block. Parking the sedan at the curb, he got out and walked to the porch. The screen door was locked. He heard voices and walked to a patio at the rear of the house where two young women and a young man were sitting at a table covered with a serape. They looked tearful and drawn. The man got up. He had wide shoulders, muscled arms.

Casey showed his badge. "Beverly Hills Police Department. I'm Detective Casey."

"I'm Rosa's brother. The coroner's investigator was just here."

"I'm sorry for your loss."

"Who killed my sister?"

"We think it was a burglar."

"My mother has a bad heart and fainted when we got the call. She wants to talk to you."

"Certainly."

Hernandez led him into a small, dimly lit living room. Children's Crayola drawings were affixed to the walls with clear tape. An elderly woman in a yellow sundress was lying on the sofa.

"Mom, Detective Casey is here from the Beverly Hills Police Department."

She opened her eyes and sat up unsteadily. Her lips were pale, grayish. She had short gray hair, sharp features, and dark circles under her eyes.

"I'm Esperanza Hernandez."

"There's no need to get up," Casey said. "I'm very sorry for your loss, ma'am."

She said to her son, "I will speak privately with Detective Casey for a moment."

Her son left the room.

"If you prefer," Casey said, "I can come back some other time."

"My husband died last year." Her voice cracked. "But I'm glad he's not here to go through losing a child."

"Did Rosa talk with you about her work at the Gloria Channing residence?"

"We talked about everything. Rosa was my best friend. She lived here and she was paying the second mortgage. I borrowed on the house to pay my husband's medical expenses; then, because of my health problems, I had to quit my job."

"Did Rosa ever say anything about suspicious people coming around the Channing house?"

"No."

"Did she mention seeing anything unusual there?"

"She complained about Gloria Channing."

He spoke softly. "What was the problem?"

"Slow pay."

"Rosa was owed money?"

"Can you imagine Gloria Channing, a movie star living in a big Beverly Hills mansion, not paying her housekeeper on time—sometimes being three weeks late in paying a salary?"

"How long did this go on?"

"For the past year. Rosa had to ask her repeatedly for her paycheck. The gardener had the same problem. Gloria would fire gardeners when she owed them a lot of money, figuring they wouldn't complain to the police because they weren't citizens. Can you imagine a rich movie star doing something that selfish and cruel to one of their employees?"

Esperanza looked like her daughter. The resemblance was uncanny, a striking familial likeness.

"Did Channing ever tell Rosa about her financial situation? About why she wasn't able to pay her on time?"

"Rosa said she thought it had something to do with Bobby Lanza. When Gloria was out of town, Bobby would hang out at the swimming pool. He went swimming in the nude. He once touched Rosa. She told him to keep his hands off her. Rosa complained to Gloria, but Gloria didn't do anything about it. Bobby was still there at the pool sometimes. Rosa told me she thought Gloria was crazy for letting him hang around the place. She had the impression that Bobby might have been giving Gloria money."

"Can you think of anything else Rosa told you about Channing?" She shook her head. Casey took out a business card, handed it to her. "I'll keep you informed about the investigation, Mrs. Hernandez. Feel free to call me if you have any questions…"

"Your picture was in the newspaper. I have a good memory. You're the detective who was wounded in the big Beverly Hills jewelry store robbery. You killed three robbers in a gun fight. You are a brave man. Your picture was on the television news. Do you have a family?"

"I'm divorced."

"Children?"

"No."

"Violence affects people forever. It never goes away."

He said he agreed.

"My wonderful daughter Rosa promised me she'd never let me lose the house. My son was in trouble with a gang but straightened up and was making good money working as a bellman at a hotel in Orange County, but the place closed three months ago. He has been trying to find another job. What happened to Rosa isn't going to destroy my family…I won't let it…Detective Casey, would you think it rude if I asked you a favor?"

"Not at all."

She met his eyes. "I know police detectives have connections. My son is strong, and he is a hard worker. Will you ask one of the rich people in Beverly Hills to give him a job?"

"I'll find something for him."

She reached out and squeezed his hand. "You mean that, don't you?"

"Yes."

Her eyes locked onto his. She pulled him close. "The heart doctor gave me bad news last month…I'm going to ask you something else."

"Okay."

She whispered, "When you find who took Rosa from me, I want you to deal with them the same way you dealt with the robbers who spilled your blood. *Quiero venganza*."

He whispered back, "You have my word."

"I can tell you are a good man, Detective Casey. I know that my husband would have liked you."

"You need to rest, Mrs. Hernandez."

Tears welling, she said, "*Que le vaya bien*."

In the sedan, Casey turned on the air conditioning and picked up his clipboard. Printing with a ballpoint pen, he filled lines on his daily chronological log beginning at the Channing house on Hillcrest Drive. He noted the time, the address of the Hernandez residence, and what Esperanza Hernandez mentioned about Gloria Channing. He didn't carry the clipboard to interviews because many interviewees stopped talking when detectives began making notes.

Slipping his cellphone out of its clip-on belt holder, he looked up a name in his address book, then touched the phone number. The phone rang twice.

"Beverly Crown International Hotel, Security Department."

The International Hotel was where movie stars and other VIPs paid for the most expensive rooms on the West Coast, and the chief of security was a retired Beverly Hills detective he'd once worked with. Casey asked if he could get a job for an experienced hotel bellman.

On the freeway driving back to Beverly Hills, Casey called Esperanza Hernandez. He gave her his former colleague's name and phone number and told her to have her son mention Casey's name when he called about the job. Tearfully, she thanked him.

CHAPTER FOUR

Casey parked in front of the Channing residence; Kristina Sutherland stood in the driveway next to the Ford SUV. Its doors and trunk were open. He got out of the car and walked up the driveway. She wore blue rubber gloves and was holding a large white envelope.

She said, "Did you come up with anything?"

"Rosa told her mother Channing was in financial trouble and that Lanza was a jerk."

"Well, I have something here. While Lanza was having his Ferrari serviced at a dealership on Wilshire Boulevard, he was using this loaner car. I called the rental company that holds the title. They gave us permission to search. I found a briefcase in the trunk containing Lanza's health club identification card, some other paperwork that belongs to him, and this." She held out the envelope.

Casey took latex evidence gloves from his back pocket, slipped them on, and opened the envelope. It contained four unposed color photographs of a man and an attractive woman having sex in different positions. The shots were clear, high-quality photographic work. The female looked to be in her early thirties and physically fit. Her dyed platinum hair was styled in a distinctive and unusual inverted bob. She had green eyes and tan lines. The man was fortyish and trim. His arms and pectoral muscles were of someone who swam or played tennis. In one of the shots, a portion of what looked like a tattoo was visible on his left shoulder. His face wasn't visible in any of the photographs, as if the shots might had been selected out of a larger group.

He said, "Lanza?"

"The coroner found no tattoos on the body. It's not him. What do you think?"

"If these are blackmail shots, the guy's face not being visible might mean he was in on the shakedown."

"Blackmail. I hadn't thought of that. But it makes sense. Good observation, Legs."

"Thanks."

"I hate blackmail cases."

"You're not the only one."

Beverly Hills detectives knew all celebrities became blackmail victims at some point in their careers, that whether they were young, old, straight, gay, male, or female, they wouldn't be spared the humiliation of being shaken down for money, extorted. He was also aware extortion was difficult to prove. Without overwhelming proof of criminal intent, the LA County District Attorney's Office would refuse to file criminal charges against blackmailers. Victims often saw the blackmail payoff as the best way to ensure privacy and preserve their reputations.

He studied the background in the photographs. The room resembled a residence bedroom rather than a hotel room. Two empty martini glasses and an ashtray containing a hand-rolled cigarette butt were on a nightstand. On a chair next to the bed were underwear, a black cocktail dress, and a pair of eyeglasses with unusual, light-blue frames. Next to the chair on the white shag carpeting were men's black leather loafers, a long-sleeved white shirt, and a pair of black trousers.

He said, "Could the photos have been taken here?"

"I've checked all the rooms. None of them look like the one in the photographs. And by the way, there's something in the kitchen I want you to take look at."

They walked inside. Smudges of ferric oxide were all over the kitchen appliances, furniture, and counters. The forensic tech had opened the cupboards and dusted the entire sink, kitchen table, stove, and walls. Sutherland pointed under the dining table. Casey leaned down and saw a one-inch square of black plastic fastened to the underside with half-inch electrical tape. He unfastened the tape, removed the device, and took out its miniature battery.

"It's a listening device," he said. "Low quality, like something purchased off the internet."

She said, "That rules out the FBI and IRS."

"Blackmail photos and electronic eavesdropping doesn't fit with some cat burglar getting caught stealing."

Later, they watched two coroner's deputies zip Bobby Lanza's corpse into a plastic bag, hoist the body onto a wheeled gurney, and roll it out the doorway.

—

Marty Vollero stopped his bright yellow Audi Spyder convertible at the main gate security booth and showed the uniformed Paramount Studios guard his private investigator's license and a studio access card given to him by a former client, an actor who maintained an office in one of the producer buildings. The guard noted the number on the card and motioned him to enter. Following the studio road a hundred yards to the main vehicle lot, Vollero parked the car and turned off the engine. Using the rearview mirror, he straightened his necktie. He liked the look of the gray sharkskin business suit. He kept his hair just short enough to comb, like the sons of the rich and powerful he'd met after being retained by their parents to bail them out of jail for drunk driving or rape.

Vollero, thirty-nine, had been an academic laggard at Hollywood High School. Dropping out of Los Angeles City College at nineteen after one semester, he decided to become either a movie star, a race car driver, or a cop. He worked on a movie set catering truck, then took a few classes in law enforcement and became a Beverly Hills Police

Department officer, a job that lasted a few years until he was forced to resign.

He got out of the car and walked to Sound Stage 13, a building the size of an airplane hangar. Its tall, sliding door was cracked a few inches. Peeking inside, he saw movie crew members moving about placing lighting equipment, talking quietly, and adjusting cameras in front of a forty-foot square blue screen. The attractive Vivienne Kalen-Boudreaux sat on a folding chair reading a script. She wore a buckskin leather jacket, matching skirt, and moccasins. For the role she was playing, the movie hair stylist had dyed black her usually platinum hair. A young man whom Vollero assumed was the movie director spoke briefly with Kalen-Boudreaux. The actress got up, handed her script to a production assistant, and walked to her mark in front of a gigantic blue backdrop. The crew stopped talking and a hush came across the stage.

The director said, "Action!"

Vivienne Kalen-Boudreaux, thirty-one years old, walked two steps toward the camera and said, "I'm going back to Kansas City."

"Cut!" the director said. "Very good, Vivienne. Wonderful performance. Exquisite."

Vivienne smiled.

The director began talking to a cameraman. The crew members began moving about. Kalen-Boudreaux returned to her chair. Vollero was amused at the ritual of movie production. In Hollywood, reciting a single sentence, neither art nor science, was enough to win the award for best actor from the Motion Picture Academy of Arts and Sciences. The uniformed security guard on the other side of the set had his back turned, and Vollero pushed the door open enough to slip inside. He knew from investigating Vivienne Kalen-Boudreaux that she managed to get movie roles because she was married to a successful movie producer.

"Good morning."

She looked up at him. Her jaw dropped. "What…what are you doing here?"

"Providing protection to talent on another set. But I need to speak with you privately."

"About what?"

He whispered, "Some confidential information."

"This isn't…a good time."

"It's in your interest to hear what I have to say. I promise it will only take a second."

Her grave and thoughtful expression told him she understood that this must be serious. Grimacing, she got up from the chair. He walked with her toward the door. He was pleased. Getting her to leave the movie set was proof he'd made it to first base.

"Okay," she said as they walked the studio alley. "What are we talking about?"

"Someone is trying to market some scandal information about you to the media."

"Who?"

"Part of my job as a licensed private investigator is to maintain sources in the underworld. Some of them are involved in marketing celebrity scandal information. Now and then, when someone finds some particularly exotic celebrity information, my informers get wind of it and come to me before the dirt hits the scandal market."

Gritting her teeth, she said, "That sounds like the same thing you told my husband."

"And with my assistance, his extortion problem was resolved without him suffering any embarrassment."

"After he shelled out a ton of cash."

"The objective was to stop bad publicity. Mission accomplished."

"You *assisted* my husband and now you're offering me help with some blackmail problem? Do you expect me to believe that's nothing but a coincidence?"

"Miss Kalen-Boudreaux, my reputation among the biggest entertainment celebrities in Hollywood is that of an honest broker."

Glaring at him, she said, "That's what you say."

He'd expected resistance. It was the way the elite always played the first inning.

"My clients include studio heads, attorneys, and some of the most successful personal managers and talent agents in the entertainment business. They trust me to handle sensitive matters."

"I could really give a fuck."

He nodded. "Is it that you don't care if the photographs come to light on the internet?"

"What photographs?"

"No one has contacted you?"

"Get to the point."

He cautiously glanced about, took an unsealed envelope from inside his jacket, and handed it to her. She opened it, glanced at the photos of her having sex with a stranger, a recent one-night stand she'd met in a Beverly Hills cocktail lounge. His face wasn't visible in any of the shots.

She whispered, "You have this game all figured out, don't you?"

"To assist you, I went out of my way to obtain these photographs. But if you prefer, I'll be happy to turn them over to the police and then aid them in prosecuting anyone trying to victimize you. Is that what you'd like me to do with the information?"

"Who took these photographs?"

"Then you haven't been contacted?"

"Who the hell's planning to blackmail me?"

The negotiation had begun.

"At this point," he said, "I'm still dealing with my network of confidential informers. To go further on your behalf, I'll have to open an investigation."

"My husband wondered how you ended up bringing him the blackmail information. For all we know, you might have instigated the blackmail situation. You might be the goddamn blackmailer."

"I want you to know that I understand the confusion and regret how you must feel after your husband was victimized."

She swallowed dryly. "You have all the answers, don't you?"

The tears welling in her eyes meant he was rounding third base.

"Allow me to explain."

"Make it quick," she said angrily. "I'm supposed to be in there shooting a movie right now."

"If you don't care, or if you are seeking the free publicity that will come from the photos being posted on the internet, we have nothing else to discuss."

"That's no explanation."

"Or, when you are eventually contacted by some blackmailer, you can pick up your phone and dial 911."

Without another word, he turned and walked toward the parking lot.

"Wait."

He stopped. She caught up to him.

"Where are you going?"

"You don't require my services."

He recognized the wounded act as part of the blackmail victim decorum. Owing her career to her bloated, loudmouth husband—a movie producer twenty years older than she who would toss her out the door the moment he saw the photographs—Vivienne Kalen-Boudreaux believed she had no choice but to cooperate. For Vollero, what remained of his plan was enduring the victim's whining before she, like her husband, would finally give in and hand over a big load of cash. The rich were experts in what money could buy: the finest plastic surgeons; admission for their brats to the best universities and country clubs; the services of mayors, congressmen, senators; and protection from being smeared by the media.

She angrily whispered, "I didn't say that."

"How can I help?"

"I need…I need to have this matter handled without my husband finding out."

"I understand."

"What is it going to take to accomplish that?"

"I estimate the blackmailers will demand about a million dollars."

"I don't have—there is no way I can raise that much without my husband finding out."

Vollero, a believer in anticipating future events, had already investigated her personal finances. She had five hundred thousand dollars in a checking account under her name.

"If you choose to retain my services, I will act in your stead and negotiate on your behalf. But my guess is that because you are married to the most successful motion picture producer in Hollywood, the other side won't take less than five hundred thousand. That doesn't include my fee, a reasonable hourly rate for my services rendered plus expenses."

"When will you be able to ascertain exactly how much this is going to cost me?"

"Hopefully sooner rather than later."

"I'll give you my personal cellphone number."

"Thanks," he said. "But I already have it."

She glared at him. "Call me."

"I will. You have nothing else to worry about."

Vollero walked to the studio parking lot feeling satisfied at having hooked another paying customer. As a child, he'd made friends easily, then found himself distrusting them as he did his weak, nagging mother as well as his cold, aggressive father, a custom window salesman who told him the best customer was someone willing to pay the highest price for the cheapest window and that life wasn't about selling windows but about "finding the right customers." At the time, Vollero didn't grasp the deeper meaning. He did now.

CHAPTER FIVE

Casey drove toward the office feeling tired. He'd staggered out of bed after another night of tossing, turning, and intermittent sleep. He took a shower, dressed, and walked to the kitchen where he opened the refrigerator, found a banana, and ate it while standing at the sink. While taking the elevator to the underground garage, he got a call from Sutherland, who told him she'd identified the person who'd purchased the cellphone connected to the hidden transmitter she found in Gloria Channing's kitchen. She was already in the police headquarters' parking lot when Casey arrived. She got in the car, put her purse on the floor, and handed him a printed overhead-view photo of a woman making a purchase at a cash register.

Sutherland said, "The store manager emailed me this. She used a credit card in the name of Wanda Troxell for the phone. I ran the name. She's thirty-one and has an arrest for residential burglary. It was five years ago, and the charges were dropped for lack of evidence. She lives in Reseda. You look tired."

"I grabbed a few hours."

"It'll be interesting to see what she has to say."

Entering Troxell's address into the GPS, he followed the screen directions from Beverly Hills to the 405 and then the 101 freeways, to Reseda. Driving along Sherman Way, a commercial street lined with dingy mini-malls, massage and nail parlors, marijuana stores, chiropractic clinics, and gas stations that also sold discount cigarettes and bottled water, it occurred to him that he could be almost anywhere in Southern California. He stopped at the light at Reseda Boulevard, made a right turn, drove north a few blocks, and made another right onto a narrow dead-end residential street lined with cheap tract homes with flat roofs, wooden garage doors, and sidewalks spray painted with gang graffiti. At the end of the block was Troxell's address: a gray stucco dwelling with a brownish lawn and windows fortified with metal bars. A silver Porsche Carrera parked in the driveway looked freshly washed and waxed.

Sutherland glanced at her notes. "That's her license plate number."

Casey parked the sedan at the curb in front. They got out and walked to the door. He heard loud rock music inside. He knocked. The music stopped.

"Who's there?" a woman shouted.

"Police."

"I can't open the door because my fingernails are wet. Come to the back patio."

They followed a driveway to the back yard. A patio attached to the house was strewn with empty Lucky Lager beer cans. The house's sliding glass rear door was open, its screen closed. Troxell stood behind it, her hands outstretched to avoid smearing her nail polish. She wore a blue silk robe that draped open to reveal blue panties and a multicolor tattoo of a cobra wrapping her abdomen. Casey thought she looked both foolish and older than thirty-one. He showed her his badge.

"Detectives Casey and Sutherland, Beverly Hills Police. May we come in?"

"Why?"

"So, we can talk without your neighbors overhearing our conversation."

"What's the subject?" Troxell had a raspy smoker's voice.

"A cell phone you bought," Sutherland said,

"You must have the wrong address."

Sutherland reached into her purse, took out the photograph of Troxell purchasing the phone, and held it up to the screen. Curling her fingers, Troxell used a knuckle to unlatch the screen door. They walked in.

Troxell blew on her fingernails. "So, what's wrong with buying a cell phone?"

Casey said, "The cell phone's number connects to an eavesdropping device found at the scene of a murder."

"I bought the phone for this woman I was working for."

Sutherland said, "How did that work?"

"It's a long story."

"Synopsize it," Casey said.

"I was shopping at the Asian Pacific market on Vanowen. When leaving, I happened to look at this advertising corkboard outside on the wall and saw an ACTORS WANTED sign pinned to it. Being out of work, I called the number and asked about the job. This lady wanted to know if I was interested in a role in a student movie. I told her yes. She mailed me a movie script and over the phone I read lines for her that sounded to me like they belonged to the role of a motel clerk. She told me I had the part, and that filming would start in a few days. I called her a few days later to ask what was going on with the project—"

"We're interested in the cell phone," Casey said, staring at a movie poster on the wall. On it, a red-haired woman in a bathing suit standing next to a custom lowrider Chevrolet convertible in the middle of a barren desert. The movie title was *Desiree's Dream Car*.

"I was just getting to that. The next day, she asked me to buy her a cell phone, something she didn't want her husband to know about. She gave me the money, I bought the phone and gave it to her. I never saw her again. When I tried to reach her, the phone number had been disconnected."

"What was her name?" Sutherland said.

"Smith."

"What kind of a car did she drive?"

"I don't remember."

"How did she pay you?"

"In cash."

Sutherland said, "How long did it take you to make up that bullshit?"

"Are you calling me a liar?"

"Yes."

"If I was doing something illegal, why would I use my own first and last name?"

Sutherland smiled. "Because someone convinced you the story would fly."

"So, what are you, a human lie detector?"

Casey said, "You planted a transmitter in Gloria Channing's house in Beverly Hills."

"That's what you say."

Sutherland said, "A man and woman were murdered there."

"I don't know anything about that."

"That's a nice car parked in the driveway," Casey said. "What do you do for a living?"

"At the moment, I'm taking acting lessons."

"How do you afford the house and car?" Sutherland asked.

"By acting."

Troxell pointed to a *Zero Hour in Tulsa* movie poster on the wall depicting a curvy model in a bathing suit struggling with a fiendish clown.

"What was your role in that movie?" Sutherland said.

"Sister of the store owner in the flashback scene."

Sutherland said, "Purchasing that cell phone makes you a murder suspect."

"So, arrest me."

Casey said, "On the other hand, telling us who paid you to plant the listening device will make us friends who can get you off the hook. Otherwise, you're in the middle of a homicide investigation. Considering your felony arrest record, is that where you want to be?"

"I've never been convicted of a crime."

Sutherland said, "Who taught you the burglary game?"

"I don't know what you're talking about. If you're trying to scare me, you're going to have to come up with something a lot better than that. I'm not some wimp."

Casey said, "Have you ever been to Gloria Channing's house?"

"The movie star?"

Casey said, "Why not just answer the damn question?"

"I don't even know where she lives."

Casey said, "Okay."

"Okay what?" Troxell said.

"If that's the way you want to play it."

"What do you mean?"

"That by involving yourself in a murder investigation," Casey said. "you're playing with fire."

"You're not talking to some dumb housewife."

Casey opened the screen door.

"Where are you going?"

"To talk to the district attorney," Casey said.

"About what?"

"We'll be back."

He and Sutherland walked down the driveway to the sedan and got in.

"How'd you like her story?" Sutherland said.

"Unoriginal."

"I bet she got it from a lawyer."

"I can see that."

Casey made a U-turn and headed to Reseda Boulevard, made a left turn, and parked a block away. Using binoculars, he focused on the Reseda entrance to Troxell's cul-de-sac.

"What's the plan, Legs?"

"To see if she goes to tell the other players that we were asking questions."

"Buying the cell phone gives us probable cause to arrest her for burglary."

He nodded, "But we might not be able to get a conviction."

After spending some time discussing the facts they'd gathered during the investigation, Sutherland turned on talk radio. An hour and seven minutes later, Casey saw the silver Porsche Carrera arrive at the corner of the cul-de-sac and stop. He raised the binoculars to his eyes. Wanda Troxell was the driver.

"She's rolling," he said, handing the binoculars to Sutherland. He started the engine again.

Troxell turned south on Reseda Boulevard and entered the stream of traffic. On Sherman Way, she stopped for the signal light. The light turned green, and she made a left under the 405 freeway overpass and merged onto the 170 followed by a right at Lankershim Boulevard, a busy commercial street. A minute later, Troxell drifted left to the yellow line and swerved across the northbound traffic lanes into the parking lot of Rick's Hacienda, a large Mexican restaurant with outdoor patio seating.

Casey quickly maneuvered the car around the block and parked across Lankershim, north of the restaurant. They watched Troxell get out of the Porsche and walk to the patio, where there were only two other customers. A restaurant hostess led her to a table and gave her a menu. Troxell sat and began reading. A waiter came to her table. She spoke with him. He went inside the restaurant.

A few minutes later, a bright orange Chevrolet Corvette Stingray pulled into the restaurant parking lot. The driver parked, got out of the car, and looked about. He wore slacks and a Hawaiian shirt. Casey guessed him as thirty, six-feet tall, and one ninety. He had long, Elvis-style hair and a full, dark beard that was combed, swept back, and sprayed to hold.

"The Wolfman," Sutherland said.

"A definite resemblance."

"I wonder how much time this clown spends every day trying to look like a movie monster."

Wolfman walked to the restaurant patio and sat at the table with Troxell. Casey raised the binoculars, focused on the Corvette. He read aloud the license number. Sutherland copied it on a pad, then used the car radio to run it. The operator told them the license number was registered to a Felix Halloran, who had a felony arrest record that included car theft, assault with a deadly weapon, and manslaughter, for which he served seven years in Corcoran State Prison; he'd been released ten months ago.

"Now he's driving an expensive car," Casey said.

While Halloran and Troxell were at the table conversing, the waiter returned with a drink. After a while, Troxell glanced at her wristwatch, got up, and left money on the table. She and Halloran walked to their cars. Troxell got in the Porsche. Starting the engine, Casey followed Troxell south on Lankershim a few miles to Ventura Boulevard. Troxell made a left turn, drove a mile, and turned into the parking lot of a small shopping mall. Parking on Ventura, they watched Troxell park the Porsche in the lot and get out. Carrying her purse, she walked to a small shop with a sign over the door that read ELEGANCE.

"It's a shoe store," Sutherland said.

Casey opened the driver's door. "Keep an eye on the shop."

"Where are you going?"

"The Porsche."

Casey got out of the sedan and opened the trunk. He took out a Slim Jim car door–opening device. Hiding it under his jacket, he walked to the Porsche. Not seeing anyone watching, he tried the driver's door. It was locked. Inserting the shim between the window and frame, he managed to unlock the door. He got in and sat behind the wheel.

Closing the door, he checked under the front seat and the back. He opened the glove box, then the console, and found gas station receipts, empty glassine envelopes of the kind used to package illegal narcotics, and a loaded .38-caliber blued steel revolver. Replacing all the items in the console, he closed the lid. Looking about to see if anyone was watching, he pressed the dashboard trunk release latch, got out of the Porsche, and searched the trunk. There was nothing in it but a bathing suit, a portable hair dryer, two empty pill bottles with pharmacy labels, and a medical prescription for Valium. The doctor's penmanship on the prescription was nearly illegible. He photographed the pill bottles and prescription with his cell phone.

He returned to the sedan, got in, and handed the phone to Sutherland, who studied the digital photographs.

"The prescription," Sutherland said. "The patient's name is Anthony Flair. He was Meredith Fox's live-in boyfriend, the first person I interviewed after her murder."

"What's his story?"

"He's a gym rat who once had a role in a movie. He manages the Greenroom cocktail lounge on Sunset Boulevard but tells everyone he's the owner. The place is owned by something called the Beaumont Corporation. He probably has a business partner or two. He has two felony pinches for selling cocaine, both of which were dropped for lack of evidence."

Casey knew the Greenroom, a dive promoted as a motion picture celebrity hangout that was frequented by mostly Hollywood grifters, casting agent poseurs, actor wannabes, dopers looking for a fix, and few celebrities.

Thinking out loud, Sutherland said, "Flair, Meredith Fox's boyfriend, is connected to Wanda Troxell, who probably bugged Gloria Channing's Hillcrest Drive home…?"

"Things are getting interesting."

CHAPTER SIX

Casey made the turn from Sunset Boulevard onto Hillcrest Drive.

Sutherland said, "Mother and I watched a couple of Gloria Channing movies on TV. In one of them, Channing plays a divorced fashion model on vacation in London, where she spots her high school sweetheart feeding the pigeons in Trafalgar Square. The movie dragged. The other movie was the one where she plays a pet shop owner with amnesia. I found it boring, but Mother insisted on watching it until the last scene. She's the same way with books. Like it or not, she reads all the way to the last page."

Casey parked the sedan at the curb in front of the Gloria Channing residence. The front lawn sprinklers were watering in great, automatic semicircles. To arrange the meeting with Channing, he'd called her personal assistant, Courtney Wellstone. He and Sutherland got out of the car and walked to the front gate security stanchion. Holding his police identification card to the camera lens, he pressed the button on the speaker box.

"Good morning," Gloria Channing said over the speaker. "Please come to the front door."

The gate lock buzzed and automatically opened. They walked up the driveway to the porch. Channing opened the front door. They exchanged pleasantries, and Casey introduced Sutherland.

"We're sorry about Mr. Lanza and Ms. Hernandez," he said. "We just have a few questions."

"My lawyer, Loretta Molinari, wanted to be here with me today, but I told her it wasn't necessary. She wasn't pleased. Come in."

Once they were inside, Channing closed the door. A movie website Casey had checked listed her age as forty-eight. Her makeup and hair were perfect, like she'd just gotten out of a makeup chair to perform in one of her movies. She was undeniably beautiful, with dark hair and a lush golden complexion. But her once piercing green eyes were dulled and puffy, like she might have had Botox injections to hide a few wrinkles.

"Molinari has been an attorney for a long time," Sutherland said.

Casey knew Molinari specialized in celebrity clients and was often hired to defend when they were charged in complicated criminal cases.

Channing motioned them toward a bright, red sofa. They sat. She took a chair facing them. She said, "She's seventy years old and still works sixty hours a week. Years ago, Loretta talked me into making *Black Wings*, a project that ended up on cable TV a week after release. The director was a charlatan who incessantly talked about himself, the characters in *Star Wars*, crossing a threshold that cannot be exited and flying out of a locked room, and other weird visions. He wanted everyone to think he was the new Alfred Hitchcock rather than a nerd with a studio deal." She glanced at her wristwatch. "I'm ready to answer your questions."

Casey considered Channing's small talk a distraction, indicating she might have something to hide. Most celebrities didn't chat with police officers. He said, "How long had Mr. Lanza been living here?"

"Two weeks. I mentioned to him that I was going to Paris. He asked if he could stay here while his condominium was being remodeled. I couldn't think fast enough to come up with an excuse as to why he couldn't stay here, so I agreed."

Sutherland said, "How would you describe your relationship with Mr. Lanza?"

"Since our divorce, Bobby would give me a ring now and then just to touch base. He's always been good at small talk."

"You didn't call him?" Sutherland said.

An expression of concern crossed Channing's face. "I guess you might say that it was a one-way relationship. Rather than hang up, I'd usually chat for a minute or two. Bobby and I have—*had*—a long past. Allowing him to stay here was foolish of me."

Sutherland asked why.

"Because now, after what happened, I'm sure the press jackals will begin making up false stories about me and about what happened here."

Casey said, "How did Mr. Lanza make a living?"

"Before we were married, he spent some time as an assistant entertainment director on a cruise ship, sailing back and forth from Los Angeles to Puerto Vallarta. After the marriage, I realized that he was selling cocaine and meth. I didn't know anything about that for more than a year. Bobby's clients were movie people. He never got caught. Before the divorce, I tried talking him into entering a drug rehabilitation program, but he wouldn't listen. Recently, when I was out of town, I've allowed him to use my swimming pool. But he started inviting over his friends from the Greenroom—that's a jazz bar on Sunset where he spent time. I finally told him I didn't want him bringing strangers over here."

"Was he still selling dope?" Sutherland asked.

"That's possible. But he certainly wasn't going to tell me anything about that kind of thing. I made it a point of not asking him about his personal finances. I feared it would lead to him asking me for money, which he often did. I once gave him ten thousand dollars. A month later he asked me for another ten. I stopped taking his calls for a year, but he created reasons to stay in touch. He'd call and hang on the phone telling me his sob stories, I frequently would just cut him off."

Sutherland said, "Are you aware he recently purchased a Ferrari sports car?"

"Uh, yes."

"Where'd he get the money?"

"I don't know."

"You didn't ask him?"

"No."

Sutherland said, "If my ex-husband bought himself a Ferrari, I'd certainly ask him about it."

"Bobby lacked personal pride," Channing said in a bitter tone. "He was a loser who managed to poison everything and everybody. I still can't believe he's dead. I feel like I'm reading a movie script that doesn't make sense. As I sit here telling you about him, I feel stupid. I can't help but think that if I would've only said no to marrying him, I'd have lost nothing, and my life would've been much better. Now I'm sitting here worrying about that kind of false stories the press will be creating about me."

Casey imagined her reciting dialogue, practicing lines from a romance movie script. He asked, "Who killed him?"

"I don't know."

"Take a guess."

"I assume it was some burglar who came in through the sliding glass door and stole all my jewelry."

Sutherland said, "In Beverly Hills, burglars seldom choose their targets at random."

"Some of them specialize in breaking into the homes of celebrities they know are out of town," Casey said. "They often have inside information about the residents."

"Well, I don't know any burglars."

"What about Mr. Lanza?"

"Look, Bobby hung with a rough crowd. And whenever he met anyone, the first thing he told them was that he'd once been married to me. I was his claim to fame, the calling card he used to impress his barfly friends."

Sutherland said, "Was he having problems with anyone?"

"If he was, he never told me. And when we spoke, he never mentioned names."

Casey said, "How do you feel about what happened to him?"

"What happened…just isn't right. I genuinely wish I could help you find whoever is responsible."

Sutherland said, "What about you? Have you been having problems with anyone?"

"How might that pertain to your investigation?"

"Maybe someone came here to harm you," Sutherland said, "and ended up killing your ex-husband."

"No one…no one has ever threatened me…do you ask everyone these questions?"

Casey said they did.

"It's not uncommon for people to get murdered by killers making mistakes," Sutherland said.

Channing used a handkerchief to dab her eyes. "This is so…utterly grotesque."

"When did you last see Mr. Lanza alive?"

"All these questions make me feel like I'm being violated. Not that I don't understand you have a job to do."

Casey said, "Have you ever had any serious disagreements with Mr. Lanza?"

"Not since the divorce."

"Did you know the publicist Meredith Fox who was murdered?" Sutherland asked.

Channing furrowed her brow. "Not really. I was shocked when I heard the news about what happened."

Casey said, "How would you describe the nature of your relationship with her?"

"Years ago, Meredith was hired to do publicity work for one of my movies. The studio had her arranging television and magazine interviews. I don't remember the exact details."

"When did you last speak with her?"

"I don't remember. Does what happened to Bobby have something to do with Meredith Fox?"

Casey said, "Did you and Bobby have any mutual friends or acquaintances?"

"I don't think so."

"Did Bobby know Meredith Fox?"

"If he did, he never said anything to me about her."

Sutherland said, "Did you and Bobby ever discuss the Meredith Fox murder?"

"My lawyer warned me the press would have a field day with Bobby getting killed here. She predicted horrible, false stories would be written and that they'd make me look bad. I hope the Beverly Hills Police Department isn't planning some big press conference about what happened here. That will do nothing but stir things up."

Casey said, "We have nothing to do with decisions regarding press coverage."

"Is there anything you can do to help me avoid the unfavorable publicity that might come from this?"

Sutherland said, "If I were you, I'd have your attorney call Chief of Police Slade and share your concern. The chief will listen."

"Thanks for the suggestion."

Sutherland asked again, "Did you and Bobby happen to discuss the Meredith Fox murder?"

"Not that I recall."

Casey said, "We found an eavesdropping device in your kitchen."

"I don't understand."

Channing was still avoiding eye contact. Casey decided he didn't trust her.

"A hidden electronic device triggered by the sound of conversation that automatically transmits to a cell phone. We tested the device and determined that it's operational. Someone has been spying on you."

"For how long has this…?"

"There is no way to know," Sutherland said.

"I feel totally violated."

Casey said, "Can you think of anyone who has a reason to spy on you in this way? Are you involved in any recent civil litigation or disputes involving money?"

"No."

"Do you know Wanda Troxell?"

"Who?"

"Troxell. Has anyone by that name ever been here?"

"No."

Casey said, "When did you last see Mr. Lanza alive?"

To Casey, her earlier failure to directly answer the question had to mean something. She'd answered most of the questions without hesitation and generally came off as believable. But Channing was an actor. If she had no respect for Bobby Lanza and avoided his calls, why had she allowed him to spend time in her home?

"He stopped by shortly before I left for France. I don't remember what we talked about."

Casey said, "When the first officer arrived here, a car Mr. Lanza used to drive was parked in the driveway. We searched the trunk and found some photographs."

Sutherland opened the envelope and handed the porno photographs to Channing. She coldly glanced at them.

"Do you recognize anyone?" Casey said.

"No."

Channing handed the photographs back to Sutherland. She slipped the photos back into the envelope.

Casey said, "Was Mr. Lanza involved in blackmailing anyone?"

Channing said, "Has someone made allegations about that kind of thing?"

"Lots of people have been interviewed," he said.

What was referred to in police circles as the "know it all" interviewing technique, exaggerating the amount of investigative information already gathered, frequently had the effect of persuading witnesses to tell what they were reluctant to share.

Staring blankly at her palms, Channing said, "Why did you come here? Is there something else going on?"

"Nothing other than a double murder," Sutherland said.

Channing spoke sheepishly. "I've told you everything I know. I honestly have no idea who may be responsible…"

"As an international movie celebrity," Casey interrupted, "it's understandable you'd be concerned how what happened here might affect your public profile. But that isn't going to stop the district attorney from serving you with a subpoena requiring you to testify before the LA County grand jury. If that were to occur, you can imagine how the media will magnify and distort everything."

Focusing on the coffee table, Channing wrung her hands. Her lower lip began to quiver. Casey guessed she'd decided holding back was riskier for her than talking.

"I've heard rumors about Bobby," she said. "But I have no way of knowing whether they were true."

"What rumors?" he asked.

"That he might be involved in extorting money from celebrities. That's all I know."

"If you suspected he might be involved in criminal activity, why allow him to stay here?"

There was a long silence. Casey wondered whether she'd decided to call her lawyer.

"I had no choice," she said.

He asked why.

Channing spoke softly. "Bobby…Bobby was blackmailing me."

"Over what?" Sutherland said.

"An incident that happened a long time ago, something no one else knows about. I'm not going to say what it was. That is no one's business. He demanded a lot of money to keep quiet."

Casey said, "Did you pay him?"

"It turns my stomach to think about how many times I gave Bobby cash. Every so often I would get sick of being used and confront him. Then he'd threaten to ruin me, and I'd give in. It happened again and again. He had a name for blackmail. He called it the 'Beverly Hills Polka' and told me if I refused to dance, I'd be eaten alive by the tabloid press. He said it with a smile. I find talking about this utterly degrading."

Sutherland said, "He made you, the woman he once married, into a victim. No one on the planet Earth would blame you for wanting to get back at him."

"I'm not a killer."

"Did you tell him how you felt about what he'd done to you?" Sutherland said. "No one could blame you for threatening him, or for that matter, striking back."

"I never did anything like that."

Sutherland said, "Have you ever discussed killing him?"

"No."

Casey said, "Or hiring someone to murder him?"

"Never."

Casey said, "Who wanted him dead?"

"I don't know! And I had absolutely nothing to do with his murder. I didn't realize until after I married him that he was…from a different world. That he was *bent.* I'd never met anyone like him. When we first met, I liked his looks. I thought we'd make a nice couple. I was wrong—I was foolish and immature."

Casey sensed Channing knew more but decided it wasn't the time to push further—that doing so might steer her to call her attorney, who would stop her from talking. He glanced at Sutherland, who gave a nearly imperceptible nod.

"Unless you have questions for us," Sutherland said, "we'll be going now."

They stood to leave.

Channing got up and then walked with them to the door and opened it.

"Loretta Molinari isn't going to be happy when I tell her I talked to you. But I don't care what she thinks. I'm still in a state of shock because of what happened. My assistant arranged for me to stay somewhere else, but I told her nothing would stop me from being in my own home. I'm not superstitious. What happened, happened. I fully intend to move on with my life. I'm not going to let some incident I didn't cause hinder me for the rest of my life. In a strange way I feel a sense of relief that his burden is no longer hanging around my neck like some lead weight."

Casey handed her his business card. "If you think of anything, we'd appreciate a call."

"Of course," Channing said.

Exiting the house, Casey and Sutherland walked down the driveway to the car and got in.

"Eyes like diamonds," Sutherland said,

"Huh?"

"That was the title of one of Gloria Channing's romance movies. She plays a fashion model who wants to be a movie star. Her agent comes up with the phrase 'eyes like diamonds' to use in her publicity. She becomes famous because of it, leaves the agent, and returns to her high school sweetheart. Then in the last scene she returns to the agent, and they drive toward the houseboat near Mount Shasta, where they first met. Eyes like diamonds. But today her eyes looked more like two burn holes in a blanket."

Casey said, "Or high on something, probably pills."

"Maybe because she knows that she's over on the big screen, passé."

"She definitely wasn't overwhelmed with grief at the murder of her ex-husband. He'd been blackmailing her."

"Legs, there was a time she put on a wedding dress and married him. Women don't forget that. She should have showed emotion." Sutherland smiled. "Like she did in *Mystery Girl,* when she found the dead chimpanzee."

He smiled, "She sounded rehearsed."

"Channing wasn't going to meet with the cops without first talking to Loretta Molinari. Molinari would want her to separate herself from Lanza but appear cooperative...without making us suspect her. She might have been repeating a script Molinari gave her."

"Channing is worried about adverse publicity."

"How did her assistant react when you interviewed her?"

"Courtney Wellstone wasn't exactly falling apart at the seams. And like Channing, she didn't express anger."

He knew it was common for relatives and friends of murder victims to express anger at an unknown killer as well as grief.

"Now that you mention it, when I delivered the bad news about Meredith to her boyfriend Anthony Flair, he didn't shed any tears. At the time, I thought it unusual."

He said, "There's something else going on with these people."

For the first time, Casey felt like he had a feel for the case.

CHAPTER SEVEN

As soft fingers of late afternoon sunlight streamed delicately through the windows of the secluded Malibu Canyon office, Vivienne Kalen-Boudreaux said, "This weekend I was sunbathing by the pool when I fell into a twilight nap and imagined being alone on the deck of an enormous private yacht anchored outside Cannes during the film festival. It was a perfect, sunny day and I was standing on the prow, feeling the sea breeze and the rolling movement of the boat. Looking toward the shore, I saw something moving in the water. At first I thought it was a fish. But as it came closer, I realized it was a woman swimming toward the yacht, a strong swimmer. She looked familiar, like someone I once knew but had forgotten, but I couldn't make out who it was. She climbed aboard the yacht naked, and when she swept her wet hair back I realized the woman was me. Without so much as a glance, she picked up a towel and left the deck. I went below to look for her. I felt her presence, but no one was there. She'd disappeared. Then I was suddenly startled awake by the sound of someone diving into our swimming pool.

Vivienne had beguiling dark eyes; pouty, sensual lips; a rounded, attractive chin; and skin carefully tanned with the help of cocoa butter. She came to Dr. Desmond Eckersley's office five days a week. Within the entertainment community, visiting a psychiatrist was both common and a mark of success. Eckersley saw clients paying for his time as proof of their naïve belief that having someone *listen* would, like religion or yoga, magically free them from the satanic curse of anxiety. Her therapy ramblings were little more than a way to remain focused on what to her was the most fascinating and compelling topic on Earth: Vivienne Kalen-Boudreaux.

That was no concern to Eckersley. She, and his other clients, were wasting their time—not his.

He wore blue-tinted eyeglasses, an Armani jacket, an Italian-made white shirt, and diamond cuff links. He believed dressing the part of celebrity psychiatrist helped him uncover secrets. When his clients closed their eyes he wanted them to recall the image of the successful medical practitioner and scientist. Assiduously monitoring his weight and personal habits, he shaved carefully and cautioned his barber about cutting his hair too short. Though not a golfer, he belonged to the Bel Air Country Club, where celebrities could see him in the dining room and bar. He believed he needed to look mature, healthy, and successful.

"Why the dream?" he asked.

As expected, her brow furrowed in concern. Avoiding eye contact, she got up from her chair and walked behind his desk to stare at the enormous, built-into-the-wall glass aquarium containing rare fish and aquatic plants. She wore a short skirt, unusual silver bracelets, earrings, and a wedding ring with a gigantic diamond. He didn't need to ask about the new bracelet she wore. She'd get around to telling him about it like she had her phobias, alcoholism, drug abuse, and pathological promiscuity. Eckersley, thirty-eight years old, imagined her as a screamer, flopping back on his desk and spreading her legs for him, then dramatizing an orgasm like she did everything else in her life.

"New stress factors."

"Such as?"

"For the rest of the day, I wondered whether the inner workings of my brain were trying to tell me something I needed to know. Then I got a warm feeling telling me the dream was about reincarnation, a spiritual awakening. Nothing in the world can convince me it wasn't a true, revelatory experience. I got out of bed last night unable to sleep, put on my running shoes, and ran for more than three hours in the dark. When I got back to bed, I was exhausted but still couldn't sleep. I relived my relationship with Ursula, my high school drama teacher. I attended school in Switzerland. Ursula was British, the daughter of a well-to-do family. I was lonely as a teenager, and I adored her verve and irreverence. I found myself dressing like her. Because she didn't use lipstick, I threw mine away. We bonded. And when I told her my mother wanted me to return to the US for the summer and I didn't want to go, Ursula told me I could spend the summer with her at a beach house her family owned in Saint-Jean-de-Luz. I readily agreed. Because of my age, I never gave a thought to any ulterior motive she might have. I saw her as the independent, creative woman I wanted to be. She wrote a letter to my mother on school stationery and suggested I be allowed to attend a summer scholarship camp in southwest France. Because she didn't care about me, my mother thought it was a wonderful idea. I was pleased and excited that the unapproachable Ursula, who kept her distance from the other teachers and students, wanted to be with me. It warmed my heart.

"The first day in Saint-Jean-de-Luz she showed me her beautiful beach cottage with my own enormous bedroom. We put on our bikinis and went surfing at Erromardie. That evening at a beachside café, we had a delicious dinner with lots of wine and then sheep's milk ice cream for dessert. Ursula became super friendly and warm. We made love the first night. Though surprised at Ursula's actions, I felt neither repulsion nor fear. Ursula was the most attractive teacher in school, and everyone looked up to her. To me, her explanation allayed any hint of deviance. She told me we weren't like the lesbians who wore mannish clothing—that we were women who'd chosen to be affectionate to one another. She asked to touch my breasts. She told me I was more beautiful than she'd ever imagined. At first I held back, but then I put my arms around her. She whispered to me that she wanted us to become comfortable with one another. At night, I looked forward to the sex, but during the day all I wanted was to be Ursula's friend.

"We drove to a restaurant in Biarritz and some men approached us and offered to buy us a drink. I loved the idea, but Ursula didn't. That's when I realized Ursula was a full-fledged lesbian. I was interested in the men at the beach and wanted to sneak away with one of them, but I couldn't risk angering Ursula. She taught me to surf and bought me expensive clothes. In August, when she told me she'd accepted a teaching position in Germany and wasn't returning to Switzerland, I knew I was free, that back in Switzerland I wouldn't have to fight her off. It was a perfect summer, and my first experience with gay sex. I enjoyed the bedroom activities, but it wasn't the real me. In a way, I'd spent the summer performing."

He stared at her as she returned to her chair. "I asked you about the new stress factors you mentioned."

"I knew you wouldn't let it go. It was a single factor. I…*acted out* as you might call it."

The perky, beautiful, Vivienne Kalen-Boudreaux was about to offer Daddy Eckersley another solemn, self-centered confession.

"In what way?

"I went to Wilfredo's."

"I see."

Admiring her sexy profile, he waited for her to explain. Her habit was to impart events in her life as one might choose shiny trinkets from a display case. Her life, like those of all his other clients, had pieces missing. And only some of the events they described were true. Dreams and shameless lies played a big role in the therapy business. He didn't lose sleep over unanswered questions. Listening to her for months, he'd observed that though she was more generally open than his other clients, she scrupulously avoided any discussion of her early childhood. She chose rather to dwell on insignificant topics like her idea for a movie: a female astronaut returning from a space station and landing in the cone of an extinct Hawaiian volcano. Her jabbering was little more than evidence of the same pathological self-indulgence he saw in his other clients.

Staring at her hands, she nervously licked her lips. "I feel comfortable there on Thursday nights when there is a big crowd in the bar. It's become my favorite place. I like the feeling of anonymity. I met someone."

Meeting someone was her euphemism for anonymous sex. She used cover names to keep her partners from learning she was married to the titan of movie producers, Norman Molitor. Her risky sexual behavior stemmed from the dark heart of her self-sabotaging energy, an obsessiveness causing everything else in her life to fall by the wayside. He saw her as insatiably bipolar, always compulsively pushing to the next higher level in the same way addicts constantly require more drugs. Years ago, she'd have been called a nymphomaniac.

She'd told him how she dropped out of college to marry a stockbroker, how they quickly became bored with one another and began experimenting with couples swinging, and how while hubby could take or leave the multiple partners experience, she found it breathtaking and fulfilling. She'd waxed on about being unsure whether the longing in her stemmed from getting away with something forbidden or a gratification she derived from having sex in front of strangers. He was sure of one thing: for Vivienne Kalen-Boudreaux, being the center of attention was exciting. Having convinced the stockbroker to have an open marriage, she found a new life of sexual adventure, including carefully planned and vetted threesomes and orgies. The marriage ended when hubby left her to marry a woman who starred in a successful TV cooking show.

After a bitter divorce, Kalen-Boudreaux married a wealthy realtor she met at a pool orgy. During a month when the new hubby was busy in his New York office, she added to her daily schedule time for anonymous sex with men she met online and through dating services. Their marriage ended at a late-night party at a realtor convention in Jamaica, where he accidentally overdosed on fentanyl and his heart stopped.

To allay her grief, she drove to Santa Barbara and attended a "Sunset and Twilight Meditation" weekend meditation retreat owned by a former child star. There, she met Norman Molitor, the Academy Award–winning producer of the blockbuster action flicks *Stripes and Stars* and *Bayonet*, each of which grossed more than a billion dollars worldwide. They began what she described as a "torrid affair." After Norman divorced his French starlet wife, he married Kalen-Boudreaux in a private ceremony held at the Bel Air Hotel in the presence of select members of the Hollywood elite, including representatives of the world press willing to kick back to the groom a cut of the wedding photo profit.

The marriage was a shot in the arm to Kalen-Boudreaux's floundering acting career. To please her ego, Molitor cast her in some character role in each movie he produced and appointed her to paid positions on the boards of three charitable foundations he and his accountant controlled. Now his production company paid a top studio hairstylist to come to their Beverly Hills home every other day to maintain her platinum-tint hairdo. Though she believed the slight darkness under her eyes gave her what casting agents called *depth*, when it came to playing roles, such as harried housewife, FBI agent, or desperate mom seeking her lost daughter, Eckersley had viewed her performance in one of Molitor's movies and observed that she couldn't act.

"And?"

"Wilfredo's was crowded when I arrived. I sat in the corner at my usual table. A younger man sitting nearby struck up a conversation with me. I'd never seen him there before. He said his name was Anthony. He told me he'd graduated from Brown University and then did graduate work at Cambridge. He said he was a professional mountain climber and the technical advisor for a couple of award-winning television adventure documentaries. He was handsome and well-spoken. I could tell he was attracted to me. After a few drinks he invited me to his apartment in Brentwood. We had sex. He was extremely attentive and went down on me. The orgasm was so good I thought the top of my head was going to blow off. Afterward, he drove me back to Wilfredo's to pick up my car. I tried to call him the next day but the number he'd given me had been disconnected. I just assumed he was married. I considered it a pleasant experience…until yesterday."

"What happened?"

"Yesterday, while I was shooting scenes at Paramount, the private investigator my husband had dealt with during his blackmail crisis stopped by to see me. He showed me some color photographs of me having sex with the man I met at Wilfredo's and then gave me this song and dance about the photos coming to his attention through his personal intelligence network and how he could stop them from getting out. He wants money."

"How did you leave it with him?"

"I told him I didn't want Norman to find out and I needed time to think about it."

"The man you met at Wilfredo's—who is he?"

"All I know is that his name is Anthony and that he has a tattoo of a black panther on his upper left arm. I questioned the people at Wilfredo's. No one had ever seen him before or since. It's obvious the people who blackmailed my husband are now trying to do the same to me."

She looked nervous and doubtful, as if questioning whether telling him about the blackmail approach might be a terrible mistake.

"What do you see as alternatives?"

"If Norman finds out, my marriage will be over. It's not that he doesn't know I have affairs. But if I create bad publicity for him, he'll file for divorce to create a smokescreen. That's what he did when he caught his second wife in bed with his stepson. Then he reported her to the IRS for cheating on her taxes. Then she reported his tax cheating to the IRS. I dread having to pay a blackmail demand. But if I refuse, I know I can be destroyed by the media."

He said nothing for a while to make her think he was cogitating, sorting data in his medical wisdom supercomputer.

"Are you able to pay what Vollero is asking?" he said softly, in a clear and deliberative tone.

He assumed asking the question wouldn't raise suspicion. She'd openly discussed with him her husband's blackmail problem and what he had paid to make it go away.

"I have a trust fund under my name, and I can come up with five hundred thousand without Norman finding out. But I don't want to pay. I consider it a degradation."

Having already decided to cough up the money, now she wanted her *listener* to sanction her plan and lead her to the crystal-clear water.

"Of course, there is always the other way."

"To what are you referring, Doctor?"

"The police."

"Impossible," she said.

"Many would consider it a reasonable course of action to take when being victimized by an extortionist."

"The one thing I cannot do under any circumstances is go to the police or the FBI and create the risk of the photos coming to light. That is out of the fucking question."

"I understand," he said after the appropriate pause.

"I've thought of asking my lawyer for assistance. But I'm afraid she might tell my husband. I wish you weren't my psychiatrist, and that you could help me."

"Vivienne, I want only what is good for you, but I am limited in my role as a physician."

"I need help."

You came to the right place, he thought, without a smile. Sexually stimulated by her weak and forlorn expression, Eckersley pictured her under him on the sofa.

"Under the canon of medical ethics," he said, "I'm not allowed to offer that kind of guidance."

"There is no other person on Earth who I can talk to about this mess—no one I fully trust."

"But I feel safe," he said, "in unofficially advising you what I might do if I found myself in a similar situation."

"Please."

"I would pay the money," he said. "If it were me, I'd pay the money as soon as possible."

"You would?"

Focusing on her eyes, he said, "Everything considered, that is the only rational way out of the problem. Peace of mind is what money is for. Use it to free yourself from this trap. Deliver the cash and be done with this psychological burden that has become an obstacle for you."

"What if I pay and the private investigator or someone else returns later and threatens me again with the same photographs? What if they make another demand for cash?"

Eckersley had anticipated the question.

"That problem may never present itself."

"It's a possibility."

"We live our lives on the plane of time, the present. No one can predict the future. You need to live in the present and act quickly before this blackmailer tars you and ruins your life. Delivering the money will enable you to move down the road."

Staring at the aquarium for more than a minute, she said, "I believe I understand what I need to do."

"There is no other way to handle the problem. Pay the money and remain self-confident and vital."

She glanced at her Rolex Datejust. "Two o'clock," she said. Briefly fluffing the bottom edges of her platinum hair helmet, she picked up her purse. "Today was good. I feel like I'm making progress. I'm releasing some of the anxiety."

He got up, walked with her to the door, and opened it. She boldly met his gaze.

"See you day after tomorrow," he said.

"Thank you for helping me see the bottom line, Doctor. Thank you for saving me."

Waiting for her to say something else, he felt a sexual stirring.

"You're welcome," he said, without a hint of emotion.

She departed the office. Closing the door, he pondered how many more blackmail demands he'd be able to convince her to pay before she'd finally refuse. He moved to the window and watched her walk to her shiny silver Bentley.

CHAPTER EIGHT

Casey exited the sterile-looking, ultramodern Beverly Hills Police Headquarters' Records Bureau. Following the first-floor hallway toward the stairs, he walked by the community relations office. The door was open. An extremely attractive, thirtyish brunette was at the desk, talking on the telephone. She glanced up, smiled. He smiled back.

He climbed the stairs to the second-floor detective squad room, passed Captain Dollinger's empty glass-walled office, and sat at his desk, next to Sutherland's.

"I'm becoming a Gloria Channing expert," she said.

"Really."

"When I got home last night, my mother was watching another one of her movies. Channing in the role of an airport customs officer who falls in love with a guy smuggling parrots from Guyana."

"So, you watched it?"

"I got bored, but Mother enjoyed the colorful parrots."

Casey said, "Have you met the new community relations officer?"

"Yes. Ellen Brady. She transferred in from the Phoenix Police Department."

"What's her story?"

"Single, straight, and keeps to herself," she said, then lowered her voice. "But if I were you, I'd stay away."

He asked why.

She whispered, "One of the records clerks saw her jogging with Dollinger."

"Thanks for the smoke signal."

Sutherland said, "I just spoke with Meredith Fox's bank. Her business account shows large deposits, wire transfers from a bank in the Cayman Islands—one for $460,000, another for $700,000."

"Probably blackmail payoffs."

Dollinger walked into the squad room holding a mug of coffee. He followed the narrow aisle between cubicle's, grabbed a wheeled chair from an empty desk, and sat. "The chief just got a call from Loretta Molinari claiming you violated Gloria Channing's rights by interviewing her without counsel."

"Molinari likes to show off for clients," Casey said.

"Now the chief wants a daily briefing on the investigation. What's the latest?"

"Channing told us Lanza was blackmailing her," Casey said.

"Over what?"

"She declined to say."

"Understandable," Dollinger said. "Have we eliminated Channing as a murder suspect?"

Sutherland said, "I made some calls to verify she was in France at the time of the murder."

"What about her personal assistant, the one who made the original call from the scene?"

Casey said, "Courtney Wellstone was with two female friends on the night of the murder. Both corroborated her alibi."

Sutherland said, "The lab guy just called. As we expected, the rounds that killed Meredith Fox were fired from the same gun that killed Bobby Lanza."

Casey said, "The photos from Lanza's car, the listening device in Channing's kitchen being planted by a woman connected to Fox's boyfriend, and wire transfers to her account from an offshore bank, looks like blackmail activity."

Dollinger said, "Fox and Lanza as shakedown artists murdered by some blackmail victim?"

"Possibly," Casey said, Sutherland agreeing.

Dollinger sipped coffee. "Anything else?"

"At the moment, that's about it."

"That's pretty much what I ran down to the chief. She wasn't overwhelmed. In fact, she said that it sounded to her like we didn't have jack shit."

It wasn't the first time Casey had listened to the frustrations of supervisors. During complicated investigations, supervisors always thought they knew more, that if they'd personally interrogated the suspects, they'd have gotten more from them—that if they'd personally supervised the crime scene, they'd have found more clues. They were seldom correct. The truth was, there was no accounting for why some cases were solvable and now and then, a few were destined for the cold case file. Casey's instinct was that the case was solvable, but attempting to articulate why would sound foolish. He said nothing.

Dollinger finished his coffee. "Last night I was at a liaison meeting and ran across an FBI supervisor I've known for years. I asked him if he knew of any extortionists who were shaking down movie celebrities. He told me there were two the bureau were aware of: a Chicago hood who just died last month in Brazil, where he was hiding from a federal warrant. The other suspected blackmailer is Marty Vollero."

Vollero, a retired detective, had resigned from the Beverly Hills Police Department a few years earlier to build a successful celebrity protection and private investigation business based on publicity he gained from appearing on television news programs, commenting as an expert about crimes involving the rich and famous.

"I once helped him on a case for a couple of days," Sutherland said.

"I never worked with him," Casey said, "Does the bureau have any specifics on him?"

"Just that Vollero has been tiptoeing around the edge of some recent celebrity extortion cases that the FBI was aware of. He contacts blackmail victims and offers help with their problem. Sometimes he shows up before the blackmail pitch, plays an 'I come as a friend' act; sometimes he comes in after. One of the shakedown victims was convinced he knew too much about their blackmail problem to not have been involved. The bureau isn't sure whether he's an extortionist or is just trying to drum up private eye business."

Sutherland said, "I can see Marty Vollero weaseling around town like that."

"Vollero got in trouble right before he resigned," Dollinger said. "Chief Braun handled the problem and then buried the file. That was the way he handled internal problems."

During a career lasting nearly sixteen years, former Chief of Police Braun eschewed his deputy chiefs and commanders and preferred instead to handle sensitive matters personally. Braun had come from the detective bureau and saw detectives as the core of the department. Braun rode a white horse every year in the annual Hollywood Santa Claus parade and spent his days speaking at Chamber of Commerce luncheons and ribbon-cutting ceremonies. He got involved in crime investigations only when it raised his public image in some way or another. Married to the rich widow of a man who owned two Los Angeles sports teams, Braun held opulent St. Patrick's Day parties designed around her Olympic size swimming pool and invited members of the Beverly Hills City Council, and his many and varied motion picture celebrity pals.

"Vollero hires off-duty and retired officers to work his VIP protection capers," Sutherland said.

"Have either of you worked for him? Either of you been in contact with Vollero since he left the department?"

Casey and Sutherland answered in the negative.

Dollinger said, "I see Vollero as a possible suspect. Find out if Vollero was involved with our victims." Glancing at his wristwatch, Dollinger said he had to run to a meeting, then got up. "By the way, the chief told me to be sure all the reports in this case are kept under lock. Because of the Gloria Channing angle, the press will surely be nosing around."

He got up and walked back toward his office.

"Marty Vollero," Casey said. "What's the bottom line on him?"

"When he was here, he didn't have a lot of friends. He would borrow money from partners and never pay it back."

"I never heard that."

"And he was a major liar. When he first came on the job, he told everyone he was a semi-pro boxer. But he'd never been in the ring. He's one of those people who should have never been hired. He was the kind of guy you couldn't talk to without him twisting what you said to make it sound like an insult, and he had some inner need to put people down. Marty Vollero is a basic scumbag."

"What got him fired?"

"Do you remember the patrol officer who found the dead suicide victim who had the three hundred grand in cash?"

"The body found in the car parked on Lomitas Avenue?"

"The officer found the stiff while on patrol, took the money home, and then put in his retirement papers the next morning."

"How was Vollero involved?"

"He was having an affair with the patrol officer's wife. She told Vollero her husband brought home the cash."

"Vollero turned him in?"

"Marty confronted the officer and demanded half the poke. When the officer refused, Vollero reported him to Chief Braun. Internal Affairs served a search warrant, found the cash, and arrested the officer. For reasons not connected to that incident, Braun hated Vollero and was looking for a way to get rid of him. Braun was happy when Vollero resigned on his own."

"How do you know all this?" Casey asked.

She whispered, "Don Braun."

"He told you?" Casey whispered back,

"He was my boyfriend for nearly ten years. He told me everything. We trusted one another."

"I wasn't aware."

And Casey appreciated her telling him about the relationship. They were partners and nothing was more important than being able to trust one another.

"It was our secret. No one in the department ever found out. The first time he asked me out, I was working patrol and had only a few years on the job. I figured: why not? We were both single and the age difference didn't matter to me. Donald Braun was a real gent, a cool dude. We'd fly up to San Francisco for the weekend and he'd take me to dinner at the Tadich Grill. Don knew what was going on in the department, including his nickname among the troops—'Don Juan' Braun. He got a kick out of it. He was the only officer I ever dated. My mother would have killed me if she'd known I was dating a white man, much less the chief of police. She's old school, a church lady. Don knew everyone and he took care of his friends. I never asked him for a favor, but he promoted me to detective. When I thanked him, he just smiled. Then a week later he replaced me on his social schedule with that movie actress who talks like Sigourney Weaver. It broke my heart. I was really hurt. But I should've known that we weren't going to go on forever. Looking back at it now, Don was always a gentleman. And he was also a damn good dancer. When he retired, he left the department with more friends than enemies."

Casey said, "Dollinger looked stressed out."

"To keep Slade from firing torpedoes in our direction, we're going to have to come through."

"We'll solve the homicides."

After a silence, Sutherland said, "Legs, can we talk for a moment?"

"Sure."

"I know it's none of my business, but I understand what shooting trauma can do to a cop's mind. I went to a few AA meetings years ago and it cured me of drinking altogether. I recommend the group meetings."

Casey liked and respected Sutherland as a detective but didn't need her advice. He liked to drink and occasionally drank too much. But while drinking, he was the same man as he was sober. When alcoholics drank, they changed, became unpredictable, and couldn't be counted upon in difficult situations. That wasn't Casey. He would work out his problems in his own way. He believed the recurring nightmares about the jewelry store shooting, which were like the ones he experienced after combat as an Army sergeant in Afghanistan, would become less frequent with time and finally drift into the restricted information vault in the back of his mind.

"My drinking is under control."

"Not really. And when you get hit with another liquor beef, as your partner, Dollinger can charge me with failure to report and I can end up behind the eight ball with you."

"I'm not planning on that."

"If it happens, he won't hesitate to make room for two on the stolen car desk. He'll sink us without blinking an eye. The last thing I want is to end up in the trick bag."

He smiled. "That's not going to happen."

"I'm worried. And I just wanted to make sure you know where I'm coming from."

"I won't let you down." He smiled. "So, let's get out of here and go find out what Vollero has to say."

"You don't need me to talk to him," she said, looking disappointed that he hadn't readily taken her advice.

CHAPTER NINE

In the underground garage of the Gamewell Building, a modern five-story office structure east of Vine Street near the Vampire Wax Museum, Casey parked in a space marked VISITOR. In the ground-floor lobby, he checked an office directory attached to the wall. VOLLERO INVESTIGATIONS was listed in Suite 201A.

Rather than take the elevator, he jogged up two flights of stairs to a wide corridor lined with doors that had the same shiny block lettering. The businesses gave off a show-business vibe: Ivy Hill Cinema Partners, Quebec Filmgate Associates, Big Movie Inc. He imagined the renters as would-be producers, film school graduates who spent the day cold-calling novice screenwriters to convince them to allow a free option on a screenplay they could later use as bait to lure movie investors. At the end of the hallway, the door to 201A was unlocked. Casey walked into a large reception area where rows of autographed celebrity photographs in identical faux bronze frames hung on the walls.

"Good morning," said an attractive young woman at the reception desk. "May I help you?"

Casey showed his badge. "I'm here to speak with Marty Vollero."

"Do you have an appointment?"

He said he didn't.

"May I tell him what this is about?"

"Police business."

"I'll see if he's in."

"You don't know?"

Maintaining her smile, she got up, walked into an inner office, and came out a few seconds later.

"Mr. Vollero will see you now."

Casey walked into a spacious workspace. Vollero sat at a white desk with nothing on it but a white phone, a white laptop computer, and a large white marble ash tray. Sunlight coming in through a large window looking down at the busy Hollywood Freeway illuminated a white-tiled floor and three walls lined with white bookcases filled with white folders. On the other was a framed color photograph of Marty Vollero in full Beverly Hills police uniform.

"Casey," Vollero said without standing. "When I was working the burglary desk, you were leading in robbery arrests."

"Congratulations on your new career."

He recalled Vollero at a desk in the corner of the detective squad room. Now, instead of a cheap suit, he wore a Brioni sports jacket and a hand-stitched white shirt open at the collar.

"My years in the police department were spent developing my outside interests," Vollero said. "I didn't care about making arrests, and neither did anyone else. When I resigned, I already had my investigation business fully operational." Vollero motioned him to the chair in front of the desk. Casey sat. "How long have you been back on duty since your jewelry store shooting?"

"A few months."

"You're feeling okay?"

"Back to normal."

Vollero picked up a gold cigarette case, opened it, took out a smoke, and flamed it with a thin gold lighter engraved with MV. "I saw you on TV receiving the department medal of valor," Vollero said, smoke rising from his mouth. "From what I've read, you deserved it."

"Thanks. I won't take up too much of your time."

Casey took out a copy of Bobby Lanza driver's license and handed it to Vollero.

"What's this?" Vollero said.

"Do you know him?"

"The face doesn't ring a bell."

"Gloria Channing's ex-husband, Bobby Lanza."

"I saw the story on the news," Vollero said, handing back the photograph. "You must be investigating his murder."

"Have you ever done any work for Lanza?"

"Why do you ask?"

"Someone told me he'd recently hired a Hollywood private investigator to do some work."

The white lie was a test. Police interviews were never about the absolute truth but rather were about the truth provable in a court of law. The questions were irrelevant. Only answers mattered.

Vollero smirked. "So, must be showing the photo to every private eye in Hollywood?"

"That sounds like a yes."

"I don't answer client questions."

"Even if they are murder victims?" Casey said.

Vollero had failed the test.

"My customers are guaranteed confidentiality."

"Have you heard any rumors about who killed him?"

"You're asking the wrong private eye."

Casey smiled affably. "Your television commercials claim that you're the Hollywood investigator who knows what's happening on the street."

"I'm glad to hear someone believes my publicity, but I know nothing about the Lanza murder. Seriously, who gave you my name?"

"Did you know Meredith Fox?"

Vollero furrowed his brow. "I'd love to help you, Casey, but most of my work involves protecting celebrities. If I knew something, I'd not only tell you, but I'd call a big press conference and tell the entire world. Success in this business is about marketing, maintaining a big public profile."

"Have clients retained you to investigate anything related to extortion?"

"I handle all kinds of investigations," he said. "What's going on, Legs? Is someone trying to put a jacket on me?"

Casey smiled. "Nothing like that. I'm just trying to solve a whodunit."

Vollero smirked. "Who told you I was doing work for Bobby Lanza?"

Vollero had something to hide. On-the-level private investigators weren't defensive when questioned. Casey wondered if Vollero might have been a crook during his entire stint with the police department.

"Sorry if you've gotten the impression that I'm trying to put you on the spot. I'm not."

"You're here because someone pointed a finger at me—someone who's out to screw me. One of the drawbacks to this business is being forced to take sides in business disputes, make enemies, sometimes of people I've never even met. I never discuss my investigations...unless it benefits me. I'd love nothing more than to solve this case for you... if I can get some press for it. In fact, on second thought, I'm going to ask around for you and see what I can find out. Maybe I can get you promoted."

"Thanks."

"You may think I'm joking, but I'm not. You seem like a nice guy, and it would do nothing but benefit my business. Every time I release information to the city news service, I get calls from potential clients. Do you have any other questions?"

Casey said he didn't.

"I'd love to spend more time with you, Casey, but I'm really slammed today."

"Thanks for your time." Casey said as he got up to leave.

"Good luck with your investigation."

"I'll need it."

Vollero walked with him to the door. "Any of the cops who worked with me will tell you I'm solid. By the way, if you're ever looking to earn some extra bucks, when I protect movie stars, I employ lots of off-duty police officers. And I pay better than any other private eye in Southern California."

"Thanks for the offer."

"Feel free to give me a ring."

Casey took the elevator to the underground garage and spent the next few minutes searching all three parking levels for Vollero's name on one of the reserved parking space signs. Finding nothing, he returned to his car and drove to the office.

CHAPTER TEN

Casey and Sutherland finished writing reports and then briefly discussed tomorrow's agenda before calling it a day. Driving out of the department parking lot at 7:00 p.m., Casey felt like a drink. In fact, after years of using alcohol to relax after the workday, he *needed* a drink. But instead of driving to the Nightwatch or one of his other hangouts, he decided to drive home and get some sleep. He'd had insomnia since the jewelry store shooting. At first, he assumed it stemmed from the prescription drugs he'd been given while recovering in the hospital. Recently, he connected the sleep problem to drinking. Using liquor as a sedative led to more nightmares.

He drove by the Los Angeles Country Club on Wilshire Boulevard, some high-rise apartment houses, and through an intersection while the light was yellow. Glancing at the rearview mirror, he saw the signal light turn red. A silver Honda SUV speeded through the intersection without slowing, then swerved to the curb and stopped.

A minute later, near UCLA, he slowed before Gayley Avenue and made a right turn. Glancing in the rearview mirror, he saw the same silver Honda SUV following him. He made a left turn, then another left. The Honda SUV dropped back but remained in view.

He turned into the driveway of a Gateway supermarket on Westwood Boulevard and navigated into a marked space in the parking lot. Walking to the rows of shopping carts at the entrance, he took one and rolled it through the doorway. He stopped at a display rack next to the tinted front window. Outside, the silver Honda SUV was parked at the curb. The driver wore a baseball hat and sunglasses.

He watched the store entrance for a minute to make sure no one had followed him on foot. Abandoning the shopping cart, he walked along a display aisle to a door at the rear of the store marked EMPLOYEES ONLY. He went into a high-ceilinged storeroom where wooden pallets were stacked with cases of canned goods in front of a delivery dock. He crossed the room and took the steps to the alley. Making sure no one had followed him out of the store, he moved to the sidewalk.

Approaching the Honda SUV from behind, he saw that the driver's side window was down. He drew his gun at the door and raised it to window level.

"Why are you following me?"

The driver startled, turned toward him, and took off her sunglasses.

"Orders," said the department's community relations officer, Ellen Brady.

"Whose?"

"Your boss, Captain Dollinger."

Casey holstered the gun. "Who's on the surveillance team?"

"Just me."

"He sent you alone to tail me?"

Brady opened the door, got out of the car. She wore tight jeans, a loose-fitting blouse, and sandals.

"I told him you'd spot a one-car surveillance. But he chose not to take my advice."

"What's the mission?"

He assumed she'd decline to tell him rather than reveal what Dollinger told her.

"He wants to know whether you are drinking liquor while on official duty. Or at least that's what he told me."

Oddly, Ellen Brady didn't look the least bit frazzled over the confrontation. She was a seasoned cop.

He smiled. "I wasn't aware community relations duties included surveillances."

She shrugged. "Ask Dollinger."

She was handling the incident like a professional. He liked her attitude.

"Ellen, can we talk off the record?"

"That's probably not a good idea. What's the game?"

"No games," he said, "and I promise not to mention anything to Dollinger."

"One question."

"Go ahead."

"Will you join me for dinner?"

He needed to determine whether there was something more to the surveillance.

"Maybe some other time."

He wondered if he'd misjudged her.

He smiled. "As the community relations officer, it would be a good opportunity for you to meet the owner."

"I'm new to the department. For all I know, taking sides between you and Dollinger might be career suicide. Sorry."

"I'm on my way to Roget's, a three-star Beverly Hills restaurant. And no one has to know."

"Sure."

"While you were investigating me, surely you must have learned that I'm not a department rat," he said. "Besides, everybody has to eat."

She studied him momentarily, then took off the baseball hat and dropped it into the car.

"Only if I pay my own way."

"Deal."

Driving the Honda, she followed him to Roget's. Leaving their cars in front, they got out and handed their keys to a valet parking attendant.

They walked to the entrance, a red door with gold lettering next to a semicircle window of thick, nontransparent glass in box frames built to thwart photographers.

"I'm not dressed for this place," she said.

"Neither am I. But it's no problem. The owner is a friend."

He opened the door. They walked in.

The hostess said, "Good evening, Mr. Casey." She waved at the bar where Roget, in suit and tie, was in conversation with some guests.

Roget graciously hurried to him. "Detective Casey. Thanks for coming."

Casey introduced Brady as his colleague. Greeting her warmly, Roget took them to a table and removed a RESERVED sign from it. They sat. A head waiter rushed to the table with wine, then departed.

She said, "Isn't this the restaurant where that movie was made?"

"*Presidential Envoy.*"

"That's the one."

"Roget was ready to sell the place when a producer asked to rent it to film some scenes. They shot here for two weeks. Now people come in every day just to see the place."

"How do you know Roget?"

"A disgruntled employee tried to torch the place. I happened to arrest him."

"Lucky you."

He raised his wineglass to hers. She smiled. They sipped.

"Ellen, what caused you to leave Phoenix PD?"

"My husband was killed chasing a fugitive."

"I'm sorry."

"I decided I was finished with law enforcement and began studying to be an emergency room nurse. After the first semester, I missed being a cop...and Beverly Hills PD was recruiting officers, so I made the call."

"How did you end up with the community relations job?"

"My resume listed a public relations position I had before I joined Phoenix PD. The admin officer convinced me I'd like the duties. I figured why not? You'd have refused the position."

"Something you learned while investigating me?"

"Along with a few other things."

"Such as?"

"You got the nickname 'Legs' when you were a rookie and chased a burglar on foot for three miles."

"The helicopter was grounded because of fog."

Smiling, she opened her purse and took out a copy of a newspaper article, handed it to him.

POLICE OFFICER FATALLY WOUNDED

Yesterday afternoon, two veteran Beverly Hills officers exchanged gunfire with three robbery suspects inside the Golden Phoenix Jewelry store on Rodeo Drive, the exclusive shopping area for the Beverly Hills elite.

In a press conference held in the department's pressroom, Beverly Hills Captain of Detectives Clifford Dollinger explained that Beverly Hills police detectives Michael Casey, 34, and Albert Zepeda, 43, were conducting a routine interview in the store when armed men entered the front door, drew guns, and attempted to rob the storeowner. The detectives attempted to arrest the robbers and a gun battle ensued. Both detectives were wounded during the shoot-out and transported to Cedars-Sinai Medical Center, where Detective Zepeda succumbed to his wounds during surgery. Detective Casey remains hospitalized in critical condition.

The three robbery suspects, whose names were not released pending notification of their next of kin, were pronounced dead at the scene. Records indicate all three were released from San Quentin State Prison in late June. Los Angeles police officials reported that the suspects were suspected of committing three similar jewelry store robberies in the Downtown Los Angeles Diamond District during the past 60 days and were on active parole status.

The Golden Phoenix Jewelry store has been in business at the same Beverly Hills location since 1947. An employee of the upscale store who wishes to remain anonymous stated, "The officers saved my life."

Casey handed it back. She slipped the article back into her purse.

"You're a hero," she said.

"Actually, we were there because I'd been tipped that the place was going to be robbed."

"After your months in the hospital, you returned to duty, got married, divorced a few months later, then had a drinking incident and ended up riding a desk until you were assigned the Bobby Lanza murder. Your peers respect you and the supervisors see you as a rulebreaker."

"Anything else?"

"You like liquor, women, jazz, and gambling—in that order. And you have trouble sleeping. Did I miss anything?"

"I'm on the wagon."

"Except wine?"

He shrugged. "Wine isn't hard liquor."

She smiled. "How did you get that scar at the corner of your lip?"

"When I was twelve years old, a friend challenged me to play burn 'em in, a hardball game that involves one player pitching a fastball at the other, then after each pitch, taking a step closer to one another. We began exchanging fastball pitches at forty feet. When we were eight feet apart, he threw his best fastball. It bounced off the top of my glove and split my lip."

"Your friend won the game?"

"No, I picked up the ball and stepped forward ready to pitch. He quit."

"I imagine that attitude helped you get through your recovery time in the hospital."

"Bullet therapy got me through it."

"What's that?"

"Realizing that what happened to me had nothing to do with fate, bad luck, or not praying the Rosary. That getting shot, like being caught in a tornado or an earthquake, had no philosophical meaning."

She furrowed her brow. "So you don't believe in anything?"

"Except what I can see."

She sipped wine. "I'm not sure I understand. But I'm sorry your partner was killed in the shooting."

Casey didn't know what to say. He'd never known what to say about it—the survivor guilt still haunted him.

"We should order," he said. "The fish is always great."

While enjoying a three-course gourmet French dinner, he avoided any discussion of the murder investigations. They talked about how there were no good movies to see, how police pay was inadequate, and why the American public had lost its ability to use reason and logic in favor of following internet fads. While chatting, he detected no hidden agenda in what she said or in any question she posed. He mused about Ellen Brady's twice-tempered steel demeanor and wanted to know her better.

He said, "What do you think of Captain Dollinger?"

He figured the subject was appropriate. Cops commonly ask one another about superior officers. If she was involved in a relationship with him, the question gave her an opportunity to let him know whether he should ask her out again.

"Legs, any gossip you've heard about me sleeping with him is fiction. I ran into Dollinger a few times while jogging, but there is nothing personal between us."

"I didn't mean to imply anything."

She raised her glass. "Here's to…community relations."

"I'll drink to that."

It was after midnight when he went through the ritual of trying to pay for the expensive dinner and Roget refusing to accept payment.

They walked outside to the valet parking station. Attendants hurried to get their cars.

"Legs," she said, "are you going to get me in trouble for accepting a free dinner?"

"We tried to pay but the owner refused to accept our money."

Shaking her head, she had an amused expression. The attendant arrived with her Honda, got out, and left the door open with the engine running.

"Thanks for the nice evening."

"Let's do it again sometime."

His words sounded awkward, like they'd come from someone else.

She touched his arm, just a brief touch. "See you."

She got in her car and drove off. What puzzled him was whether Ellen Brady denying a personal relationship with Dollinger was the truth or an obligatory falsehood. He guessed she'd tell Dollinger her surveillance had failed and that Dollinger, having initiated the internal investigation, wouldn't mention anything to him. Police supervisors responsible for keeping an eye on their subordinates weren't required to explain internal affairs investigations to anyone but the chief.

A minute later, the attendant arrived with Casey's car. Casey tipped him for both cars, got in the sedan, and drove out of the lot. Arriving a few minutes later at the Wilcox Arms, a five-story apartment building near UCLA, he drove into the underground garage and parked his car in his assigned space. Riding the elevator to the fifth floor, he walked along a carpeted hallway and unlocked the door to his furnished one-bedroom apartment that cost him more than half his monthly pay.

He went in, closed the door, and walked to the large living room window. As he was staring across Wilshire Boulevard at another high-rent apartment house, his mind was on the soft-spoken Ellen Brady, who'd registered a ten on his sexual approach meter. He thought about Dollinger, the cautious bureaucrat who'd sent Ellen Brady to watch him, fearing that if Casey got drunk and crashed a city car, Dollinger would be blamed for lack of oversight.

Casey's cell phone rang. The display screen read ANTOINETTE VAN PATTEN. He didn't answer. The ringing stopped. He checked messages. There was only one, from her.

"Hi, Legs. Just a call to touch base. I was thinking about you and wanted to see how things were going. Call me if you feel like it. I'd love to hear from you."

Having heard that she'd recently broken up with the choreographer, he erased the message.

In bed later, he closed his eyes and tried to clear his mind and fall asleep but saw the tiny security cubicle in the Golden Phoenix Jewelry store on Rodeo Drive where he and his partner Al Zepeda were anxiously staring through a large, one-way mirror into the shop's well-lit main showroom: white carpeting; bleached marble, walls with flowing lines and swirls; a stained-glass window; enormous display cases filled with diamonds, rubies, and sapphires; and a majestic golden eagle chandelier presiding over everything. The hidden room was the perfect place for a robbery stakeout. The display counters and the front door were visible. The robbers walking into the establishment from Rodeo Drive were within gun range.

His iPhone vibrated. A text message read: *they just left the motel and are on their way.* He showed the message to Zepeda, seated on a stool balancing a Remington 12-gauge shotgun across his lap and eating peanuts out of a small cellophane bag. Zepeda slipped the bag into his jacket pocket.

A minute later, the front door of the jewelry store swung open and three masked robbers ran inside and began shooting. The sound of rapid gunfire and shattering glass mixed with that of a siren wailing. Casey was in the speeding ambulance choking on his own blood. The next day, Chief of Police Slade woke him in his room at Cedars-Sinai and whispered to him that Zepeda had been killed by "friendly fire," a bullet from Casey's own gun, and that she believed Casey needed the truth but that no one else had to know.

He got out of bed, walked to the kitchen, and drank two shots of Seagram's V.O. whiskey, hoping to drop off to sleep without another rerun of the trauma dream. Returning to bed, he picked up the TV remote control from the nightstand and browsed channels. Stopping on a boxing match, he watched fighters display good footwork, head movement, feinting, and jabbing while an overly zealous referee kept breaking up clinches and giving unnecessary commands. Neither fighter had enough punching power to win. The key to the sport was being able to knock out an opponent. No champion ever won a belt without having a knockout punch.

He stopped next on the biography channel and watched an old interview with Gloria Channing. Seated on a sofa in front of a movie poster depicting her alone in a European train station, she was interviewed by a young man wearing aqua designer eyeglasses. She talked about the five days she spent filming a drowning scene at the Burbank Studios water tank, festival groupies she'd met when filming a horror movie in a producer's Lake Como home, and a director who demanded the actors take vitamin pills each morning during the shoot. Bored with the entertainment industry bullshit and feeling the effect of the whiskey, Casey pressed the OFF button on the remote. Closing his eyes, he hoped to drop into slumber.

CHAPTER ELEVEN

Marty Vollero drove north on Interstate Highway 5 near Dodger Stadium, veered right onto the off-ramp, and followed Los Feliz Boulevard west to Vermont Avenue. Turning right onto Observatory Drive, he drove up a hill to the entrance of Griffith Park, the largest urban park in the United States and one of the few spaces in Los Angeles that wasn't covered by buildings or asphalt. Past the Greek Theater, an outdoor amphitheater used for summer concerts and other events, he parked his car across the street opposite the theater box office and cautiously looked about. His experience as a Beverly Hills police officer had taught him to be aware of his surroundings. He glanced at his wristwatch, a gold banded Patek Philippe Calatrava. He was on time for the meeting, but he expected Wanda Troxell to be late. As a rule, he didn't trust anyone, and she was a "smokehead," which only further limited his trust in her.

His aunt told him as a child that his cynical outlook stemmed first from his father and then his mother abandoning him at an early age. As Vollero saw it, whatever the reason, attentiveness benefited him. Fifteen minutes later, staring in the rearview mirror, he saw the silver Porsche park behind him. Wanda was behind the wheel. She got out wearing white shorts and a matching halter top, walked to his car, opened the passenger door, and got in.

She said, "Do you have something against meeting at a nice restaurant or a bar?"

"I've explained the situation to you more than once."

"No one is going to see us together. Even if they did, there's no law against talking to someone."

"Someone seeing us together gives them the opportunity to make up stories."

If she were to get arrested and testify that he'd paid her to break into houses and businesses to gather information for him, he'd deny it and claim he'd never met her. It would be strictly his word against hers. He wanted to avoid witnesses taking the stand and corroborating their meetings. Looking at reality from a jury's point of view was a security practice that had served him well.

She smiled pallidly. "Like someone might not see you when you come over to my house and fuck me?"

"I park my car around the corner."

"Someone could see you walk in the front door."

"You and I have a successful business relationship. I laid out the rules. You agreed. Now that you're on easy street, driving a new Porsche, do you really want to risk all that?"

"You're the one living in a big house in the Hills, not me."

"Wanda, you called and told me you had a problem. I've taken the time to get in my car and drive here. But I have a busy schedule and I don't have time to play games."

"All I said was why can't we talk somewhere other than in a fucking car?"

"I'm here to help, Wanda. I'm listening."

"Two Beverly Hills pigs came to my house."

"Names?"

"Detective Casey and his female partner. I forgot her name."

Surprised and concerned, Vollero said, "So what did the detectives want?"

"They asked about the transmitter I installed in Gloria Channing's kitchen. When I laid on the cover story about buying the phone, they didn't buy it."

The hair on the back of his neck tingled. "What makes you think that?"

"They called me a liar. And they had a picture of me in the telephone store."

She'd probably smoked a lid of dope beforehand.

"I told you to have someone else buy the cell phone."

"I needed the money and just wanted to get the job done. I'm not perfect like you, Marty."

"I'm disappointed."

"You told me planting the bug involved nothing but a civil case. The cops said two people were murdered. If I would have known that I'd have told you to find someone else to take care of your shitty little errand. I didn't know this would turn out to be some murder thing. I had no idea. You lied to me."

"Why the attitude?"

"Because the cops are trying to frame my ass."

"They were bluffing."

"Don't sit there like some know-it-all. The pigs told me I'm going to need a lawyer."

"They have nothing."

"You have no way of knowing that."

"I was a cop, baby. I know their game."

"First of all, I'm not your baby. And second, you're not talking to some rich lady who lost her cat. I'm in trouble. The cops weren't just blowing smoke. They are going to come back and try to get me to talk. They are going to fuck with me. I could see it in their eyes. They're fixing to lay shit on me. You've gone and got me involved in a big, fucking murder twist."

She was high. He'd warned her about getting high and making mistakes.

"When was the last time you used?"

"Marty, whether I have a taste now and then is none of your business. You don't own me. And I'm not your fool. Dope is a way for me to relieve anxiety.... Another way is for people to pay what they owe me so I can make my fucking house payment. That would be a real stress reliever. You owe me five thousand dollars for planting the transmitter, and now I'm in trouble for doing something for you that I haven't been paid for. I'm being royally fucked, and I don't like it."

"Have I ever not paid you?"

"Slow pay is no pay. And while we're at it, what happened with Bobby Lanza? Did you know he was gonna get gunned down at Channing's house? Since I'm the one in the damn hot seat, I think I have a right to know."

For the past couple of years, she'd been a valuable tool in helping him build his business. He'd chosen to use her because of her reputation for keeping her mouth shut. Others had warned him about her mean streak. He'd never seen it but had noticed signs that she was using OxyContin again. He'd never seen her this worked up. Now that he had, he recognized her attitude as dangerous. He could see that Wanda wasn't going to take a fall—not for anyone.

"I give you my word that when I offered you the Channing transmitter job, I had no idea anything was going to happen to Lanza. I didn't even know Lanza was staying at Channing's house. What happened to him was as much of a shock to me as it was to you. The bug I asked you to plant had nothing to do with any murder. It related to a movie contract between Gloria Channing and her movie studio. It was strictly a routine business dispute thing."

"I want my money."

"I'll have the cash I owe you day after tomorrow. And thanks for bringing this to my attention, Wanda. I'm tied up on working a big case in Palmdale and realize I failed to take the time to explain things to you as I should have."

"I don't want the cops putting this murder on me."

"Avoid them."

"They walked in on me, Marty. And they were pushy. They seemed hot to make an arrest. They probably think they'll get promoted for solving the murders."

"You'll get your money, and I'm adding a bonus for the stress I've caused you."

She cocked her head. "How much?"

"Another grand."

"Make it two."

"Okay. Total of seven grand. You deserve it. In the meantime, avoid talking to the cops."

"You don't have to tell me that. I'm not stupid."

He said, "Are you interested in an easy job that would benefit you personally?"

"You know I need money. What's the gig?"

"An apartment."

"What's in it?"

"A personal item belonging to the tenant."

She asked what he meant by a personal item.

"Something that if found somewhere else could be traced to him—a printed identification card, a key, or some personal jewelry item the police could later easily trace back to him."

"Sounds to me like you're trying to frame someone."

"I call it routine private investigative work. I need a yes or no."

"What's in it for me?" she asked.

"Five grand."

"Where's the apartment?"

"Near UCLA."

"I'll take it."

He took out a gold fountain pen, uncapped it, and copied an address from his cell phone onto a blank 3 x 5 notecard. Handing the card to her, he slipped the pen back into his shirt pocket.

She stared at the address. "Who lives in the apartment?"

"Detective Casey. You can get inside and do what's necessary while he's on duty."

"What do you have planned for him?

"Something that will be to your benefit, Wanda."

She smiled. "Marty, the way you always seem to have something up your sleeve is creepy."

"Relax."

"I'll call you when I have the goods."

"I look forward to hearing from you, baby."

"Marty, I don't like it when we argue. I hate that tone you get in your voice."

"This will all blow over soon and things will be back to good ol' normal."

"I hope so." She opened the passenger door and got out of the car.

In the rearview mirror, Vollero watched her walk to her Porsche and get in. She made a U-turn, drove south toward Vermont, and out of the park. He appreciated her bluntness. And he didn't have to do any cogitating about what course to take with her. The talented, valuable, and closemouthed burglar Wanda Troxell had become a clear and present danger.

CHAPTER TWELVE

Casey steered the sedan into the underground garage at the ten-story Switzer Garden apartments in Wilshire Boulevard's "Condo Canyon." He and Sutherland got out in a marked visitor's space on the first level and took the elevator to Meredith Fox's seventh-floor condominium. Sutherland knocked. A minute later, Anthony Flair opened it holding an oversized Superman coffee mug.

"Sorry to bother you, Anthony," Sutherland said, "but I have a few more questions."

Flair said, "Have you figured out who did it?"

"Not yet," Sutherland said. She introduced Casey as her partner. "May we come in?"

"Uh, I was just leaving."

"This won't take long," she said. Casey followed her inside.

Looking unsettled, Anthony Flair closed the door. His hair was pulled up in a man bun. His face and arms had a burnt orange sunlamp tint. He wore fitted jeans, ostrich leather boots, and a sleeves-rolled designer T-shirt outlining puffed biceps, oversized pectorals, and abdominal muscles. Casey assumed his unusual torso and bulging eyes were the result of steroids.

Flair said, "I'm still in a state of shock over what happened. I've been in a fog, trying to figure out what it all means."

"I'm sorry to hear that, Anthony," Sutherland said. "Mind if we sit?"

Flair motioned to a black sofa. They sat. Flair sat on a matching sofa facing them. "The last time we spoke, I asked you about the .38-caliber revolver found in Meredith's car."

"She bought the gun for protection after being robbed while she shopped on Rodeo Drive and then took some shooting lessons with it at the Beverly Hills Gun Club."

"Yes," Sutherland said. "I checked the department files. Meredith never filed a robbery report."

"I'm just going by what she told me. A lot of people in Beverly Hills carry guns for protection."

"No doubt."

"Detective, is Meredith's murder…solvable? Will you eventually be able to make an arrest?"

"That's the plan," Sutherland said.

Flair fidgeted. "Like soon?"

"That depends," she said. "So far we've spent a lot of time talking to those who knew her. We're taking things by the numbers, being as thorough as possible. We've learned a lot about Meredith. The people we've interviewed have been very helpful. Because we don't want to get in a hurry and miss some important detail, we're taking our time."

"Meredith knew a lot of people, but she was lonely."

Casey said, "Is that what she told you?"

"Not in those exact words."

Casey thought Flair looked uncomfortable.

"Then how did you form the opinion?" Casey said.

Flair looked taken aback, irritated at the question. "For one thing, she hated small talk. Meredith was all business."

"How do you mean?" Casey asked.

"I auditioned for the lead role in the remake of *Son of Spartacus*, but it didn't work out. I told Meredith. She used her studio connections to get me a role in a Salome Vergara movie called *Risotto Vacation*. It was my first and only role. In a scene filmed at Burbank Studios, I played a bistro waiter who served Vergara a tray of oysters when she was sitting at a sidewalk table in Verona. Meredith told me it was going to be a speaking part, but it didn't turn out that way. I was convinced Meredith was my ticket to Hollywood success, but once when she was in a bad mood she told me she considered me nothing but a quality piece of ass."

Maintaining a straight face, Sutherland said, "How did that make you feel?"

Flair sipped from the coffee mug. "Sometimes I think I should accept that she was just using me to impress her business contacts. I still can't imagine Meredith getting murdered. Now I doubt everything." He smirked. "But I had nothing to lose by moving in here with her."

Casey said, "When did you first meet Wanda Troxell?"

Flair studied him momentarily before saying, "The name doesn't ring a bell."

"That's strange," Casey said. "She knows you."

"She told you that?"

"Anthony," Sutherland said, "we didn't come here to answer questions, just to ask them."

Flair said, "Well, *la di da*."

Casey said, "Do you think this is a game?"

"Me?"

"We're looking for Meredith Fox's killer. Usually, the only people who don't want to help are on the suspect list."

"I find your questions disorienting."

Sutherland said, "Lying to the police is a crime, Anthony. People get put in jail."

"I'm not lying."

"What's your relationship with Wanda Troxell?" Casey said.

"What did she say about me?"

Casey said, "Why not just answer the question?"

"I might have hooked up with her one night."

"You don't remember?" Sutherland said.

"I own the Greenroom on Sunset Boulevard. Wanda is one of hundreds of women I've met there when they stop in for a drink. I get along with women, and sometimes I take them home. In my book, fucking a few female customers is one of the benefits of owning a bar."

Casey said, "What do you know about Wanda?"

Flair blinked rapidly. "Unless I'm mistaken, she orders chardonnay wine spritzers. That's about it."

"Why the games?" Casey said.

"I'm not playing any—"

"I'd think a big, successful businessman like you," Sutherland interrupted, "would want to help us catch the person who murdered his lady."

"Where does it say that I know anything about this shit? You're talking to the wrong guy. The newspaper said Meredith was the likely victim of a carjacker."

There was a long silence, during which Flair sat staring at the detectives.

Casey said, "Thanks for your time."

"What, that's all?"

"Do you have anything to add?"

Flair said, "I think somebody mentioned to me that Wanda once got arrested in Beverly Hills."

Sutherland smiled demurely. "Not exactly a news flash," she said.

Casey said, "Does the name Bobby Lanza mean anything to you?"

"Nope."

"He was killed at Gloria Channing's house," Casey said.

"Oh yeah, Channing's ex-husband. I think I read something about that online."

Casey decided he was being too cautious, that the investigation needed a boost.

"Anthony," Casey said, "I'm going to tell you something, a fact that if it got out could harm the investigation."

"I won't say a word."

"The same weapon may have been used to kill both Meredith Fox and Bobby Lanza."

Flair licked his lips. "Now I feel like I'm living in some kind of horror movie."

"If there's anything you've been holding back," Sutherland said, "now is the time to spit it out."

"I've told you everything."

"Did Meredith ever mention Bobby Lanza's name to you?" Sutherland asked.

"No."

Casey said, "A lot of information has been coming in on the case. We've learned a great deal about the homicide victims. In fact, we're learning more about them every day."

Flair cleared his throat. "I think Meredith knew Lanza."

"What was their relationship?"

Flair sipped coffee. "I'm not sure."

Casey said nothing. He and Sutherland would wait.

"The, uh, first time I met Bobby Lanza was when he came here one night to see Meredith."

Sutherland said, "She introduced you to him?"

"She didn't even tell me his name. She said they needed to talk in private and asked me to leave—not just go to another room but leave the condo so they could talk in private—so I went outside and took a walk. When I got back, Lanza was gone."

"What did Meredith tell you about him?" Casey said.

"Nothing."

Sutherland said, "Really, now? You didn't ask her what the hell was going on?"

"She told me she had a right to her own secrets and that she didn't like the idea of me pressing her for information. She told me what they were talking about was none of my business."

"She filled you in," Casey spoke scornfully.

"What you believe or don't believe means nothing to me."

"You were her man, Anthony," Sutherland said. "She told you everything. That's the way things work."

"Meredith said Lanza was divorced from Gloria Channing and that Channing won an Academy Award because the reviewers fell in love with the scene in her first movie where she was gang-raped by the African tribesmen working for the big-game hunter—"

"Cut the bullshit," Casey said.

Flair glowered at him. "Meredith told me she and Bobby were involved in some business deal. She didn't say what, just that they were making money together and it was their secret, and she wasn't going to tell me because she'd promised not to tell. There. That's all I know."

"*Making money together?*" Casey said. "That doesn't sound like the way people talk."

"Well, that's what she said."

"What did it mean to you?" Casey said.

"That they were working a deal, money. I didn't press her for information. I'm not investigating anything. I could give a flying fuck what Meredith was up to with Lanza."

Casey saw Anthony Flair as one of a hundred thousand other showbiz hangers-on existing in their own personal reality show, dreamers nourished by social media, dope, and wishful thinking. He also saw him as a wormy Hollywood dope dealer.

Sutherland smiled. "Why didn't you say that earlier?"

"Because I don't want to get involved, that's why. I have enough problems. Since what happened to Meredith, I've been in a fog, walking around in a circle asking myself what it all means. Look, if you don't have any other questions, I need to get busy. I'm moving out of here today and have things to do."

"Where are you going?"

"I've rented a place near the Beverly Center."

Casey exchanged a glance with Sutherland.

"We'll be going now," Sutherland said.

"No more questions?"

"For now," she said. "Sorry for bursting in on you unannounced."

Casey and Sutherland stood to leave.

"Will someone notify me when you arrest the person who murdered Meredith?"

"You'll be the first to know," Casey said.

They walked to the elevator landing. Casey pressed the call button. The doors opened. They got on. The doors closed.

"*I've been in a fog*," Sutherland said, mimicking Flair, "*trying to figure out what it all means.*"

"He might as well have 'Dope Dealer' tattooed on his forehead."

"Where do you see him fitting in, Legs?"

"He was living with a Hollywood publicist who had to know about the blackmail game."

"Him and his stupid-looking man bun. If he took off that rubber band, a thousand insects would probably fly out."

Casey smiled. "You're talking about an actor who played in a scene with Salome Vergara."

"Well, excuse me."

CHAPTER THIRTEEN

Dr. Desmond Eckersley left his office at the end of the day and drove along Malibu Canyon while Debussy's "Prelude to the Afternoon of a Fawn" emanated from the powerful stereo speakers in his Mercedes-Benz AMG sedan. He believed classical music facilitated creative thinking. Reaching the Pacific Coast Highway, he slipped on his Persol sunglasses to shield himself from the eye-singeing pink twilight illuminating the coastline. He turned north and a minute later he reached a mini mall frequented by residents of the nearby Malibu movie colony. He saw Marty Vollero's bright yellow Audi Spyder parked in front of a vegetarian restaurant. Vollero was seated behind the wheel, waiting for him.

Eckersley parked next to the Audi; turned off the engine.

Vollero got out of his car and into the Benz. "Greetings, Doctor."

"I like your wheels."

"I had it up to a hundred fifty miles per hour last week."

"I'll bet you did."

Vollero took out his gold cigarette case and lighter.

"No smoking," Eckersley said.

"I forgot."

"Not really."

Eckersley considered Vollero boorish and vulgar, but he valued his punctuality and attention to detail. He'd first retained him after receiving a threatening letter from a former patient. Vollero handled the problem by having the letter writer arrested. Recognizing Vollero's potential in the game of celebrity tag, Eckersley had cautiously asked him whether he'd be interested in "consulting on sensitive celebrity matters." Vollero quickly grasped what he was getting at. Their business relationship was cemented when Vollero delivered him his cut of shakedown money paid by one of Eckersley's clients, a successful and loquacious male star of romance movies who'd been arrested for raping a young girl and managed to hide the incident from the press.

Vollero slipped the cigarette case and lighter back into his shirt pocket. "What's this valuable information you have for me?"

"First things first," Eckersley said. "What's the latest on the homicide investigations?"

"The Beverly Hills cops have nothing. Detectives are walking around confused."

"How can you be sure?"

"People tell me things."

"Beverly Hills police officers?"

"Take it from me, Doctor. You and I have absolutely nothing to worry about."

Eckersley said, "That's the same thing you told me before you brought Fox and Lanza into our tent."

"When faced with celebrity refuseniks, Meredith Fox was our insurance. She knew the biz and was there to sell secrets to the scandal sheets at the market price. Sure, I cut her in. But what we got in exchange was her expertise in dealing with a backup market for us. And, at the time, Lanza was a reliable errand boy who handled sticky situations so that you and I didn't have to get our hands dirty."

"Reliable?" Eckersley said.

"No one could have predicted that he'd get greedy and begin rehashing our victims. Or that he would be able to talk Meredith into going along with him."

"They rocked the boat."

"And I fixed the problem once and for all," Vollero said angrily.

"They took money out of our pockets, Marty."

"What is this, a straightening session?"

Eckersley disliked getting together with Vollero but recognized that when it came to discussing business, telephone conversations and even cleverly coded email messages were too risky. He knew that many of the biggest celebrities and entertainment lawyers overlooked Vollero's less-than-stellar reputation so they might utilize his ability to successfully gather sensitive information on wives, husbands, and business enemies. He was a known quantity and the only private eye who somehow managed to illegally wiretap homes and businesses without getting caught. Defense lawyers regularly used the wily ex-cop to create believable fictitious information they used in court to free criminal defendants. Eckersley saw him for what he was: a useful sociopath focused on becoming as rich as the people he was blackmailing. His knowledge of both the Hollywood underworld and the celebrity overworld was invaluable.

"Not at all, Marty."

"For a moment there, I thought you'd gotten me confused with one of your fucked-up, incest-bred clients."

"Nothing personal—I'm here to discuss business. I'm only pointing out that Fox and Lanza might very well have brought us down."

Vollero smirked. "When I told you I could convince Lanza to kill Meredith, you didn't believe me."

"It didn't seem logical."

"I thought psychiatrists were supposed to be able to predict human behavior."

"I never said—"

"Lanza jumped at the chance," Vollero said. "The two cockroaches have been eliminated. The ship is back on course and the headline is 'POLICE BAFFLED.' Our business is in the black. And you never so much as even met Fox or Lanza. You have nothing to worry about."

"Marty, you could have been a psychiatrist."

"Impossible."

"Why?"

"I'm not crazy enough."

"But you'll never make it as a comedian," Eckersley said with a gracious smile.

"So, what's this important development you said you have for me, Doctor?"

"It's about Norman Molitor's latest sex slave: the beautiful Vivienne Kalen-Boudreaux."

"I can't bear the suspense."

"Vivienne has made her decision for Christ."

"Another home run," Vollero said. "How sweet it is."

"A word of warning: she made a point of sharing her concern about being hit with a rehash."

"I'll be sure to emphasize that I'm talking a one and done. And we can wait a couple of months before hitting her with a sequel."

Eckersley smiled. "If she has any doubts about what to do, she can talk things over with her psychiatrist."

Vollero laughed. "It pays to seek the advice of a professional." He glanced at his wristwatch. "It's time for me to get back to the office." He grasped the door handle. "Don't let those crazy millionaires get you down."

"Have no fear."

Vollero got out of the car and closed the door. Eckersley accelerated out of the driveway onto the Pacific Coast Highway with the breeze rushing in through the windows. For a split second, he imagined Aspen in February, cutting easily through fresh, powdered snow on an early morning downhill ski run.

CHAPTER FOURTEEN

At 7:00 a.m., Casey drove by Anthony Flair's red Chevrolet Camaro parked on Ogden Drive in Hollywood, in front of the well-kept, pale-green house Flair had moved into the day before. It had a large front porch, a front lawn, and a garage. A few years earlier, before large foreign conglomerates stopped building homes and instead cornered the market on rental property, it would have been considered middle-class affordable. Now it was considered upscale. As in most of LA, cars lined the streets because there weren't enough garages.

Casey parked his sedan in the middle of the block, the only available space. Keeping an eye on the Camaro, he used his police radio to check with Officer Mark Fukunaga, who was parked in a police cruiser around the corner on Stanley Avenue. Casey spent some time writing in his log report for the previous day, then turned on the commercial radio and listened to jazz while reading internet news on his cell phone.

At 2:06 p.m., Anthony Flair exited the front door. Casey picked up the radio microphone and thumbed the transmit button.

"Exiting to the Camaro."

"Roger," Fukunaga said.

Flair got in the Camaro, started the engine, and drove north toward Sunset Boulevard.

Casey said, "Coming your way."

The Camaro stopped at the corner stop sign and then turned left. Seconds later, Fukunaga's police car rounded the corner onto Sunset Boulevard. Remaining at a distance, Casey trailed Fukunaga as he followed Flair west. A few minutes later, the Camaro crossed the

Hollywood border into Beverly Hills. Fukunaga turned on the cruiser's red light and sped close to the Camaro's rear bumper. The Camaro swerved to the curb and stopped.

Casey parked in front of a furniture store on Sunset. Through his binoculars he saw Fukunaga get out of the police car, walk to the Camaro, and lean down to the driver's window to speak with Flair, who handed him his driver's license. They talked for a minute. A second squad car arrived and parked next to Fukunaga's car. A uniformed officer got out with a German shepherd on a leash. The officer walked the dog around the Camaro for a while. The dog sat near the trunk.

Fukunaga ordered Flair out of the Camaro. Flair complied. Fukunaga searched the trunk, removed a brown paper sack, opened it, and showed the contents to Flair, who turned around and put his hands behind his back. Fukunaga handcuffed him, led him to the other squad car, and opened the rear door. Flair got in. Fukunaga closed the door. The K-9 officer and the dog got in the front seat and drove off with Flair.

Seconds later, Casey received a text message from Fukunaga that read: *TWO OZ COCAINE, LOADED .45 IN TRUNK.*

In the multistory Los Angeles County Jail, an imposing gray edifice near Union Station in downtown Los Angeles, a sliding door of bars opened in the visiting area. Anthony Flair, in jail denim, walked up to a raised desk and handed a printed form to a uniformed sheriff's deputy. The deputy glanced at the paperwork and pointed him toward a wall of cubicles used by law enforcement officials for interviewing jail inmates. Flair walked to private cubicle eight. The door was open. Casey was sitting at a table.

"Come in," he said.

Flair, pale and needing a shave, didn't move.

"Who told you I'd been arrested?"

"I saw your name on the department arrest log."

"A cop named Fukunaga pulled me over. He had a dog sniff my car for marching powder."

"I read the report."

"You had me arrested."

"Why would I do that?"

"You think I know who murdered Meredith. You think I'm holding back information."

"Sit down, Anthony."

Flair didn't sit. "This is nothing but a squeeze play."

"It's a friendly visit."

"I don't have to talk to you."

"Anthony, you know you have nothing to lose by listening to what I have to say."

"If you think I'm some punk who goes around spilling the beans, you're wrong."

"Sorry to have bothered you, Anthony."

"What?'

"You heard me."

If Flair meant what he was saying, all he had to do was walk out of the interview room. He was acting.

"That's it?"

"If you don't want to sit down and chat for a minute or two, you can return to your cellblock."

"I'm not…I'm not saying I might not be willing to do something." Flair walked in, sat at the table, and formed his hands into a steeple. "Okay, what's in it for me?"

"Help with your dope case."

"Because I had a prior arrest for sales, I need this case to disappear. Otherwise, it's not worth me sticking my neck out."

"Everything depends on what you have to offer."

Flair swallowed dryly. "Bobby Lanza hung out at the Greenroom. He would come in and run his mouth trying to convince everyone he was a slick Hollywood dude, an insider instead of a born loser. He was all about maintaining a smokescreen. He'd talk about having speaking parts in movies, but it was all a lie—a false front. The closest he ever got to a movie set was driving Gloria Channing to a studio lot. He had no friends. He'd brag about having been to dinner with this or that celebrity. Later, when the celebrity would come in, I'd ask them about Lanza and they'd tell me they'd never heard of him. When people questioned his bullshit, he never got embarrassed. That was Bobby Lanza, a no-pride stiff. People either laughed behind his back or squawked about money he owed them. His claim to fame was having once been married to Gloria Channing, who is nothing but a has-been."

"Who killed him?"

"What makes you think I would know that? Why are you asking me this shit?"

"You get around," Casey said. "You talk to people. I'm betting you've heard something."

Flair licked his lips. "Lemme get this straight. If I help you, then you will have the district attorney wash my dope case?"

"That's how it works."

Chewing on his lower lip for a moment, Flair said, "The word on the street is that Lanza got in a cross with someone—an argument over some loot. That's how he got killed."

Casey said, "Do you expect me to talk the district attorney into unlocking the door for that?"

After a long pause, Casey glanced at his wristwatch. A look of concern crossed Flair's face.

"I don't know whether this has anything to do with it, but for the past year or so, Bobby was asking a lot of questions about this or that celebrity."

"He was looking for dirt?"

"Movie actors come into the Greenroom. Bobby thought I knew all of them on a first-name basis. Sure, I know some celebrities. But it's not as if they call me up every night and ask me to dinner."

"Why would Bobby Lanza be seeking information about movie stars from anyone?"

"I got the impression he was looking for shakedown goodies, something he might use for a twist."

"Blackmail?"

"That doesn't mean he was. I'm offering up the facts as I know them. It was a constant topic for him. But Bobby was always asking questions. And in the past couple of months, instead of waiting for someone to pick up the tab, he was throwing money around, buying rounds of drinks, and coming in with high-maintenance broads."

"You think he was collecting some payoff?"

"He bought a couple of new cars—for cash. Some of the regular customers were under the impression that he was shaking down movie stars. That was the talk. But I didn't believe it."

"Why?"

"Because I hear that kind of thing all the time and also because I didn't think Lanza had the brainpower or the balls to pull off a big celebrity shakedown."

"Who were his partners?"

"He never mentioned any."

Flair's eyes rolled upward now and then as he spoke, his body language indicating deception. As an actor, he'd never be in line for an Academy Award. Casey took out the sex photographs found in Lanza's car and put them on the table.

"The photos were found during the homicide investigation. Do you recognize the woman?"

Flair smiled. "No, but I'd like to meet her. By the way, are you still interested in Wanda Troxell?"

Casey picked up the photographs, slipped them back into his jacket. He wasn't going to give Flair the opportunity to play the stool pigeon game by manipulating insignificant bits of truth into self-serving lies. Flair either knew something or he didn't.

"Is there something you want to tell me about her?"

"At the moment, the word on the street is that she might have been working with Lanza."

"Doing what?"

"Setting up blackmail capers."

"How?"

"By helping him frame some celebrity marks."

"Who are we talking about?"

"Uh, I don't have any specifics. But it involved breaking into movie stars' homes to steal secrets and plant microphones, that kind of thing. Wanda's first old man taught her the locksmith game. For her Beverly Hills jobs, she always had inside information. When she is on her way to do a burglary, she dresses like a housekeeper and takes a bus. She walks out with the swag in her purse and gets on a bus again. She never uses a car."

"What else do you know about Lanza?"

"Nothing."

"Anthony, that's not enough information to get you out of jail. You're playing games. If you want to get out of jail, you're going to have to dig a lot deeper."

"Look, there's only so much I can do to help you while I'm locked in a cell."

"What are you saying?"

"People talk to me. They tell me things. And when I ask questions, they know they can trust me. I have a good rep."

"What's your point?"

"If you'll agree to get my case dismissed and let me out, I can find out who murdered Bobby Lanza."

The offer made sense. Flair was connected to the murder victims, and Casey had engineered the arrest to get him to tell what he knew. Casey saw nothing to lose.

"How long would it take you to get the scoop?"

"Maybe a day or two."

Casey had more than one LA County deputy district attorney who owed him favors. And asking for help in solving a murder was never an unreasonable request. He guessed the odds of Flair coming up with enough information to solve the Lanza murder as fifty-fifty. Considering that the longer the case lingered the more difficult it would be to solve, and that putting the case on Flair had been relatively easy, Casey decided to take the bet.

"Here's the deal: I get you out. If you get me enough information to solve the Bobby Lanza murder, I'll have the charges against you dismissed. If you don't come through, you ride the cocaine beef without help."

"You set me up," Flair said, staring vapidly at him. "That's why I'm in here, right?"

"You weren't framed. And by cooperating now, you have everything to gain."

"If I come up with the goods, you'll have my dope possession case dismissed from the docket?"

"That's what I'm telling you."

"I'll take the deal."

"When you hit the street, call me every day."

"No problem." Flair got up from the chair. "But I still think I'm getting hosed."

Flair walked from the cubicle to the cellblock door. The visiting room deputy pressed a button. The door of bars slowly opened.

Trudging through the cellblock doorway, he turned and glanced back at Casey as the door closed.

Casey walked to a door on the other side of the visiting area. A guard unlocked the door. Exiting the visiting area, Casey crossed the lobby to the jail administration office. He wrote Anthony Flair's name on a printed Law Enforcement Information Request Form and handed it to an attractive uniformed deputy who came to the security window. She took off her eyeglasses.

"Hi, Legs."

"Dora."

Dora and some of her female friends, all cops, were regulars at the Nightwatch, a popular East LA cop bar.

"I look different when I wear glasses, don't I?

"You look beautiful either way."

"Where are you hanging out these days, smooth talker?"

"Nowhere. I've been tied up on a case."

She slipped the eyeglasses back on to read the administrative form, then touched keys on a computer keyboard. The printer activated. She tore printed paper from the machine, dropped it into the security box, and pushed the box toward him. He took the paper; read it. Anthony Flair had only one visitor since being booked into custody: Martin Vollero. Casey felt like cheering.

"Thanks, Dora."

"Last Friday night was a big retirement party at the Nightwatch. All the regulars were there. How long until you clear that case you're working?"

"It can't go on forever."

"After I gave you my telephone number, you never called me."

"Uh, I was married at the time."

"My phone number hasn't changed, smooth talker."

"Thanks, Dora," he said and then walked toward the exit.

CHAPTER FIFTEEN

At 2:30 a.m., Casey was driving east on Sunset Boulevard near Crescent Heights. Because of the hour, the usual heavy nighttime traffic had dissipated. It had been a week since Casey arranged with the district attorney's office to have Flair released from the county jail on a personal recognizance bond. Flair had called him once, a few hours after being freed, to report that he'd made some phone calls to people he believed might have information. Since then, Flair wasn't answering his cell phone or returning email messages.

On his right, the Greenroom cocktail bar had no sign, only a stenciled letter G over the door—a clever advertising touch that made customers think it was a celebrity haunt. Because of the hour, customers were exiting and walking to their cars. Casey made a right turn at the end of the block, then another right into an alley leading behind the bar. Anthony Flair's Camaro was near the rear exit.

Casey parked his unmarked police car near it and watched the last few customers depart the bar. Forty-six minutes later, Flair came out, stunned to see him there.

"What are you doing here?"

"We had a deal."

Flair glanced about as if to see if anyone was close enough to hear what he was saying.

"I was just going to call you."

"You have something?"

"I'm working on some leads."

"Don't say I didn't give you a chance."

"What does that mean?"

"The deal is off, Anthony. You'd better hire a lawyer."

"I swear to you I'm being straight."

"You're on your own."

Lowering his voice, Flair said, "Wanda Troxell…she knows who killed Lanza."

"Who told you that?"

Whispering angrily, Flair said, "I promised to gather information for you, not rat out my sources."

"More games?"

"I'm honestly doing my best."

Casey said, "What makes you believe you're smarter than everyone?"

"Bobby Lanza owed Wanda money."

After a pause, Casey said, "Here we go again, inch at a time."

"Lanza owed her a cut from one of the celebrity shakedowns. Now that he's dead, Wanda is trying to collect what she's owed from Lanza's partner in the shakedown business."

"I don't hear a name."

Flair spoke hesitantly, as if he knew Casey might not believe him. "I'm working on that. I swear."

"That's all?"

"The way the blackmail guy delivers cash to Wanda is to drop money somewhere and then call her and tell her where to pick it up. He doesn't trust anyone. The cat-and-mouse stuff is the guy's way of not getting caught."

"Sounds fishy."

"My source is reliable," Flair said.

"What else does your *source* say about Lanza's partner in the blackmail business?"

"Just that they were doing some heavy deals. I'm talking six-figure scores."

"Did Lanza's partner kill him?"

"That's possible."

"And so is reincarnation."

"I'm working for you every minute of the day. It's not my fault that what I'm finding out comes in dribs and drabs."

"You've given me nothing."

"I just found out that the blackmail guy who was working with Lanza is meeting with Wanda tonight. He's going to meet with her for dinner."

"Where?"

"At the Chez Dominique."

Casey knew of the place but had never been there. "The restaurant in Topanga Canyon?"

"That's the only one I know of."

"What's going to happen there?"

"Lanza's partner, whomever he is, is supposed to pay Wanda what she is owed."

"Not exactly a smoking gun."

"That's not my fault. I'm working my ass off to fulfill my part of the bargain."

"Keep your ears open," Casey said coldly.

"Can I go now?"

"See you soon."

Flair walked to his car, got in, and drove out of the alley. Casey didn't like the sound of the information and he didn't trust Anthony Flair, but if Wanda Troxell was meeting with someone who'd been involved with Lanza, Casey needed to identify him.

—

Casey drove by the Chez Dominique restaurant in the Santa Monica Mountains near Topanga Canyon Boulevard on Riding Trail Avenue, an upscale log cabin big enough to seat a hundred diners. Sutherland was following him in an unmarked city Toyota. He parked off the road just south, out of sight of anyone in the restaurant or its parking lot. Sutherland parked behind him. They got out of their cars and locked them before trudging north through the woods to a vantage point providing a clear view of the Chez Dominique restaurant and its parking lot filled with luxury cars.

Sutherland took binoculars from her purse and focused them on the restaurant.

"She's here," she said as she handed Casey the binoculars.

He raised them to his eyes. Through the large restaurant windows, he could see customers at tables inside. Wanda Troxell was sitting alone at a table near the front door.

"Flair's information is on the money so far," he said, lowering the binoculars, "but I still don't trust him."

"Neither do I."

"I can't figure out what he's up to."

Sutherland said, "Maybe he's really trying to get his case dismissed."

"Then why the games?"

"Your guess is as good as mine, Legs."

"We could be on a wild goose chase here. Maybe he doesn't know a damn thing. Maybe he knows Wanda and told her to come here."

She said, "If we're lucky, some new player will show up. Hell, maybe she's waiting for Marty Vollero."

"If Wanda told Flair she was meeting a blackmail player here, it means Flair is in on the game."

Sutherland said, "I read somewhere that the owner of this restaurant is a TV sitcom star who paid an architect a million dollars to design the exterior to complement the environment."

"A log cabin and acre of trees cut down for a parking lot doesn't sound like a green idea to me."

Sutherland said, "Guess who called me on the drive up."

"Dollinger?"

"He asked how the case was going. I told him that we were still plugging away. Then he asked how you and I were getting along. When I said okay, he asked me if you were drinking liquor during duty hours. When I said you weren't, he seemed miffed, as if he doubted my word. Then he told me not to tell you he'd called."

He nodded. "Thanks for trusting me enough to tell me."

He liked Sutherland. But he wasn't sure she wasn't reporting to Dollinger. Casey had seen such betrayals in high-pressure investigations. Then he scotched the thought as foolish. If he couldn't trust Sutherland, he couldn't trust anyone in the department.

She said, "If the situation were reversed, you'd tell me."

"Without hesitation."

"So, what do you think is going on, Legs?"

"Chief Slade assigned me to this case. Maybe Dollinger is trying to prove she made a mistake."

"I can see him doing that."

He said, "I thought you and Dollinger got along."

She elevated her eyebrows. "What's that supposed to mean?"

"Just that he wouldn't have assigned the Meredith Fox homicide to someone he didn't trust."

"Maybe. But a couple of months ago, I complained to him that he was giving all the big cases to his golfing buddies. He assigned me to the Meredith Fox murder because it was a high-profile case and he was worried that if he gave it to one of his pals, I might squawk to the chief."

"Makes sense," Casey said.

"The problem with Dollinger is that he's been on the job too long. He knows that his chances of moving up the ladder ended the day Chief Braun retired. Dollinger fears retirement. He can't picture himself having nothing to do but feed pigeons in the park."

He smiled. "The ego thing."

"Chief Braun considered Dollinger nothing but an ass-kisser. He barely tolerated him, but the old fox never let on. Dollinger still pictures himself as the Braun's right-hand man."

Casey focused the binoculars on the front window. Troxell, sitting at a table near the door, was talking on her cell phone. During the next few minutes, well-dressed customers arrived at the restaurant, left their cars with a valet, and went inside in twos and threes. The dining area began to fill.

A Chevrolet Corvette entered the driveway and stopped at the valet station. The parking valet opened the door. Felix Halloran, who'd met with Troxell at the Mexican restaurant when he and Sutherland had been watching her, got out of the car. He wore Levi's, a green sports shirt, and red tennis shoes like the kind basketball players wear to movie premieres and personal appearance gigs.

"The Wolfman," he said.

Casey handed the binoculars to Sutherland. She focused on Halloran, who was walking into the restaurant.

Sutherland said, "He's sitting with Troxell at her table."

"Do you read Halloran as someone involved with blackmailing celebrities?"

"Not really," she said, staring through the binocs. "If he tried to blackmail me, I'd wonder whether it was a Halloween joke. This means Anthony Flair tricked us into getting him out of jail and we're wasting our time. Wolfman just left the table."

The front door opened; Halloran came out.

Casey said, "He isn't staying for dinner."

"Should we follow him?"

"You stay on Troxell," Casey said. "I'll follow Halloran."

"Catch you later, partner."

Casey jogged to his car and got behind the wheel. A minute later, Halloran drove his Corvette out of the parking lot and turned east. Casey made a U-turn and discreetly followed him to Topanga Canyon Boulevard. Halloran turned left.

Casey followed, allowing him to get ahead. Driving north with the headlights off, Halloran slowed at the edge of a heavily wooded area a quarter mile later and then steered to the right shoulder of the road and stopped. Casey drove by. The road curved, and he maneuvered the sedan behind some tall shrubbery, hidden from anyone driving by. In the moonlight, he watched Halloran get out of the Corvette. He was holding a cell phone to his ear. Halloran walked to the trunk and slipped the phone into a trouser pocket. From the trunk he removed what looked like a shopping bag. Closing the lid, he glanced at his wristwatch and then walked east, into the woods.

Casey took a small flashlight from the front seat console. Without turning it on, he shoved it into his pocket, got out of the car, and quietly closed the door. To avoid being seen, he jogged along the edge of the woodland to the Corvette and then cautiously followed Halloran's path into the woods. Moonlight shining through tree branches enveloped him in a surreal patchwork of shadows. Hearing nothing, Casey followed a trail about fifty yards to the edge of a narrow clearing. He saw the shopping bag Halloran had been carrying on the ground. The stillness reminded him of Afghanistan. Drawing his gun, he walked to the bag and picked it up. It was empty.

A gunshot exploded bark chips from a tree next to him.

Dropping to the dirt, he low crawled into the shadows. He touched his head and face. Thankfully, everything was still there. Two more gunshots whizzed through the trees. Halloran had drawn him into a kill zone. He glimpsed the fire flash, guessed it was no more than forty yards away. Rather than indiscriminately returning fire,

Casey remained in the shadows and began low crawling in a circular path toward the area where he'd seen the muzzle flash. Halloran was a bad shot. He'd blown the element of surprise when Casey had been within his sights and was within handgun range.

Another shot rang out. The sound of the slug hitting a tree told Casey Halloran hadn't changed his aim. Buoyed by Halloran firing in the same direction unaware Casey had moved, Casey crept slowly toward him in darkness. From his right, he heard crunching leaves, the sound of footsteps. Casey stopped. The crunching halted. Halloran was hunting him. Imagining Halloran drawing a bead on him in the darkness, Casey slithered next to a tree and lay prone. His heart was beating wildly.

Scanning the terrain, he focused on a shadow about thirty feet away. Seconds later, he saw it move. Crawling closer, Casey realized he was looking at Halloran's dimly lit profile. Halloran took another step into a narrow shaft of moonlight and Casey caught a glimpse of his gun. Halloran was holding it in front of him with both hands, but he was aiming the wrong way. In the darkness, Halloran had gotten his wires crossed. Standing, using a tree for cover, he was aiming away from his target.

Planting his elbows in the dirt, Casey felt a chill. He grasped his gun firmly with both hands and concentrated on steadying the barrel. Resting his right index finger on the trigger, he closed an eye and aimed squarely at Halloran's torso…then, realizing that killing him would foreclose any chance to learn what Halloran knew about the murders, Casey changed his mind. Adjusting his aim to Halloran's left tennis shoe illuminated by moonlight, Casey squeezed the trigger. The gun fired. The slug striking Halloran's foot knocked him to the ground with an animal-like shriek that echoed through the trees.

Struggling to his feet while firing rounds in the wrong direction, Halloran dove into the woods and hobbled away. His gun at the ready,

Casey followed the sound of uneven footsteps crunching dry leaves. Casey followed the sounds through the darkness using one tree at a time for cover. The hobbling sounds got faster. There was a silence. Casey stopped to listen. Seconds later, he heard a car door slam and ran toward the sound. Near the moonlit edge of the woods, Casey heard tires squealing. Emerging from tree cover to the roadway, he saw Halloran's Corvette was gone. Casey keyed Sutherland's number into his phone.

She picked up on the first ring. "Hey, Legs."

He said, "Where are you?"

"Still at the restaurant. Troxell is leaving."

"Let her go. Halloran led me into a trap and started shooting. He's wounded but escaped."

"Are you injured?"

"Negative."

"Thank God…that bastard Flair set you up."

"Flair must have figured we'd watch Troxell to see who she met with."

"That's what it sounds like."

"Flair's a major player in the murders. He knows everything."

"You were right about blackmail investigations being complicated."

"Partner, this one just got a lot simpler."

"What's the plan?"

"We find Halloran, lock him up for attempted murder, and then offer him another chance to sing."

"I like it."

Back at the office, they briefed Dollinger, then began calling hospital emergency rooms to determine if Halloran had sought treatment for his gunshot wound. Obtaining no positive results, they checked police, public utility, DMV, and probation department databases trying to ascertain Felix Halloran's current whereabouts. It was nearly 8:00 a.m. before they came up with his home address.

Casey and Sutherland took the freeway route to North Hollywood. Winding through North Hollywood's suburban Valley Village, they found Bouldin Avenue, a narrow street lined on both sides with multiunit housing. Halloran's address, a recently renovated apartment house with a red brick front and iron grilles covering the windows of its first-floor apartments, had a driveway in front leading down into an underground garage. Casey parked the sedan two doors away. They got out of the car and walked to the garage gate. Inside, Halloran's Corvette was parked facing the wall.

They checked a resident directory next to the apartment house entrance. Halloran's name wasn't listed. Casey pressed the RESIDENT MANAGER button.

"Management office," a man said through the intercom.

"Police officers," Casey said.

"What is it?"

"We need to speak to you in person."

"First floor, number 103."

The speaker buzzed and Casey pushed open the glass door leading into a lobby. They walked to 103. A sixtyish man standing in the doorway wore a purple golfing shirt, yellow Bermuda shorts, and a white baseball hat. Casey and Sutherland held out their badges.

"What's the problem?"

Casey showed him a prison photograph of Halloran. "Do you know this person?"

"Never laid eyes on him."

Sutherland said, "His car is parked downstairs."

"What's this about?"

"Murder."

"Uh, Mr. Halloran told me some bill collectors had been bothering him."

"Which apartment?" Casey said.

"304, third floor at end of the hallway."

Sutherland said, "Does he have anyone else living in the apartment with him?"

"Not that I know of."

"Have you seen him today?"

"No."

Casey said, "We need the key."

"Are you going to arrest him?"

"If you warn him," Sutherland said with a glare, "you'll be going to jail with him."

"Okay, okay."

The manager went inside, returned with a key, handed it to her. Walking up two short flights of stairs between floors, they reached the third-floor landing. One of the doors jerked open and a young boy stuck his head out and said hello. He wore a Spider-Man costume.

"Hello, Spider-Man," Casey said.

The boy smiled and pulled the door closed.

They paused at the door to apartment 304. Next to it on the floor was a clear plastic delivery bag containing two bottles of wine. Casey put his ear to the door. Hearing nothing, he tried the handle. It was locked. Sutherland handed him the key. He drew his gun. Sutherland drew hers. He knocked. No sound came from inside. Inserting the key, he slowly turned the lock and pushed open the door. The living room coffee table was overturned, its drawers removed and upended. The doors to an entertainment center were open, its contents strewn across the floor.

"Police officers!" Casey said.

Guns drawn, they followed the short hallway to an open door. The room was bare. In the corner, a barbell and some weights were on a plastic-covered exercise mat. They walked in. Sutherland cautiously opened the closet door. It was empty. They moved to the adjoining bedroom. The door was closed. Casey tried the handle. It was unlocked. He shoved the door open. The light was on. Halloran lay next to the bed, unmoving. A rope wrapped his bruised neck. His eyes bulged in a mask of strangulation. He wore shorts and a white T-shirt. A bloody towel wrapped his right foot and ankle.

"What the fuck?" Sutherland said.

Holstering his gun, Casey knelt and touched Halloran's neck. No pulse.

Sutherland said, "Somebody was probably here waiting for him to return from murdering you. Seeing Halloran's wound, they realized there was nothing else to do but get rid of him."

"Bad luck for the Wolfman. And bad luck for us."

The armoire and nightstand drawers in the bedroom were open. Personal items covered the floor: socks, a key chain, an electric razor, a leather bag, and a purple baseball hat with an embroidered Sand & Sea Casino logo. Casey picked up a well-worn black leather wallet lying on the dresser table. In it were twelve one hundred–dollar bills and a Show Girl Cabaret Gentlemen's Club membership card in Halloran's name.

The closet contained men's trousers and shirts on hangers. On the floor were men's shoes, two sets of golf clubs, and a baseball bat covered by clothing items in clear plastic bags with laundry receipts attached. Trouser pockets had been turned inside out. The bathroom medicine cabinet contained shaving items, a tin box filled with Band-Aids, a tube of toothpaste, and a container of foot powder.

In the living room, Casey looked through the items on the carpet: a two-week-old newspaper, two decks of playing cards, a cheap vase, and some unopened advertising mail addressed to Halloran. Sorting through a coffee table drawer that had been left open, he found a flyer for a pizza shop and a roll of duct tape. There were no family photographs, utility bills, business papers, personal letters, travel receipts, medical prescriptions, business cards, phone books, computers, or cell phones.

Sutherland said, "They took the time to get rid of anything we could use to connect him to anyone."

"Protecting the blackmail operation."

They walked to the kitchen. Casey opened the refrigerator. No weapons or contraband were on the shelves or in the drawers. Sutherland opened the cupboard under the sink. The trash receptacle was empty. Casey's phone rang. Dollinger's name was on the screen.

Casey touched ACCEPT, then SPEAKERPHONE. "Casey," he said. "Kristina is on with us."

"Where are you?"

"Halloran's apartment. He's dead."

"You killed him?"

"Negative," Sutherland said. "It looks like someone strangled him to death."

Dollinger said, "I just got an interesting call from the Los Angeles FBI agent in charge asking if we were looking for Halloran. When I asked why he wanted to know, he told me Halloran was an active FBI informant."

"What kinds of cases?" Casey asked.

"When I asked the question, he gave me the runaround," he said. "Is anyone else in the apartment?"

"Negative," Casey said. "And the apartment manager says Halloran lived alone."

"Clues?"

"There's no sign of forced entry."

"Someone he knew…have you notified LAPD?"

"Not yet," Casey said.

"I'll notify LAPD North Hollywood homicide from here. Do you two need anything?"

Casey said they didn't.

"Keep me informed," Dollinger said.

"Will do." The cell phone returned to silent.

Sutherland smiled wryly. "If Wolfman was an FBI rat, I wonder if he told them he was planning to kill you?"

Casey slipped the phone back onto his belt. "If so, they probably classified the information top secret."

"Legs, someone once told me half the criminals in the country are FBI informers."

His mind was racing. "What was Meredith Fox doing at the Beverly Mandarin hotel?"

"Before leaving her condo that morning, she told Flair she was going to Warner Brothers for a business meeting. But the timeline shows her driving straight from the condo to the Beverly Mandarin garage. I checked the garage security cameras. It showed her arriving, then driving to the rooftop parking level where there are no cameras. That's where they found her."

Thinking out loud, Casey said, "Wanda Troxell wired the Gloria Channing estate for eavesdropping, but Wanda didn't kill Lanza and Rosa Hernandez. Flair manages the Greenroom, where Lanza was a regular customer. Lanza was blackmailing Channing—"

"Marty Vollero has been nosing around blackmail victims."

"And Meredith Fox's boyfriend, Flair, who is connected to Troxell, knows Halloran…who tried to kill me."

"What are you getting at, Legs?"

"We know who's involved in the blackmail game, but when it comes to the murderers, they've managed to stay one step ahead of us since day one. And we're still not over the target."

"Any ideas?"

"Not at the moment."

CHAPTER SIXTEEN

Chief of Police Donna Slade leaned back in her comfortable leather executive chair and studied Dollinger, standing in front of her desk, wearing military pressed trousers, a long-sleeved starched white shirt, and a pale-blue necktie that she guessed might've been an expensive holiday gift from management at one of the Beverly Hills clothing stores.

She said, "Were Casey and Sutherland aware Halloran was an FBI asset?"

"They had no idea."

"This case gets more convoluted every day."

"The other way to look at it," Dollinger said, "is that with detectives gathering more information, it's getting less complicated."

To her, Dollinger's compulsion to say the self-evident was irksome. She saw it as his mousey, passive way to indicate he considered briefing her on the case nothing but an unnecessary formality. He was silently telling her that when it came to real policework, he didn't think it possible she could ever know as much as he.

"What's your personal take on it?" she asked.

Setting the scene for her, Dollinger said, "One of the blackmail players hires Halloran to kill Casey. When Halloran botches the contract and gets shot in the leg, they know it's just a matter of time before he'll be apprehended and then questioned. Rather than risk him naming names in exchange for leniency, they decide to get rid of him."

"Have we identified all of the blackmail players?"

"That's not clear."

"Nothing is clear?"

"I wouldn't go that far."

"Who's the prime murder suspect?" she said.

"Probably Vollero."

"Evidence?"

"We have nothing against him at present, but his luck can't last forever."

"Who said?"

"Chief, either he or one of the other players will make a mistake."

"We're still at square one."

"The moment something breaks, Casey and Sutherland will be there to bag the players."

"In the meantime, the crooks are dealing the cards. Is that the way you see this?"

"Not at all."

"Because I intend to run for sheriff, the mayor and the city council members have been talking behind my back, stirring up rumors about the two murders. They keep pressing me for an arrest. What should I tell them?"

"That everything that can be done is being—"

"Do you feel confident about solving these homicides?"

"I believe something will break."

"I have confidence in our people…"

"You do? I recall you telling me you had reservations about Casey. Now you're betting he can solve three homicides. What has changed?"

"He and Sutherland are making progress."

"Progress? I don't see jack shit."

"I'm carefully supervising…"

"You need to turn this case around."

"I intend to go over everything with the detectives."

Her eyes flashed anger. "Forget the happy song and dance, Dollinger. I don't intend to be jawing about this case a month from now. You're going to have to show me something soon." Her phone rang. Picking up the receiver, she said, "Hello, Mayor…yes. I was just going to call you…."

She gave Dollinger a disconsolate wave to end the meeting.

—

Casey awoke to someone knocking on his apartment door. The luminous numbers on the nightstand clock indicated 5:17 a.m. He got out of bed, slipped on a robe, and took his gun from the nightstand drawer. Walking to the front door, he leaned close to the peephole. Chief of Police Donna Slade stood in the hallway. She wore a gray jogging outfit and a matching baseball hat. Putting the gun down, he opened the door.

"Good morning," she said. "We need to talk."

"Sure, Chief." He opened the door. "Come in."

"Is anyone else here?"

"No."

"Thanks." She walked inside. "I thought a personal visit would be better than a closed-door meeting in my office. I hate giving the department gossipers an opportunity to create rumors."

"May I make you a cup of coffee?"

"No, thanks. I'm on my way to the firing range—if I expect my officers to qualify with their weapons every month, I have to set an example. There's talk about whether the state marksmanship qualification should be made more difficult."

"I've heard the same rumors. But I'll bet that's not the reason you're here."

She walked to the window and stared down at the street. He'd heard the rumors that accompanied her from the LAPD—how she screwed her way up the ladder all the way to deputy chief. He'd also been told by trusted friends in the LAPD that the rumors were untrue, but he knew there was no way for her to squelch the talk. It was common in police departments. Commanding two separate LAPD divisions, she cleared up a lot of corruption, something the gossipers always omitted. The truth was police departments were the last government bureaucracies that were still men's clubs. He assumed Slade's peers spread the rumors about her: the inexperienced, strutting command drones who talked behind her back after failing to get in her pants.

She turned to him. "I've been reading all your homicide reports that make it to my desk. From the paperwork, it looks like the three murders are still whodunits."

If she was here to officially remove him from the Lanza case, he was prepared to aggressively argue the facts and try to change her mind.

"Kristina and I have been working every—"

"How are you getting along with Dollinger?"

"No problems that I'm aware of."

"Good. And I understand you've met Brady, the new community relations officer. Have you developed any solid information that didn't make its way into your written reports?"

"Not that I can think of."

She said, "I'm told that the Fox and Lanza murder books are locked up along with all the original case notes."

"Because of the celebrity press angle, Dollinger thought that was a good idea."

"I want to see everything."

He said, "You've asked Captain Dollinger?"

"I don't want him to know."

She was checking on Dollinger, probably with the intention of replacing him and appointing some other captain to command her detectives. Rather than question Casey in her office, Slade stopped by to make sure no one could overhear what she was saying.

"Why?"

Chief of Police Slade, cleverer than he had guessed, was coldly putting Casey on the spot.

"That's none of your business."

"Dollinger ordered us to keep the reports under lock and key."

There was no easy way out. Casey was boxed in. Whatever he said was going to harm him. It looked like he was destined to end up back in the punishment barrel, filing stolen car reports and dreaming about making a second career comeback.

She said, "I've gotten the impression that I'm not being kept fully up to speed."

"Sorry to hear that."

He immediately realized his poor choice of words. The remark sounded condescending.

"I want you to make copies of the murder books and all the case notes, then drop them off at my home."

"Without telling Dollinger?"

"Or anyone else."

"Dollinger ordered us not to share the information or go over his head."

Though he preferred not to take a position in the fray, if Casey wanted to keep his job, he had to side with Dollinger. Though he respected Slade and appreciated that she'd put him on investigating cases, in November she was likely to be elected LA County sheriff and leave the Beverly Hills Police Department. In a practical sense, the odds of Casey being able to remain on the job were better if he crossed Slade rather than Dollinger, who'd still be captain after her departure.

She smirked. "Tough guy Detective Legs Casey is suddenly afraid of disobeying an order?"

Without a witness, there was no way she could sustain firing him for insubordination. He said nothing.

"Forget it," she said. "Others will fill me in." She walked to the door, opened it. "Mention this visit to Dollinger or anyone else and you'll find yourself driving a patrol car from midnight to eight."

He hoped she'd realize her mistake in trying to involve him in whatever problem she was having with Dollinger. Then another thought crossed his mind: Dollinger wasn't sharing information with Slade because he believed she was corrupt, that maybe Slade's husband or one of the donors to her political campaign had reached out to her for inside information on the murders. Maybe Dollinger was resisting. Whatever the reason, the homicide investigation had become hazardous both to Casey's career and his life.

—

On his narrow apartment balcony, Casey was sizzling two steaks on a small barbecue grill when Ellen Brady came from the kitchen carrying two martinis and handed one to him.

"Thanks." He sipped.

"Too strong?"

"Perfect."

Earlier in the day when he'd called to invite her for dinner, she seemed pleased. And tonight she was much more talkative and at ease than at Roget's restaurant. Casey guessed that she'd informed Dollinger that Casey had detected the internal affairs surveillance Dollinger had ordered. But Casey wasn't sure. Dollinger, whom he would have expected to call him in to discuss the matter, hadn't said a word. Casey's best guess was that Brady told Dollinger about her failed surveillance but omitted telling him about having dinner with him at Roget's. To Casey, it didn't matter. He found Ellen Brady stimulating. She'd been on his mind since they met.

During conversation about the Beverly Hills Police Department, he shared with her a rough outline of the current homicide investigations.

She showed interest without being nosy. Brady had a first-rate mind, and he found himself saying things he hadn't realized he felt. Her natural good looks and her long legs were pleasant to look at. She was that kind of self-assured woman who always looked stylishly turned out, as if her clothing might have been designed solely for her. He couldn't tell what she thought about him.

He said, "How well do you know Donna Slade?"

"My total contact with the chief is one ten-minute interview during my first day on the department."

He smiled wryly. "It wouldn't surprise me if you were working for her."

Brady sipped her drink. "My chain of command is two admin officers and Dollinger, who from the rumors I hear is getting a lot of heat from Slade over the murders you and Sutherland are working."

"Dollinger told you that?"

She made eye contact with him. "He's never spoken to me about department politics. My information comes from the department's overactive rumor mill, mostly from traffic officers and clerks in the records bureau. It's certainly not from the detective bureau. The detectives here don't talk because they think everyone is secretly working for some television gossip reporter."

He smiled. "With good cause."

"But I've heard detectives talk about you."

He asked what they were saying.

"They wonder how after returning from a suspension you were selected to investigate a sensitive homicide case."

"I was on mandatory medical leave, not a suspension."

"Whatever you call it, it's still unusual."

He shrugged. "I'm not the first officer to get a break."

She smiled broadly. "It won't be a break if you fail to solve the homicides."

"Tell me about it."

The oven buzzer sounded.

"My potatoes," she said, hurrying to the kitchen.

During a leisurely dinner they sipped red wine and talked easily while listening to a blues album. After dessert and cognac, she insisted on doing the dishes. He liked her. And unless he was mistaken, she felt that way about him. He told himself that if she was romantically involved with Dollinger, she had a right to her secret, but eventually it would come out. If so, Casey would deal with it. In the meantime, nothing could stop him from pursuing her. He put on some dance music, and they slow danced in the living room for a while. Later, they went to the bedroom and made love. Ellen Brady, the first woman he'd dated since his divorce, was sexy, uninhibited, and playful.

In bed in the early morning darkness, he was startled awake by the shooting nightmare. Ellen was snuggled next to him, sleeping soundly. The illuminated face of the clock read 2:19 a.m. Avoiding waking her, he sat up, got out of bed, and shrugged on a robe. In the living room, he stared out the window at the city lights and ruminated about each fact gathered during the investigation as if he were packing them in a big suitcase before a long trip, including the listening device found in Gloria Channing's kitchen, the porno photographs found in Lanza's car, Channing's admission that she'd been paying blackmail money to Lanza, and Vollero's reactions while being interviewed. It was an unusual case, but he knew there was no such thing as a conventional homicide.

Ellen walked into the living room. "You need to get some sleep."

He turned to her. "Sorry if I woke you."

"What are you thinking about?"

"The murders."

"What's wrong?"

"Something's missing."

"Complicated investigations sometimes get better on their own."

"You know that's not true."

"You'll solve it."

"Not if the facts—the theory of the investigation—was off the track from the beginning."

"There is such a thing as a lucky break."

"I'm not so sure." She put her arms around him and whispered, "Come back to bed."

Returning to the bedroom, they made love again. Ellen went back to sleep. He got up, showered, shaved, and put on his clothes. He kissed her as she slept, then left the apartment, got in his car, and drove to police headquarters.

CHAPTER SEVENTEEN

Casey dialed numbers on the combination lock securing the filing cabinet in the detective squad room where he and Sutherland stored the Fox, Lanza, and Hernandez murder paperwork. Gathering from the top drawer the three murder books containing the original daily chronological logs of every investigative activity he and Sutherland had performed during the homicide investigations, he picked up all the notes, investigative reports, and other documents, including scraps of paper torn from newspaper margins and scribbles made in his pocket notebook. Taking everything to his desk, he plopped it all down. Alone in the morning stillness, he spread the paperwork out and began carefully reviewing everything. His penmanship on the handwritten notes was sloppy but readable.

He adjusted his computer screen and spent some time comparing his original crime scene notes with the typed reports in the computer file. What he faced now was being stranded on a plateau where the combination of only a few facts and a general lack of evidence had begun to overwhelm the mission like a fast-replicating black mold. The murder investigations had stalled. His years as a cop had taught him the danger of the natural tendency to want to fit facts into theory. Facts, real events and things, the currency of his profession, were what would unveil the truth. Before proceeding further along the same exploratory track, he needed to determine whether he'd misinterpreted or overlooked something important, whether somewhere along the line, wires had inadvertently gotten crossed.

At 6:00 a.m., he finished reading the notes and reports and began concentrating on Sutherland's paperwork, including the charts she'd created listing the times and dates of calls from Fox and Lanza's monthly telephone bills to others who'd been interviewed during the investigation. He saw nothing in the documents he considered significant. Then, thumbing through the phone number spreadsheets, he noticed some calls dialed from Lanza's cell phone to Gloria Channing's personal assistant, Courtney Wellstone. Telephone company records indicated that Wellstone made hundreds of calls to both Bobby Lanza's landline and cell phone numbers. Making a note of the discovery on a yellow notepad, he sat back in the chair and stared at the paperwork for few minutes before wading through it again.

After a while, he stood and stretched. He turned on the coffeepot in the office lunchroom. With a paper cup filled with black coffee, a stale donut he'd found in the produce drawer of the lunchroom refrigerator, and a candy bar purchased from a vending machine, he returned to the desk and reread Sutherland's report of her initial interview with Meredith Fox's boyfriend, Anthony Flair, and compared it with the reports of the interviews with Wellstone and Gloria Channing. He studied the Fox, Lanza, and Hernandez autopsy reports, then the photographs found in Lanza's car. Thumbing to a fresh sheet of lined paper in his notebook, he wrote the most puzzling aspects of the homicides as follows:

1. *Who wanted Meredith Fox and Bobby Lanza dead?*
2. *Who are the man and woman in the blackmail photographs found in Lanza's car?*
3. *Why the frequent phone contact between Courtney Wellstone and Bobby Lanza?*

He found reviewing the information piece by piece reassuring, but he knew he hadn't found any master key to solving the murders. He walked about the office, taking a bite of the stale donut and dropping what was left of it into the trash container next to the desk. He unwrapped the candy bar and slowly took a bite. It too was dry. Tossing it, he wiped his hands on a paper tissue. He picked up from the desk an old booking photograph of Anthony Flair taken three years earlier in Los Angeles, when Flair had been arrested for being drunk in public.

Casey spotted it then, the connection he'd been missing—something that made the entire document review worthwhile. Pleased, he sat back in the chair and allowed the case images to flicker in his head again, including the crime scene on Hillcrest Drive as well as the interviews with Courtney Wellstone, Esperanza Hernandez, and the hammy Gloria Channing. Returning to the lunchroom, he refilled his coffee cup before walking back to the desk.

"What are you doing here so early?" Kristina Sutherland said, walking in from the hallway toward her desk.

"Looking for clues."

"Find any?"

He picked up the file page displaying Anthony Flair's booking photographs—a headshot, right and left profile—and handed it to her.

"The left profile shot," he said, "upper arm."

Her eyes widened. "He has a leopard tattoo."

"Flair is the guy in the blackmail photographs."

—

At 2:41 a.m., after a brief summer shower, Casey drove by clothing stores whose night-lights illuminated display windows filled with faceless, life-size manikins wearing colorful Armani sports coats. Sunset Boulevard glistened in the reflections from high-power mercury streetlamps. It was the beginning of "burglar time"—when everyone was sleeping and only felons and cops roamed the streets. Driving to the eastern edge of the Sunset Strip, he slowed in front of the Greenroom.

Anthony Flair's Camaro was parked in front. Because of the hour, the place was closed. Flair had been avoiding his phone calls.

Casey parked in the alley behind the bar and walked to the back door. It was locked. He knocked loudly and waited a few minutes before using his phone to call Flair's cell number again.

"Whatsup?" Flair said, answering after five rings.

"I'm outside, Anthony," he said. "We need to talk."

"Is everything okay?" Flair sounded nervous.

"I need to run a few things by you."

"I'm busy."

"Open the back door." Casey ended the phone call.

Flair opened the door a minute later. He wore slacks and a dark sports coat with an open-collar white shirt.

"What do you want?" Flair said.

"Who else is here?"

"No one. The cocktail waitresses left a few minutes ago. I'm finishing up the count."

Casey walked in. Flair followed him along a short hallway and past a door marked OFFICE. Pushing aside a black curtain, Casey entered the dimly lit bar area. Chairs were stacked seat down on cocktail tables. Mirrored walls reflected a black granite cocktail bar with illuminated bottle racks, black leather chairs and booths, and a baby grand piano used by the jazz musicians who played there Friday and Saturday nights. An oversized Champagne glass on the piano was a tip container. There was the aroma of marijuana, the universal scent of crime. Casey sat at the bar, near the cash register and some stacks of credit card receipts.

Flair asked if he wanted a drink.

Casey said, "Big crowd tonight?"

"Huge."

"Who was playing?"

"Les Roberts at the piano. He has a lot of followers. The place was wall-to-wall packed, standing room only. Mostly TV and movie people: studio bitches, basketball players, and half the confidence men in LA running down their bullshit to one another. That blonde who sings at the Dresden Room stopped by. People love her. Everyone was drinking like hell. Some TV writer and his girlfriend were drinking shots of Jagermeister and chasing it with white wine. Watching them, I almost gagged."

"Your dope case isn't going to be dismissed."

"You have a strange sense of humor."

"I'm serious."

"By giving you the information about Wanda meeting with someone, I fulfilled my part of the bargain. My attorney says all the dope charges against me should be immediately dismissed."

Flair, who'd set him up to be killed, wasn't shaking in his boots. Casey no longer doubted whether Flair was involved in blackmail and the murders. He was a varsity player.

"You'd better ask your attorney whether he has experience defending suspects charged with murder."

"What about our deal?"

"Things have changed."

Flair asked in what way.

"I admire your confidence," Casey said. "I was going to say that you should have stuck with peddling cocaine. But you botched that, too. You've put yourself in an uncomfortable position."

"In what way?"

"Believing that you could actually get away with setting me up to get whacked."

"We have a deal, Casey. You gave me your word. And I've done what I promised."

"You aided Halloran in trying to murder me. And you just became a prime suspect in the Hillcrest Drive murders."

"You're out of your mind."

Casey took from his inside jacket pocket Flair's left-profile police booking photograph, handed it to him.

"Two years ago, I got arrested for drunk driving," Flair said after glancing at it. "So what?"

"Your leopard tattoo matches the one in the photographs found in Bobby Lanza's car."

Flair handed back the photo. "Millions of people have tattoos."

"Most murders are committed by people living under the same roof. You were living with Meredith. And you admitted to being the last person to see her alive."

Flair's complexion took on an ashen cast; perspiration had formed on his upper lip. "I didn't kill her."

Casey slipped the photograph back into his jacket. "Good luck on convincing a jury of that."

"You're actually going to frame me for her murder?"

"Your other problem is the shooter."

"I don't know what you're talking about—"

"Felix Halloran was an FBI rat. The Feds have photos and recordings of everyone he talked to."

"You don't scare me."

Casey said, "It's not pretty. If the blackmail guys killed Halloran because he botched the hit, you might be next."

"Fuck you. And fuck the Beverly Hills Police Department."

"I'm going to walk out of here now. The next time you see me, I'll have arrest warrants in my hand, meaning you're headed either to the main line in San Quentin or the morgue."

"I...I can solve the murders."

"Oh, have I captured your attention?"

"You'll have to talk to my lawyer before I agree to anything."

"It's too late for that."

Flair looked surprised. "Why?"

"By setting me up, you advanced from the featherweight to the heavyweight division."

"There's no way you can solve the murders without me."

"Life isn't perfect. And I get a paycheck every two weeks."

"I've been working for you."

"Bullshit."

"I'll have some information soon."

"The ship has sailed. For you, it's either plead guilty, go to trial, or tell me who killed Bobby Lanza."

"I swear I don't know."

"The woman in the porno shots. Who is she?"

"I don't know her name."

"Who took the photographs?"

"I have no idea."

Casey got up, walked toward the door. It wasn't a bluff.

Flair said, "Bobby Lanza talked me into the photograph caper."

Casey stopped, returned to the bar, and sat on a stool. "I'm listening."

"He showed me a picture of her that had been cut out of a magazine. He told me she was rich and that she used different names when she was out on the town looking to get laid. When he first asked me if I was interested, I said no. Then I changed my mind and called him. It was a chance meeting caper. When he said all I had to do was fuck her, I thought he was joking. But he wasn't. He told me there'd be nothing to it, that the woman was a nympho. Lanza just needed some photos to use as the twist in the shakedown."

"What was your cut?"

"I never got paid."

"How much did he offer?"

"Twenty grand. Lanza was in the shakedown business, but I wasn't involved in any of that. After the secret photo play, I never saw her again."

"What was her name?"

"Bobby didn't tell me and I didn't want to know."

"What was her first name?"

"When I introduced myself, she said her name was Vivian."

"Did Meredith know about Lanza's offer?"

"I expected her to be jealous when I told her Lanza wanted me to jump a broad for him. But when I told her he offered me twenty grand, she wished me luck and said it was 'just guys,' meaning that she considered it strictly business. She wished me luck. For Meredith, twenty grand for anything wasn't going to interfere with our relationship."

"Then what?"

"She was sitting at a table in Wilfredo's. I introduced myself and a couple of hours later she and I were in this condo in Brentwood that Lanza had rigged with pinhole cameras and motion-activated recording equipment. Bobby told me it was all legal; that in a place they were renting, people could take any kind of pictures they wanted."

"What else did Lanza say about her?"

"Nothing," Flair said. "He didn't give me her last name because he thought I might accidently use it and spook her. All I was thinking about was the twenty thousand bucks. Whatever Bobby and Meredith were up to with their celebrity tag game was strictly their deal. If they were blackmailing rich people, that was their thing—not mine. I'm not into that kind of shit. And I didn't violate any law by throwing a jump on this bitch. None whatsoever."

"You never got paid?"

"When I asked Lanza for the money, he did a slow pay act. I complained and he got irritated. When I heard somebody killed him, I knew right then I'd never get my money.... There, I'm fully cooperating with your investigation, and you can see I haven't done anything illegal...and I didn't kill Meredith. Why the hell would I do that? And I swear to God I didn't set you up. I don't even know Halloran."

Casey had tired of listening to Flair say the plausible while hoping to keep himself out of the deep water. "You're such a liar."

Flair hesitated, then said, "Halloran asked me to tell you that Wanda was meeting with someone. I didn't know what he was going to do. I swear I had no idea."

"How did you know Halloran?"

"He was a regular customer here. And, uh, he had something going with Wanda. He told me that he was going to meet Wanda at Dominique's. I knew they had something going. It was simple as that. I didn't set you up. I told you the truth as I knew it."

"You're not leveling with me."

"The hell I'm not. And I'm going to find out everything for you. I want to have all this over. I'm going to talk to some people and get the scoop for you."

Casey got up and walked toward the exit.

"I'll call you tomorrow," Flair said.

"I won't hold my breath."

CHAPTER EIGHTEEN

While Casey edged the sedan slowly forward in bumper-to-bumper rush hour traffic on the northbound Hollywood Freeway, Kristina Sutherland was shuffling through her notebook.

"You're right," she said. "Flair's phone bill shows calls to Wanda Troxell, Halloran, and Lanza, and two calls to Marty Vollero's office."

"Vollero hires Halloran to kill me, then tells Flair to set me up for the hit at the restaurant?"

"I can see that."

He found going over the facts with Sutherland helpful. "At the murder scene, when I spoke with Courtney Wellstone, she was cooperative, but I came away suspecting she knew more. Now she isn't answering my phone calls."

"Maybe she's busy being Gloria Channing's personal assistant, peeling her grapes."

"While Channing sits next to her Olympic-sized pool waiting for some big director to send her a movie script…"

Sutherland laughed. "A *personal assistant*, that's what I need. Someone to take my car in for an oil change and deal with my mother when she gets in one of her nasty moods."

Near Universal Studios, Casey swerved onto an off-ramp leading to Ventura Boulevard in Studio City, a suburban/commercial enclave bounded on the north by another freeway and to the south by Mulholland Drive in the Hollywood Hills. Following the car's GPS map, Casey navigated two blocks north of Ventura Boulevard to a cluster of hillside homes. On Lemoore Street, in front of a dual-level modern with a three-car garage, Courtney Wellstone's Cadillac was parked in the driveway. He parked the sedan behind it.

They got out and walked to the door. He knocked and heard footsteps inside. Expecting someone to open the door and tell him she wasn't there; he was surprised when Wellstone opened it.

She grimaced. "Hello."

Casey introduced Sutherland and said, "Can you spare a few minutes?"

"What's the problem?"

"We're still investigating the Bobby Lanza murder."

"I've told you everything I know."

"May we come in?" Casey said.

"I don't have a lot of time."

"Nor do we," Sutherland said.

They walked by her.

Staring at them, Wellstone closed the door. She wore a designer T-shirt, palazzo pants, and no makeup. A counter separated the living room from the kitchen. A hallway led to bedrooms. The view from the living room window was a portion of the enormous Universal Studios complex. She motioned them to a sofa. They sat, she perched on an upholstered chair. The furniture looked new. Casey thought Courtney Wellstone was living well for a personal assistant to an actor whose career was on life support.

"I'll get to the point," he said. "When you and I talked, I came away with the impression that you were leaving something out."

The expression that crossed Wellstone's face was a mixture of condescension and impatience. "It was the first time in my entire life that I'd been questioned by the police."

"It also occurred to me that you might not be aware that withholding information can get people into a lot of trouble."

"I don't understand."

"Having gathered a lot of information since I spoke with you," he said, "we have a better overall picture of what was going on. I wanted to offer you an opportunity to…clear things up."

Wellstone had a puzzled look.

Casey had no evidence to prove she knew more. It was nothing but a hunch.

She said, "I feel like you're treating me like I'm some kind of criminal defendant."

Casey said, "We're only interested in the truth."

"If you suspect me of something, under the law I have the right to know what it is."

She didn't know what she was talking about, but Casey knew nothing good could come from pointing that out.

"We consider you a witness who might be able to shed some light," he said. "Nothing more."

"You're making a big mistake if you're looking to fix responsibility for the Bobby Lanza murder on me."

Sutherland said, "Telling us the truth, everything you know, is the best way to erase misunderstandings."

"If you like," Casey said, "we can forget about our first interview and start fresh."

Wellstone looked stunned. "Is it that someone mentioned something about Bobby and I being…close?"

Though no one they'd interviewed had mentioned anything like that, Casey didn't hesitate to nod.

"When did it start?" Sutherland said.

"I don't see that as anyone's business."

"Two people are lying dead in the county morgue," Sutherland said, staring coldly at her. "This isn't like watching TV. You don't get to change channels."

"You're raising your voice. It makes me uncomfortable."

Sutherland said, "Why not just answer the goddamn question?"

Wellstone cleared her throat, then spoke softly. "Bobby and I were dating."

Sutherland said, "Did this begin before his divorce from Gloria Channing?"

"Bobby and Gloria weren't getting along for months. Bobby asked me out to dinner. At first, I wouldn't go; then I changed my mind. We began seeing each other secretly. He promised to marry me after he divorced Gloria, but that didn't happen. Things just continued along. After their divorce was finalized, he strung me along, kept making excuses. I was a fool. I finally realized he wasn't going to commit and I broke off the affair. He acted like he was shocked, but by that time, I knew he was dating other women. Then our relationship gravitated into what you might call sort of an on-again, off-again thing."

Hearing the emotion in her voice, Casey said, "What was Bobby doing at Gloria Channing's house on the night of the murder?"

"I don't know."

"He didn't tell you?"

"And I didn't ask."

Sutherland said, "Let me get this straight. You're having an affair with Bobby Lanza for years. He suddenly moves into his ex-wife's house, and you don't ask him what's going on?"

"I…didn't want to…cause an argument."

"That would be a perfectly reasonable answer," Sutherland said, "except that it doesn't make any sense."

"Ours was a physical relationship. Nothing more and nothing less. Look, I knew Bobby wasn't a particularly trustworthy person. But this is Hollywood. I think you know what I mean by that."

"The day before Lanza was murdered," Sutherland asked, "was the relationship on or off?"

There was an uncomfortable silence in the room. The distant hum of a leaf blower rose from the street. Casey assumed Wellstone, her eyes welling with tears, might be ready to tell them what she believed they'd already learned during their homicide investigations.

"I was always turned on by Bobby," she said. "He did it for me. I don't know why. I can't explain it." She covered her face, sobbed. Then, as if chagrined, she used the back of her hands to wipe her eyes.

Sutherland said, "Did Gloria know?"

"Our affair was a secret the whole time. Now that Bobby is dead, I find saying that oddly surreal."

Casey said, "How did Bobby pay his bills?"

"I'm not sure."

Wellstone got up, walked to the kitchen, and used a tissue to wipe her eyes and nose. She returned to the chair, sat.

"How could Bobby afford to pay for that Cadillac he gave you?" Casey said.

"The Cadillac wasn't a gift. It was just a…sort of a loan."

"The car is registered to you," Sutherland said.

"Bobby was generous."

Casey said, "Making up the story as you go along isn't going to work."

"I was never involved with whatever Bobby may have been doing to earn money."

"Bobby was living here with you, wasn't he?" Sutherland said.

"Not every night. He had other girlfriends—and, no, I don't know their names or addresses."

Casey said, "May we see his belongings?"

"He didn't keep anything here but a tennis racket."

Deciding it was time, Casey took from his inside jacket pocket a business-sized envelope, handed it to her. "We found this in Bobby Lanza's car."

She opened the envelope, and an expression of restrained anguish crossed her face. Blinking rapidly, she handed back the photos and the envelope.

Sutherland said, "Do you recognize the woman?"

Wellstone said she didn't.

Casey assumed Wellstone's failure to ask about the photographs meant she was aware of the blackmail operation. Otherwise, she'd have asked him why he showed them to her.

He said, "Did Bobby tell you he was making money blackmailing movie celebrities?"

After a long pause she said, "Absolutely not. I don't know anything about that topic."

"He told you," Sutherland said.

"Who said?"

"He told you a lot. Men share a lot of secrets with their girlfriends. He trusted you."

Wellstone said, "You have no way of knowing that."

"We're interviewing people day after day," Sutherland said. "Then re-interviewing a lot of them. We're still nosing around, asking questions and getting quite a few answers."

Wellstone said, "This is getting weird."

"Murder investigations don't disappear," Casey said. "Eventually everything comes out in the wash."

"You were helping him blackmail celebrities," Sutherland said. "That's why he bought you the car."

Wellstone stared glumly at the carpet. "Bobby didn't discuss his business dealings with me."

"Blackmail victims are rich," Sutherland said. "They hire powerful lawyers."

"So what?"

"Big-time attorneys have political juice. They can call the district attorney and exert pressure on her to prosecute. Suspects who might not have otherwise been arrested can suddenly find themselves in jail charged with lying to the police. To get out of the soup, they are forced to hire their own defense attorneys."

"All that has nothing to do with me."

"Sometimes they are acquitted. Sometimes the jury sends them to the penitentiary."

Casey said, "Courtney, you had access to the murder scene, and you had a motive to murder Bobby Lanza. Right or wrong, it's possible that you might end up in a real jam."

Wellstone got up, walked to the window, and stared out at acres of land owned by Universal Studios. "If I were to tell you everything I know," she said softly, "what happens then?"

"We can make your cooperation known to the district attorney," Casey said.

Sutherland said, "And I can tell you from experience that she isn't in the business of prosecuting friendly witnesses."

"That doesn't sound like an ironclad promise of immunity to me."

"If you cooperate, no one will prosecute you," Casey said. "We give you our word."

"I don't want to get involved."

"Hoping for the best isn't going to work," Sutherland said.

Casey thought of a question and quickly assessed the possible damage that might come from asking it. "Are you aware Gloria Channing was one of Bobby Lanza's blackmail victims?"

Wellstone's eyes flashed rage, and then her face reddened as if she'd been slapped. "Now I get it. You talked to Gloria."

Expressionless, Casey said, "You need to think about what's best for you."

"That bitch is the one who sent you. Gloria laid the blackmail rap on me, didn't she?"

"We're here to get your side," Sutherland said with a straight face.

"I know Gloria better than anyone. She used to spend twelve thousand a month just on flowers. She's always spent too much. And it's been years since her last movie. She doesn't own her home and can barely afford the rent. Bobby bragged to her how much money he was making from the blackmail game. Because she needed money, she convinced him to let her in on the operation. Of course, Bobby went along with the idea without asking my advice. That was one thing about Bobby: he's always made bad decisions."

Casey said, "What was Gloria Channing's role in Lanza's blackmail operations?"

"Bobby had her nosing around other celebrities, particularly her close contacts in the movie industry—people she'd known for years, big-name celebrities who confided in her as a friend. Like some spy, she would dig nasty little secrets out of her friends and deliver them like a Christmas present to Bobby. He would use the information from her to squeeze cash out of celebrities."

"Which ones?" Casey said.

"Solange Gazebo is the only one I know. Gloria knew her long before she became television's biggest talk show star. She vacations with her and her husband, Ivan, every year in Aspen and Zermatt, where they own homes. They invite Gloria there during ski season. Gloria always goes there every winter."

Casey said, "What happened?"

"Solange made the mistake of telling Gloria an embarrassing personal secret. Gloria then ran to Bobby with it. Then one of Bobby's associates used the secret to blackmail Solange. She ended up paying a ton of cash to keep everything quiet."

Sutherland spoke softly. "What was the secret?"

"Something that happened when Solange and Ivan were alone at their Santa Barbara home. Solange ended up paying hundreds of thousands of dollars to keep the story out of the public eye."

"We're investigating a double murder," Casey said. "We need all the information. What was the twist?"

"Gloria told me Solange Gazebo and her husband are addicted to methamphetamine."

Casey had heard rumors that Gazebo was a longtime meth addict.

Sutherland said, "A lot of people have heard that rumor."

"There's more," Wellstone said. "Solange and Ivan were in the swimming pool in the backyard of their Santa Barbara home. While they were under the influence of the drug, Ivan filmed Solange having sex with Reggie, their pet Labrador retriever. Solange, who talks too much when she's high, told Gloria all about it."

By the very nature of their profession, police officers gained access to all the varied and sundry forms of human behavior, including twisted mistakes in judgment; crimes of greed, revenge, and self-destruction; bizarre foolishness; and sexual aberrations and perversions. But for Casey, the bestiality story was something new, a landmark.

Casey said, "To work a blackmail scheme using that as a twist, Bobby would have needed the film."

"Bobby had someone burglarize Solange's house and steal the digital video Ivan made. He had the burglar break in when Solange and Ivan were in Hollywood being interviewed about the upcoming Emmy Awards."

Sutherland said, "Who handled the actual shakedown, contacting Solange Gazebo and threatening her with the film?"

"Some crooked private investigator Bobby knew. Solange paid hundreds of thousands to keep the video secret. Bobby told me that the private eye was supposed to split the payoff money with him but ended up giving him only ten grand. Bobby was so angry he cut the private eye out of the blackmail game and began blackmailing celebrities that the private eye had already shaken down. Bobby called it a 'rehash.' He was making tons of money doing that."

"Who's the private investigator?"

"Do I have to say a name?"

"Yes," Sutherland said.

"Vollero, Marty Vollero. Gloria told me she never met him. I've never met him. Bobby threatened to kill me if I ever told anyone about the blackmail stuff. But I guess that doesn't really matter now, does it?"

Sutherland said, "What was your role in these blackmail operations?"

Wellstone fidgeted, then picked at her face. "Who told you I was involved?"

Casey said, "We're not allowed to answer questions about the investigation."

"Gloria told you, didn't she? I can see her doing something like that to help herself."

Casey said, "We've talked to lots of people."

"Bobby had me doing internet research on possible victims. He gave me names to check."

"What names?" Sutherland said.

"I don't remember."

"Women's or men's names?"

"Both. Most of them were movie and TV celebrities. I would check websites."

"To learn what?"

"There's nothing illegal about going online. It was just routine research." Wellstone smiled wryly. "For all I know, he was using the information for…a magazine article."

"Do you think this is a joke?" Sutherland said.

Wellstone said, "There's no need to be rude."

"Then why don't you answer the damn question and stop playing the stupid games?"

"Bobby wanted to know if the celebrities had been involved in any lawsuits, where they did their banking, if they had offshore banking accounts. I picked up a lot of their financial information from credit agencies and the dark web. Computer research isn't illegal. What I told you about Gloria calling and asking me to go to her house to pick up a phone number, that was the truth. And when I went there, I didn't connect Bobby to the car parked in the driveway. And I swear I don't know who killed him. For all I know the killer might have been someone Bobby was blackmailing. People commit murder every day for a lot less."

Her eyes sought his, as if to ascertain whether he believed her.

He glanced at Sutherland. "Is there anything else you'd like to add?"

"No."

"Thanks for your time," Casey said.

They stood to leave and walked to the door. Wellstone opened it.

"Are you going to tell Gloria what I said?" she asked.

"Never," Casey said. "Not under any circumstances."

"What happens now?"

"We'll be in touch."

Wellstone said, "You gave me your word that you'd keep me out of this entire mess."

Casey said, "We have a deal."

Walking to the car, he thought about what Wellstone told them. As he drove away, he saw that Courtney Wellstone was standing at her living room window, looking down at them.

"I'm disappointed," Sutherland said. "Solange Gazebo is an animal rights person who has her dog on her television show with her every day."

"Channing, Wellstone, Lanza, Troxell, and Vollero were all involved with the blackmail game."

"And we're no closer to solving the three murders."

—

Casey parked downstairs and took the elevator up. He unlocked his apartment door and turned on the light. In the kitchen, he took off his jacket, opened the refrigerator, and took out bread and lunch meat. He heard a knock, walked to the front door, and leaned close to the peephole to see the elderly Mrs. Paxinou, the resident apartment manager, who lived on the first floor.

He opened the door and said hello.

"Sorry to bother you, Mr. Casey, but something happened about ten this morning that you might want to know about. I returned from the grocery store and checked the security camera monitors. They'd stopped working. I looked in the garage and found the power cord connecting the cameras had been cut. Someone had gone in there and used wire cutters to sever it. I've checked with most of the tenants, and no one has reported any theft. But the lady across the hall told me she was leaving to teach her class at UCLA when she saw a man and a woman near the elevator."

"On this floor?"

"Yes. She'd never seen them before and got the impression they might have come out of your apartment. Are you missing anything?"

"Not that I'm aware of, but I'll certainly check everything."

"Do you think I should call the police and make a report about the cameras?"

"That's a good idea. Even if it turns out to be vandalism. Do you need any help?"

"Thanks for offering, but my grandson is coming over to handle that. He is a UCLA graduate and an electrical engineer. That should qualify him to fix an electrical cord."

"Thanks for letting me know, Mrs. Paxinou."

"I haven't seen you around much lately."

"I've been working a lot of overtime."

"My mother used to tell me that life was too short for working overtime or not taking Saturday and Sunday off."

"She was right."

"Be careful at work, Mr. Casey."

"Thanks."

"Have a nice night."

"You too."

She walked toward the elevator.

He closed the door. Walking to the kitchen, he looked about for evidence of tampering. Finding none, he checked the rest of the kitchen, then the bedroom. Opening drawers in his bedroom, he didn't see any evidence of anything having been searched or burgled. But that didn't mean the apartment hadn't been burgled. He guessed the intruders were FBI agents trying to determine if he'd murdered their informant, Felix Halloran. After defeating the building's security cameras, they might have entered the apartment after picking the lock. They'd have worn gloves to avoid leaving fingerprints while searching the apartment. Luckily, he kept the Fox, Lanza, and Hernandez homicide files locked in his office.

—

Vollero, sitting at the bar in the Greenroom, checked his wristwatch. "Let's go over the conversation again," he said to Anthony Flair, seated next to him.

"I talked with her for a while," Flair said. "When I told her you were here, she said that she was pissed and that she was coming in to talk to you about something. She told me not to tell you."

The place was standing room only. The jazz piano mixed with the conversations of young actors trying to impress one another by sharing show business rumors that had nothing to do with them personally: a stuntman overdosing on the set of *Gunsmoke on Planet Mars*, the plug being pulled on a movie being filmed entirely in a storm drain in Gardena, the star of a movie about the wife of a US president undergoing a secret sex change operation.

"How did she sound?"

"Tipsy."

"You didn't say that."

"I forgot."

"Details matter."

"Marty, are you angry at me about something?"

Vollero sipped his scotch. He disliked the bar acoustics, and he disliked Flair, a weight-pumping dullard whose first job in Hollywood was as a paid escort more popular with men than women.

Wanda Troxell walked in.

Flair nodded toward the door. "There she is."

Vollero watched Troxell look about, spot him, and then edge her way through the crowd to the bar.

"Hi, Wanda," Vollero said.

"Anthony," she said, "this fucker owes me five thousand bucks."

"Is that true, Marty?"

"Sit down, Wanda," Vollero said.

Flair got up. Wanda sat on his barstool.

Vollero said, "What would you like to drink?"

"Tequila, a double."

Vollero told the bartender, who picked up a bottle from the rack, poured a double shot.

"I thought you were in Palmdale," Wanda said.

"I came back for a couple of hours to handle an interview. I'm going back shortly."

"My money, Marty. You told me that you had the cash."

"I haven't forgotten."

Wanda picked up the tequila, threw it back. She put the shot glass down on the bar. "I want my dough, goddammit."

"I should've brought the cash with me. It slipped my mind."

"You're not going to get away with stalling me any longer," she said, slurring her words. "I've had it with you."

"She needs the dough, Marty," Flair said. "She deserves to be paid."

"I was just leaving, Wanda."

"You told me you had the fucking cash. You *told* me."

"I do, at my hotel in Palmdale. You can follow me there if you like."

"To Palmdale?"

"It's not that far. "

Troxell said, "I'm drunk."

"I'll be back in town at the end of the month. Do you mind waiting till then?"

"Fuck that. You owe the money and I need it now."

Vollero said, "Anthony, how about being a gentleman and driving Wanda up to Palmdale?"

"When?"

"Right now," Wanda said.

"My car is being painted."

Slurring her words, Troxell said, "You can drive my car."

Perfect, thought Vollero.

Flair said, "It's a long drive."

Vollero said, "The lady needs a ride."

"Come on, Anthony," she said. "Don't be a donkey."

Flair said, "Okay, Wanda."

Wanda smiled broadly. "That's the least you can do for your goddamn sugar baby."

Vollero smiled.

CHAPTER NINETEEN

Casey and Sutherland were busy at their desks writing reports when Dollinger came out of his office holding in his hand a miniature digital recorder/player.

"I just received an interesting phone call," Dollinger said, pressing the PLAY switch:

"Is this Captain Dollinger?"

"Who's calling?"

"Marty Vollero, Captain. Long time, no see."

"I see you on TV all the time."

"I've learned the value of advertising."

"When are they going to make you the star of a private eye television series?"

"As soon as they offer me a role with a beautiful actress, so I'm not banking on anything."

"I'm not trying to be rude, Marty, but I have a meeting to attend in a couple of minutes."

"I thought it might be a good idea for you and me to get together for a little chat."

"About what, Marty?"

"The Bobby Lanza murder."

"What do you have?"

"I don't want to talk about it over the telephone."

"Can you come to my office?"

"My schedule is tight today. I'm flying to San Francisco this evening for a client conference."

"I can send detectives to your office."

"I'd rather explain the situation to you in person."

"Why?"

"It's important information, something that will certainly break the case open, and I prefer to deal with a command officer. I'm available today at three p.m."

"Name the place."

"The Chinese Garden at the Huntington Library in San Marino. I'll have a half hour between a meeting there before driving to the Burbank Airport to catch a flight."

"Casey and Sutherland are handling the investigation. They'll meet you there."

"Should I assume that you don't want to meet with me face-to-face because we have a problem?"

"Not at all, Marty. The best way to handle an ongoing investigation is to meet with the detectives handling it. If some problem arises, feel free to bring it to my attention."

"If that's the way you want to handle it."

"Gotta run, Marty. Thanks for calling."

"Ciao."

Dollinger turned off the recorder. "Vollero hasn't been in touch with the department since the day he resigned. What do you make of it?"

Casey said, "Maybe he's hearing footsteps."

"That's what it sounds like to me." Sutherland said. "Marty thinks he's in trouble and he wants to build up a little goodwill."

Dollinger said, "I want a briefing as soon as you find out what he has to say."

—

Casey drove south on Robertson Boulevard toward Interstate 10. For some unknown reason, the traffic was light.

Sutherland said, "Vollero might be the Mr. Big in the blackmail operation."

"A definite possibility."

"If it wasn't blackmail victims killing Fox and Lanza," she said, "it's probably someone involved with the blackmailers."

"True."

"Then I ask you this," Sutherland said. "If you were an ex-cop-turned-crooked private eye and someone needed killing, how would you go about handling the murders? Who would you hire as shooter?"

"No ex-cop would make the mistake of thinking a hitman wouldn't turn on him if things got dicey."

"Legs, what you're saying is that if there's killing to be done, you'd do it yourself."

"That's my point exactly."

"Great minds think alike," she said. "Marty Vollero might well be the killer."

He drove east through the downtown Los Angeles interchange to the outdated, narrow Pasadena Freeway. Passing though Arroyo Seco Park and the north side of the Monterey Hills, they reached the wind-up of the freeway in South Pasadena. From Glenarm Street, he drove into San Marino, a city filled with mansions that wealthy Chinese immigrants had purchased from conservative Richard Nixon donors. In the center of the mansion area was the Huntington Library Art Museum and Botanical Gardens, an educational and research institution open to the public. Casey entered by the Allen Avenue gate at the north end of the enormous property, drove into the visitors' parking lot, and parked his sedan.

He and Sutherland got out and walked to the entrance. Showing their police identification to a guard wearing a sports coat and slacks, they crossed a lawn to the elaborate, twelve-acre Chinese Garden on the grounds. Vollero stood alone near two benches and some well-tended miniature trees.

"Hello, Kristina," Vollero said, disdainfully eyeing Casey.

"Long time no see, Marty."

"The last time I saw you was in court. You were testifying in a robbery case."

She said, "Congratulations on your business success."

"Dollinger refused to meet with me," Vollero said. "He must think he's super important."

Casey said, "He told us you might have some information on the Lanza murder."

"This garden took two years to build," Vollero said without altering his expression. "It's surprising there aren't more visitors." He motioned them to the stone benches. "Sit down."

"We prefer to stand," Sutherland said.

Vollero furrowed his brow. "First of all, let's get something straight. I'm strictly a private investigator, a professional security consultant. I never involve myself in anything illegal, political, or inappropriate."

Casey said, "We'll keep that in mind."

"Are you still interested in Wanda Troxell?"

After a silence, Casey said, "What information do you have for us, Marty?"

"It's like this: after you questioned Wanda about a cell phone she purchased, she drove straight to my office and asked my advice on how to deal with you."

Casey said, "How do you know her?"

"When she was trying to beat a burglary case, she hired me to do some pretrial investigative work and came to trust me. She told me you'd threatened to arrest her. Is that true?"

Sutherland said, "Dollinger sent us here for the information you have on the Lanza case."

"Wanda told me she was involved with Bobby Lanza in what she called a 'blackmail ring.'"

"What was her role?" Casey asked.

"Lanza talked her into committing some burglaries that may have been related to celebrity shakedowns. The purpose of one of the break-ins was to install eavesdropping devices in big Beverly Hills homes."

"Who were the blackmail victims?" Casey said.

"Rich celebrities, household names. She assumed Lanza was using the information gathered by the electronics in his celebrity blackmail business."

Sutherland said, "How did Lanza pay her?"

"She was supposed to receive cash, but he stalled paying her. Lanza picked the wrong person to stiff. Wanda is a tough broad. She called him and demanded to be paid, then she drove to Gloria Channing's house, where Lanza was staying while Channing was in France. She and Lanza had a big argument about the money she was owed. Lanza threatened her. Frightened and convinced that he was going to kill her, Wanda defended herself."

Casey said, "Are you saying Wanda Troxell is the one who murdered Bobby Lanza?"

Maintaining eye contact with Sutherland, Vollero said, "Affirmative. That's what she told me."

"What did she say about the murder?"

"That she shot Lanza in the head with an automatic. Then, when Wanda was leaving the residence, Channing's housekeeper showed up for work. Wanda panicked and killed her, too. Wanda said she feels bad about that. She'd gotten herself into a cross and under the circumstances, she just didn't know what else to do. She's depressed about what happened."

Casey said, "Was anyone else present when Wanda confessed to having committed the murder?"

"It was just she and I."

Casey said, "Are you willing to testify to everything Wanda told you about the murders?"

Vollero smiled. "That won't be necessary."

Sutherland asked why.

"I talked her into telling you."

"Confessing?" Sutherland said.

"Yes. It took me a little time to convince her, but now she is willing to drive to your office and making a formal confession."

Casey said, "How'd you manage that?"

"Wanda is under the impression that you two are only days away from arresting her. She's terrified and confused. I told her I'd talk to you and pave the way for a prosecution deal in exchange for her telling you everything."

Casey had trouble imagining Troxell in a courtroom pleading guilty before a Superior Court judge.

"What's her motive in that?"

Looking Casey in the eye, Vollero said, "Because I talked her into it. I did you a favor."

"Why?" Casey said.

Vollero grinned. "You might say I find it appealing, the idea of solving a double murder—one you people are unable to solve. Like they say, once a cop, always a cop."

Casey guessed Vollero, a weirdo who'd never fit the cop mold, used the phrase frequently to promote his private eye business.

Sutherland said, "Where's Wanda now?"

"Waiting for me to call her."

"Thanks, Marty," Sutherland said. "We're happy to meet her anywhere she likes."

Vollero glanced at his wristwatch. "I'll relay the message to her. But right now, I have to be going."

Casey said, "How about calling her right now?"

"As I explained to Dollinger, I need to get to Burbank to catch a flight to San Francisco. I'm working on a priority investigation. My client in San Francisco is a man whose investment counselor ran off with his yacht and life savings."

Vollero began walking toward the steps. They walked out of the garden, along with him.

"Since this case stems from a double murder," Casey said, "would you mind taking a later flight?"

"Don't worry. My return flight arrives in Burbank tomorrow at two p.m. I'll bring Wanda to the department by four p.m. so she can lay everything out for you. And I'll be in touch after I speak with her."

Sutherland said, "Thanks," as they went up the steps leading to the parking lot.

"My pleasure." Vollero walked to his car and got in.

Casey unlocked his sedan. He and Sutherland got in.

"Headline," Casey said. "Hollywood private eye solves two Beverly Hills murders."

"Troxell didn't seem to me like a woman who'd confess to anything."

"And if she was going to, why would she involve Vollero?"

Sutherland said, "It doesn't make sense."

Vollero drove out of the lot.

Casey said, "Why would he stall us about bringing her in to confess?"

"He's a private eye. Maybe he needs time to shake some dough out of her. Or maybe you need to do a little more convincing. Troxell knows that confessing means she's headed straight to prison."

Back in Beverly Hills, Casey parked the car in the police lot and went upstairs to Dollinger's office. Casey summarized everything

Vollero told them about Wanda Troxell, and when he finished, Dollinger looked astonished.

"When you first interviewed Troxell," Dollinger asked, "did she give you any murder vibes?"

Casey and Sutherland told him she didn't.

"Let's take it by the numbers," Dollinger said. "Because of the eavesdropping device, we know Troxell was, at some time or another, present at the murder scene. And with Vollero telling us she confessed, could it be possible that some defense lawyer she hired might have retained Vollero to help create a phony self-defense plea for her?"

Casey said, "If so, why dangle the confession and then fly out of town? Why not call a big press conference and tell the world?"

"Good point," Dollinger said.

Sutherland said, "Vollero promised to bring her in tomorrow."

"We're not waiting," Dollinger said. "Her confession to Vollero gives us probable cause to arrest her for murder. Find Troxell and bring her in."

"What if she declines to be interviewed?"

Dollinger said, "Tell her what Vollero said about her. And if that doesn't get her talking, we'll file a murder case on her."

"In court," Sutherland said, "it'll be Vollero's word against hers. A jury might not convict."

Dollinger got up. "We'll worry about that down the road."

Casey and Sutherland left the office and walked downstairs.

Sutherland said, "Vollero bringing Troxell in might have made this a lot easier."

"If she confessed to Vollero, she'll confess to us."

"We're due for a break."

The freeway traffic was heavy on the way to Reseda. It wasn't rush hour and there were no accidents blocking the road, but no one was driving at more than forty-five miles per hour, an LA traffic situation normally caused by too many cars as well as trucks towing boats and trailers on the road. The scene was dystopian, with chrome and windshields glinting in the sun and angry drivers with eyes watering from the constant layer of acrid, grayish ozone. The city planners had abandoned the idea of having a functional transportation system. The trip to Wanda Troxell's home took an hour and a half.

They parked the car at the curb in front.

"No Porsche," Sutherland said.

Casey took out his phone and keyed Troxell's number. It rang a few times. No one picked up. They got out of the car and walked to the front door. He pressed the doorbell switch. They heard it peal inside. He tried the door handle. It was locked. They walked to the rear of the house. The sliding glass door was unlocked. Casey and Sutherland drew their automatics and walked in.

CHAPTER TWENTY

"Police officers!" Casey said. "Are you home, Wanda?"

The living room reeked of marijuana. He crossed the room and turned on a light. Papers, clothing, magazines, and newspapers littered the room. Down the hallway there was nothing in the first bedroom but a basketball and single-bed mattress without bedsprings. He pushed the door open to the adjacent bedroom and turned on an overhead light. The bed was unmade. Opening the closet, he detected the faint odor of mothballs. On the rod were dresses and overcoats, jogging suits, slacks, blouses, a raincoat, and other women's items. Dozens of pairs of women's shoes lined a shelf. He looked under the bed. Nothing. The bathroom was filled with women's cosmetics.

Returning to the living room, he checked some dog-eared beauty magazines addressed to Wanda Troxell strewn across the coffee table. On the floor was an Explorers Club paperweight and a pamphlet about bartending. In the top drawer of a small desk, he found paper clips in three sizes, real estate paperwork, ballpoint pens, a *Screen Stars* magazine with Gloria Channing's photograph on the cover, a paperback book titled *Solange Gazebo: My Life*, and an *Architectural Digest* article illustrated with a dozen photographs of the rooms in Channing's Hillcrest Drive home.

They walked into the kitchen. All the drawers were open, their contents dumped on the linoleum. The refrigerator door was ajar. In it was a half-full container of coleslaw, a jar of Mexican hot sauce, and a cardboard bucket containing moldy chicken wings. A cupboard door under the sink was open. Bottles of cleaning solution were crowded into a plastic box.

On the kitchen table sat a .22-caliber Walther automatic pistol and a box of Wolf Match LR ammunition, the same kind used in the Meredith Fox, Bobby Lanza, and Rosa Hernandez murders.

Sutherland said, "Is that what I think it is?"

"No wallet, cell phone, or personal computer, but she leaves a gun and ammo tying her to Lanza's murder. How convenient."

Casey took out his phone, dialed Marty Vollero's number. A message greeting came on. He turned off the phone. "Vollero is avoiding us."

Sutherland said, "From the beginning, nothing about these murders has made sense."

"Unless Vollero is lying."

"About Troxell confessing?"

"About everything."

"Oh…I didn't think of that."

—

They briefed Dollinger and obtained a search warrant for the Wanda Troxell home by listing what they'd seen in plain sight after entering the house after seeing evidence of a break-in. The sheriff's crime laboratory confirmed the gun was the one that had killed Meredith Fox, Bobby Lanza, and Rosa Hernandez, and Casey put out a nationwide wanted-for-murder bulletin on Wanda Troxell. Sutherland left the office at seven to take her mother to a church meeting.

At 8:00 p.m., Casey finished his report and locked it in the filing cabinet. Heading home, he stopped for a red light at Wilshire Boulevard. He glanced up at the rearview mirror. A white, late-model Toyota was behind him. The driver was in his twenties. He had a well-trimmed beard. Casey thought he looked familiar, then realized he'd seen the same car and driver when driving to work. He pondered whether Dollinger had assigned someone else to follow him or whether those responsible for the Fox and Lanza murders might have hired someone to replace Halloran, the unsuccessful hitman.

The light turned green, and Casey crossed the intersection. Two blocks south, he steered into the driveway of a three-story Beverly Hills public garage and stopped at its automated parking machine to watch the Toyota. It drove by, stopped at the corner, then turned right. Reaching out the window, he pressed a green button on the parking machine, took the time ticket, and drove into the garage. Following ramps up to the third level, he parked the car, turned off the engine, and got out.

He walked to the open wall and looked down at the street. The white Toyota was parked two doors north in front of a clothing store. Glancing about to make sure no one was watching, he took out his automatic, checked the magazine, and re-holstered. He descended the stairwell steps to the ground floor and exited the parking structure. The driver of the white Toyota turned his head to avoid looking in his direction. Entering a specialty wine shop, Casey looked out through its display window. The Toyota hadn't moved. He guessed if the driver was a cop, he'd have gotten out of the car and followed him by now—but a killer would wait to strike when his quarry was alone.

After a few minutes in the store, he returned to the parking garage, walked up the stairwell to the third floor, and looked down at the street. The Toyota hadn't moved. Casey steered down the ramps to the parking machine. He slipped the time ticket and a credit card into the slot, and the gate rose. He took the receipt and the card and drove out. The Toyota was gone. Driving west to Santa Monica Boulevard, he stopped for a motorcade of five white limousines exiting the driveway of the Beverly Mandarin Hotel before traffic resumed.

He drove a quarter mile to Avenue of the Stars and braked in a lefthand turn lane for the light. Seeing nothing untoward in the rearview, he wondered if he'd mistakenly presumed he was being followed. The light turned green. He turned left and drove by the multistory Century Plaza and Marriott Plaza hotels, stopped for the red light at Pico Boulevard, and glanced at the passenger side mirror. The Toyota was behind him again.

When the light changed, he swerved into the left lane and drove south on Motor Avenue. The Toyota followed. On his right was El Rancho Park, where he occasionally played tennis. He steered into a parking lot adjacent to the well-lit public tennis courts. The Toyota continued south. Casey navigated into a marked space next to a tall chain-link fence surrounding the courts and killed the engine. The driver of the Toyota made a U-turn on Motor Avenue, steered into the lot, and parked near the exit.

Casey got out of the car. Walking by the courts, he heard tennis balls being hit back and forth. He went inside the recreation center office.

A young attendant stringing a tennis racket said, "Haven't seen you here in a while, Mr. Casey."

"Been busy."

Casey looked out the window. The Toyota was in the same spot.

"Are you here to reserve a court?"

"Uh, yes, for next Saturday." Casey walked to the counter. The attendant handed him a tennis court sign-up list. Casey signed his name and handed it back. "Thanks."

"See you."

Exiting the office, he looked about. He was alone in the parking lot. Walking to his sedan, he unlocked the driver's door.

The bearded man who'd been driving the Toyota came from behind a panel truck parked in the adjacent space. Casey rested his right hand on his gun.

"FBI," the man said, holding out a leather wallet with a badge and an identification card in it. They looked real.

A woman behind him said, "Take it easy."

Casey turned. She wore a business suit and was also holding FBI identification.

"Why are you following me?"

"It wasn't our idea," the male agent said.

"What's going on?"

The woman said, "Halloran was working for us."

"I didn't kill him."

"That's what Dollinger told our agent in charge. But he isn't convinced."

"Halloran tried to kill me."

The male said, "We figured warning you about the surveillance was better than a friendly fire incident."

The explanation made sense to Casey. The agents were sabotaging their surveillance but considered the mission questionable and not worth someone getting killed by accident. Casey knew of similar rare occurrences between police agencies.

Casey took his hand off the gun.

The female agent said, "We aren't planning to put this in any report."

"I can go with that. But since we're talking off the record, have your people been nosing around my apartment?"

"Negative," the bearded agent said. "And we would know if that were happening."

"Thanks for sticking your necks out."

The woman said, "If we find out you're working for the other side, all bets are off."

Casey nodded. "Fair enough."

The FBI agents walked toward the other side of the parking lot. Casey got in his sedan and drove off.

—

Hearing Dollinger rap lightly on the office door, Donna Slade looked up from her paperwork. “Come in.”

He opened the door. “You wanted to see me, Chief?”

“I hope I didn’t take you away from anything important.”

“No problem.”

She slipped off her eyeglasses. “What’s the latest on the double homicide?”

“Still no leads on Wanda Troxell. None of her credit cards have been used. Her license plate number has been put in the system. There are no reports of activity.”

“What’s going on?”

“That’s the latest news.”

Dollinger raised his eyebrows. Like a lot of cops who felt comfortable in his job, he didn’t like being questioned. She could care less about what he found irritating.

“I’m referring to how you see things from your point of view as a detective supervisor.”

“Uh, it’s possible Troxell changed her mind about turning herself in and then, believing she was going to be arrested for murder, just decided to leave town.”

“Do you believe Vollero was telling the truth when he said Troxell confessed to him?”

“I have no evidence to the contrary.”

“Where is she?

“When Casey and Sutherland arrived at her home, they found the front door locked, the back door unlocked. Inside, there was some evidence of ransacking.”

She said, “What do you make of it?”

“That’s hard to say.”

“What the hell is Vollero up to?”

“I just sent Casey and Sutherland to ask him that very question.”

She said, "Have you considered asking Vollero to submit to a lie detector test?"

"We can certainly pose the question."

She said, "The expression on your face tells me you don't think much of the idea."

"I don't know any law enforcement officer who'd voluntarily submit to a polygraph examination."

Dollinger could barely hide his resentment toward her. She knew he was piqued at being passed over by the promotion board, who chose an outsider from another department to be chief over him. Men like him couldn't handle being bested by a woman. Like some kid who didn't make the baseball team, Dollinger couldn't get over the loss.

She said, "Come to think of it, neither would I. Have you considered the possibility that someone may have paid Vollero to frame Troxell for the murders?"

"That's possible, Chief, but I tend to consider the simplest answers first," he said coldly. "By the way, an FBI surveillance team has been tailing Casey."

"Since when?"

"Casey isn't sure, but he confronted the agents following him and they've backed off."

"What do you make of it?"

"Casey thinks the Bureau suspects him of murdering Halloran, their rat."

"Casey?"

"Halloran tried to kill him."

She got up from the desk and walk to the window. "Is that possible?"

"Minutes after the exchange of gunfire in Topanga Canyon, Casey was with Sutherland. She was with him when they went to Halloran's apartment and found his body."

"Could Sutherland be covering for Casey?"

"Sutherland is a straight arrow. I can't imagine her getting involved in that kind of game."

Slade said, "I don't see her handing up any detective who was her partner."

He shrugged. "Breaking it all down, Chief, I've seen nothing to indicate any internal cover-up."

"Is there documentation—"

"I checked both their logs."

She spoke coldly. "Three unsolved murders. A missing suspect. And now something we never expected: the FBI tailing our detectives."

"The Feds always have their feelers out for police misconduct."

She turned to him. "I know the Bureau. If they know something, they won't tell us anything until after they've made an arrest."

"Casey didn't kill Halloran, Chief. I don't think we've overlooked any internal problem."

"If he did, if Casey turns out to be a ringer, it would be the worst publicity imaginable, the mother of all shit storms. You and I would be washed down the drain."

"Yes, Chief. I see what you mean."

"Something is blocking us from solving the homicides."

"Is it possible these murder investigations are offtrack?"

"I don't see internal sabotage as a possibility, but I'm not trying to downplay any possibility. We need to look at every scenario."

"Stay on top of what Casey and Sutherland are doing," she said. "Minute by minute."

—

Twelve miles away, Casey waited in the arrival terminal of the Burbank Airport, near a Southwest Airlines baggage carousel as dozens of passengers from a San Francisco flight looked for their luggage. Marty Vollero, one of the last to exit the jetway, wore a beige summer suit, brown tie, and sandals. He was clean shaven and looked rested. Hefting a wheeled black suitcase from the conveyer, Vollero rolled it slowly through the crowd moving toward the exit. Casey followed him out to the sidewalk. Vollero walked toward the valet parking station rather than waiting at the curb for transportation.

Casey caught up to him. "How was your trip?"

Vollero stopped. "What are you doing here?"

"You said you were going to call."

"About what?" Vollero's face reflected no emotion.

"Wanda Troxell."

"I left her a phone message. She hasn't gotten back to me."

Casey said, "She's not home."

"How do you know that?"

"I checked her address."

"I was under the impression you were going to wait until I got in touch with you."

Casey said, "Who else knows Troxell confessed to you about the murders?"

"No one."

"What's going on?"

"You're asking me?" Vollero said.

"You said she trusts you. Why hasn't she touched base to ask what you learned from the cops?"

Vollero looked irritated. "My first brainwave would be that someone guilty of two murders might have second thoughts about turning herself in for a one-way trip to the joint."

"Where can I find her?"

Vollero smirked. "For all I know she might be over in Beverly Hills murdering someone else."

"Do you find humor in this?"

"Lighten up, Casey. I solved a double homicide for you. What else would you like me to do? Write the report and take it to the district attorney for you?"

"How about testifying before the county grand jury as to her murder confession?"

"Send me a subpoena."

"I'll do that."

"Anything else?"

"Not at the moment."

Vollero said, "May I ask you a question?"

"Go ahead."

"Had you been drinking before the jewelry store shoot-out where you killed your partner?"

Casey felt the heat of anger rush from the back of his neck to his face. "I don't blame you for being nervous, Marty. We're getting closer to you every day."

Glaring at him, Vollero grasped the handle of the suitcase. "Be careful out there."

"You too."

Rolling the suitcase, Vollero blended into a bustling crowd of passengers walking toward the valet parking station.

Casey walked to the nearby covered parking structure. On the second level, he unlocked the sedan and got in. Thinking about Vollero's words, he turned on the commercial radio and half-listened to the news. Sixteen minutes later, Kristina Sutherland exited the stairwell, walked to the sedan, and got in on the passenger's side.

She said, "He walked to the valet parking station, handed a receipt to the attendant. When they brought him his yellow Audi Spyder, he left a nice, big tip, got in, and drove away."

"That's what I need," Casey said, "A luxury sports car."

"In Beverly Hills, appearance is everything." She laughed. "While every other private investigator I know is in debt and scrambling for work, Vollero is driving a convertible that costs more than four years of a police salary…"

"He's lying."

"About Wanda?"

"How's this for a fact pattern: Vollero, who is in with Lanza on the blackmail game, finds out Lanza is poaching some of his blackmail victims. He goes to Channing's house, kills Lanza, and shoots Hernandez when she comes to work and sees him. He's a big player in the game."

She smiled "And telling us about Wanda confessing?"

"A deflection, away from him."

"Then you think he planted the murder gun in her house to incriminate her?"

He nodded. "That fits."

"Do you think she's still alive?"

"Unfortunately, that doesn't fit my theory."

CHAPTER TWENTY-ONE

Near the Beverly Center shopping mall, Casey parked on Willoughby Avenue, north of Melrose, in front of a two-story duplex. He got out of the car with a bottle of cabernet sauvignon given to him by Roget and walked upstairs to the one-bedroom unit Ellen Brady rented from a retired Beverly Hills officer who'd bought the place, remodeled both units, and then moved to Croatia, where the Willoughby rent money enabled him to live in a three-story oceanfront manor.

After having sex, they showered together, dressed, then went to the diminutive kitchen, where Casey uncorked the wine. While sipping it, he helped Ellen make mushroom risotto from a complicated recipe she'd cut out of a *Bon Appetit* magazine. Later, at the kitchen table enjoying the meal, she told him about meeting with two different community business groups and getting lots of questions about why more police officers weren't visible on Beverly Hills streets.

"What did you tell them?"

"The truth: that there wasn't enough money in the police budget to hire more officers."

"How did they react?"

"Not well. I wanted to also tell them they needed a new mayor and city council but decided that might not be good idea."

"I'll drink to that."

"How's the Lanza murder case going?" she said.

"Sutherland and I thought we had it solved."

"What happened?"

"A private investigator told us someone had confessed to the murders, but we can't find the suspect."

"What's going on?"

"The private eye is playing games."

"Sounds complicated."

"And increasingly difficult."

"Are you going to be able to solve it?"

"I'm not sure."

"What's the problem?"

"The chief is leaning on Dollinger for results. If something doesn't break soon, I can see him taking Sutherland and me off the case and assigning it to someone else."

"One of the records clerks told me Slade's husband is raising lots of money to be used in her campaign for sheriff."

He said, "Another reason the chief wants the murders solved quickly."

Ellen refilled wine glasses, put the bottle down on the table, and picked up her glass.

"Here's to solving it."

They drank.

"By the way," Casey said, "did you ever mention to Dollinger that I spotted you following me?"

"No."

"He didn't ask about the surveillance?"

"When he asked, I told him the truth: that you weren't drinking. Then I asked to be taken off the assignment because I didn't want to become known as a rat, that and being new to the department, I wanted to fit in rather than strangle myself working Internal Affairs."

"What was his reaction?"

"He told me he understood how I felt and that I could return to being a full-time community relations officer."

"No harm, no foul?"

She said, "The incident made me think about what I really want to do with my life. So, I drove to USC and talked to a career counselor. She told me I need two more semesters to get certified as a registered nurse. I signed up for night school. If I remain in the community relations job, I'll be able to pick up most of the school credits at night."

He was stunned. "You're planning to leave the department?"

"Legs, returning to law enforcement was a big mistake, a step backward for me."

"Maybe if you return to patrol you'll feel differently."

"I'm through with being a cop. I no longer find the profession fulfilling. Being a nurse pays more, and rather than being hated by the public, medical professionals are liked. From here on, I'm using the job to make a living while I complete my studies."

He put his hand on hers.

She smiled, got up, and sat on his lap. They kissed passionately.

—

At 3:16 a.m., Los Angeles County Sheriff's Deputy Duane Rutherford was taking his nightly nap in the back seat of his police cruiser parked off Highway 14 near Palmdale, a high desert community sixty miles from Beverly Hills. Patrolling the same area for three years, he knew the safest places to hide for his nightly snooze. He'd even developed the ability to detect his call sign from other official radio traffic while napping. He knew missing a single radio call while sleeping could cost him his police career and consequently his two-bedroom Palmdale home; Mastercraft ski boat; and wife, Maria, who'd begged him not to borrow on the house to finance the boat.

Startled awake by the radio dispatcher's voice calling "Three King Three Five," he lunged to the front seat, snatched the microphone from the dashboard, and thumbed the transmit button.

"Three King Three Five, go."

"Abandoned car, a possible stolen," the dispatcher said. "Rest Area 138. A sports car parked near the drinking fountain."

"Three King Three Five, roger."

Dropping the microphone on the front seat, Rutherford rubbed his eyes. He got out of the police cruiser. Yawning loudly, he stretched his arms and legs. He slipped on his gun belt and cinched the buckle. Behind the wheel, he used the interior light and rearview mirror to button his khaki uniform shirt and fasten the clip-on necktie. He drove onto Highway 14.

At the sign for Rest Area 138, he swerved onto an off-ramp and followed a frontage road about a hundred yards. Steering into the rest area driveway, he slowed and looked about. Because of the hour, only a few cars were there. He turned on the spotlight and aimed it at the public drinking fountain area. Driving closer, he parked behind a sports car—a silver Porsche. He walked to the driver's side window and aimed the beam of his heavy, steel flashlight into the front seat. A gray blanket covered what he guessed might be a body on the floorboard and part of the passenger seat.

He rapped the flashlight on the glass. "Wake up!" He rapped loudly again. "Police officer! Are you okay?"

Nothing moved. He used the flashlight to smash the driver's side window glass. Reaching inside to unlock the door, he pulled it open, leaned inside, and tugged back the blanket. A woman in a red shirred dress wasn't moving. Her hair was tangled as if someone had grabbed it and twisted. A reddish-purple bruise circled her neck. Her skin was cold. An Apple wristwatch with a gold band was on her left wrist.

He pressed the transmit switch on his mobile radio. "Three King Three Five."

"Roger, Three Five."

"Rest Area 138, the sports car has a female DB in it. Notify homicide."

—

Casey walked into the office, signed the duty roster, and moved to his desk.

Sutherland, who was at her computer, got up and, without saying good morning, whispered to him. "A sheriff's detective has been in Dollinger's office for the past half hour with the door closed. Dollinger just came out and asked me where you were. I told him you'd be here any minute. I've seen the sheriff's guy before. I was working a street robbery in front of the Writers Guild Theater. He and Marty Vollero were protecting some movie star."

The phone on Casey's desk rang. He picked up the receiver.

Dollinger asked him to come into his office.

"Sure," Casey said and put the phone down and turned to Sutherland. "Are you sure the guy in there is the one you saw with Vollero?"

"Positive," she said with a worried look. "Good luck."

Casey walked to Dollinger's office and opened the door.

"Come in," Dollinger said.

Casey walked in and closed the door.

Dollinger introduced him to the heavyset, fiftyish man sitting in a chair in front of the desk: Detective Sergeant Lenny Gomulka from sheriff's homicide. Gomulka and Casey exchanged pleasantries without shaking hands. "I'll let the sergeant fill you in."

Gomulka said, "I understand you've been looking for Wanda Troxell."

"Yes."

"We found her body in Palmdale last night. The cause of death is manual strangulation. We ran her name in the system along with your wanted for questioning notice. I'm assigned to investigate the homicide."

Casey figured if this were a routine inquiry, Gomulka would have called him rather than come to the office and request to speak with Captain Dollinger. Something was going on.

Casey said, "Do you have any leads?"

"Nothing at this point. I thought you might be able to help."

"I interviewed her while working a homicide investigation," Casey said. "From what we've been able to put together, it looks like Troxell was an associate of one of the victims. She may have been involved in some burglaries."

"Her car was found at a highway rest area. Do you have any ideas about who might have killed her?"

"No," Casey said, glancing at Dollinger.

Looking uncomfortable, Gomulka said, "How well did you know her?"

"She was someone I interviewed." Casey had no intention of discussing the details of the Lanza murder with him.

"We found your business card in her wallet. I assume she got it from you."

Casey nodded. "When I interviewed her."

"Did you have a relationship with Troxell outside of your official duties?"

"Negative."

"Did you ever give her anything else?"

"No."

"So, you never gave her anything of value?"

"Correct. Like I said, she was someone interviewed during an investigation."

"Do you own an Apple wristwatch?"

"Yes, I bought one about a year ago."

"Where is it?"

Casey felt his heart rate increase. "It's missing."

"Could you have given the wristwatch to Wanda Troxell?"

"No. But why do you ask?"

"We found an Apple wristwatch with a gold band on her left wrist. You are listed as the registered owner of the watch. Has she ever been in your apartment?"

Casey said she hadn't.

"How do you think she ended up dead with your watch on her wrist?"

"Troxell was a burglar," Casey said. "Maybe she broke into my apartment and stole it."

"Are you sure you didn't give it to her?"

"Positive."

"Have you been to Palmdale recently?"

"No."

"Any ideas as to why she'd burgle your apartment and steal your wristwatch?"

Casey said, "I think someone else stole it."

"Who?"

"Maybe whoever murdered her, to make me a suspect and sabotage a homicide investigation I'm working."

"Who's your murder suspect?"

"I don't have one."

Gomulka turned to Dollinger. "Is that right, Captain? No homicide suspect?"

"Are you hard of hearing?" Dollinger said, glaring at Gomulka. "That's what the man said."

"No—"

"Do you consider Casey a murder suspect?"

"Not at the moment."

Casey said, "Then why the personal visit? Why didn't you pick up the phone and call me?"

Gomulka coughed dryly. "This is just the way I conduct my investigations."

"Do you have any other questions?" Dollinger said.

"Just a few."

"Detective Casey is busy now and for the rest of the day. I suggest you call me tomorrow to see if I can arrange another meeting."

Gomulka looked chagrined. "I was just gonna ask—"

"The interview is concluded," Dollinger said.

Gomulka looked surprised. "May I ask why?"

"Because your questions sound accusatory. If you have any further questions for Casey, you can call me."

"Yeah, sure." Gomulka stood and adjusted his jacket over his gun belt. "Nothing personal. Just following leads in a routine investigation." He walked toward the door.

"I have a question," Casey said.

Gomulka stopped, turned to him. "Sure."

"Do you know Marty Vollero?"

"Uh, he used to work here, right?"

"Then you know him, right?"

"We've met."

Casey said, "Actually, you work for him."

Dollinger's eyes widened.

"Part-time," Gomulka said, "Part-time security work now and then. Like a lot of officers from other departments, including this one."

Casey said, "Tell Marty I said hello."

Gomulka gave a slight nod and departed.

Dollinger got up, closed the door. "What the fuck was that?"

"Sutherland saw him working a VIP protection job with Vollero at the Writers Guild Theater."

"What's going on, Legs?

"My apartment manager recently found some security cameras disabled on the same day a tenant saw two strangers near my apartment. At first I thought the FBI might have broken in to search the place. Now I think it was Vollero or one of his people. He might be trying to frame me for the Troxell murder."

"Why didn't you tell me?"

"Because it's just a guess."

"Did you make a burglary report on the wristwatch?"

"Negative."

"Why not?"

"I wasn't sure it had been taken. I thought I might have left it in a gym locker, and someone stole it."

"Vollero," Dollinger said. "His name keeps showing up in this investigation. And the sheriff's department is and always has been tight with the FBI."

"Interviewing Vollero about this would be a waste of time. He isn't going to say anything. What makes him dangerous is that if he is making lots of extortion money, he can afford to do whatever it takes to keep the cash rolling in. What will happen after you tell the chief about this?"

"I'm not sure."

"Marty Vollero would love nothing better than to have me taken off the case."

"I intend to explain that to her."

"I hope she understands."

"No one is going to be taken off the investigation because of Marty Vollero. That I guarantee. In the meantime, because this investigation is getting extra dicey, if the sheriff's department or the FBI attempts to interview you, decline to speak and refer them to me. I'll handle them."

"No problem."

"Now go back to work and solve these murders."

CHAPTER TWENTY-TWO

Casey sat alone in an unmarked police sedan parked on Hollywood Boulevard near Marty Vollero's office. Having arrived shortly after 9:00 a.m., he walked through the Gamewell Building's underground garage and found Vollero's yellow Audi sports car parked in an unmarked space on the first floor. Since then, Casey had been watching the garage driveway on Hollywood Boulevard, the building's only vehicular exit.

He'd found himself thinking about Ellen Brady—about her easygoing personality and about being in bed with her. He also exchanged phone calls with Sutherland to discuss homicide report details and listened to the radio news, some free PBS jazz and talk programs, until they became tedious. Turning off the radio at 2:00 p.m., he sped to a nearby McDonald's for a cheeseburger and fries then raced back to the surveillance location to wolf them down. The Audi hadn't moved from the garage. Nothing, Casey mused, could be more boring than an unproductive surveillance—and nothing more depressing than an important investigation that was stalled.

He again reconsidered the facts of the investigation. The people of interest had been interviewed, the physical evidence analyzed and catalogued. The pressure applied to Anthony Flair and Wanda Troxell failed to crack the case. Nothing was left but the theory of the case, some suspects, and a few hunches. Casey was oddly tense and impatient. The surveillance stage of an investigation wasn't the place he wanted to be. Surveillance meant time, lots of time, and the possibility of coming up with absolutely nothing new. He didn't like the feeling that came with it—the opposite of working a fast-breaking case when the facts were quickly falling into place. He recalled years earlier watching a Hollywood motel room around the clock for two days only to learn that the fugitive armed robber he was stalking had been arrested in London a week before. On the list of investigative activities, surveillance took the most time and had the least chance of case-changing success. Most often, that came from someone spilling the beans during an interview.

The secret to tolerating surveillance tedium was to adjust the mind into a timeless, bodiless zone. Living another's life wasn't the way to feel vital and alive. The trick was to be able to note the time in a log but not be affected by it, like some island lighthouse keeper. But Casey wasn't in the detached zone, and he knew this wasn't an ordinary surveillance. For him, everything was at stake. Carefully observing Vollero's activities, he was hoping to uncover fresh leads, but with media stories increasing the pressure on solving Beverly Hills's only double murder in more than twenty years, Slade and Dollinger would soon relieve Casey and Sutherland from the investigation and appoint two other detectives to take over.

At 6:03 p.m., someone drove the yellow Audi to the garage exit. Casey raised the binoculars to his eyes. Vollero was behind the wheel. The gate arm rose. Vollero drove the Audi out of the garage and onto Hollywood Boulevard. Casey followed the Audi to Vine Street, where it slowed and then came to a stop at the intersection. After waiting for the signal light to turn green, Vollero made a left turn. Casey discreetly followed him south to the signal light at Sunset Boulevard. Vollero turned right. Casey followed, dropping back to avoid detection.

A few minutes later, the Audi slowed near Fuller Avenue and swerved to the curb. Vollero parked in front of a yoga school. Casey stopped down the block. He watched Vollero get out of the sports car, drop coins in a parking meter, and then walk into a hair-styling shop next to the yoga school. Casey drove by the hair salon to gauge

Vollero's view from its front window. Deciding the Audi wasn't visible from the salon, he parked the sedan on Sunset. In the trunk, he unzipped a leather equipment bag and took out a small GPS tracker device. Having verified the transmitter was functioning, he clipped it to a magnetic holder. Slipping the device into a brown paper bag, he closed the trunk lid and carried the bag to Vollero's car.

One eye on the hair salon, he took the tracker from the bag and reached under the Audi's right rear wheel well. Hearing the thump as the tracker's magnet attached securely to the car's frame, he folded the bag, returned to the sedan with it and drove around the corner. He took out his cell phone and checked the tracker app. A blinking red icon on its GPS map indicated the locater attached to the Audi was working. Now he'd be able to monitor Vollero's activities from miles away.

An hour later, the GPS locater icon on the phone screen began to flicker then continued to blink as Vollero drove the Audi west. Using the tracking signal, Casey followed him at a discreet distance to Sunset Boulevard in Beverly Hills, then to Lasky Drive, where the tracking icon stopped moving.

Casey saw Vollero walk from the Audi to an office building and enter using the front door. An hour later, he exited the building and drove to a motion picture screening room on Victory Boulevard in Burbank, where Casey saw him enter by the front door. Vollero remained inside two hours and sixteen minutes before returning to the Audi.

Casey followed him to Abdul's Bistro in Studio City, where Vollero had dinner and drinks alone at the bar and departed shortly after midnight. Casey followed him to Cahuenga Boulevard, near the Hollywood Bowl. Vollero turned onto Mulholland Drive and began winding upward through the hills. The car icon stopped. Driving by the location minutes later, Casey saw the Audi parked inside the gate of a luxury hillside home. Noting the address, he parked up the road and switched off the headlights. He checked the address in the DMV database: Vollero owned the property.

Assuming Vollero was home for the night, Casey drove out of the hills to his apartment and caught a few hours' sleep. Early the next morning he checked the GPS icon on his phone. Vollero was still home. Casey showered, dressed, and returned to his surveillance position on Mulholland Drive. Vollero departed shortly after 8:00 a.m. Casey followed him to Sunset Boulevard in Beverly Hills and turned north onto Hillcrest Drive. The Audi stopped, parked at the curb in front of the Gloria Channing residence. It could mean several things, but Casey believed the simple answer was the best: Gloria Channing needed money, and Vollero, operating a successful celebrity blackmail ring, was swimming in it.

From a few blocks away, Casey waited an hour and eleven minutes before the GPS icon moved again. Vollero went to the Gamewell Building on Hollywood Boulevard; drove into in the underground garage. Famished, Casey drove to Sara's Taco Hut on Hollywood Boulevard and ate three tacos as he stood next to his car while monitoring the GPS tracker. Returning to the Gamewell Building, he parked in the middle of the block.

Vollero departed his office in the afternoon and drove to The Palm restaurant in Beverly Hills, where he had lunch at the bar with two attractive Latin women. Later, he drove to Murray's Clothing in Beverly Hills; he went inside and came out carrying a sports coat on a hanger. Vollero then cruised south to the 10 freeway and then drove west.

Monitoring the GPS signal, Casey remained a mile behind Vollero as he drove to the ocean and turned onto the Pacific Coast Highway. Using the locater, Casey saw the icon on the screen stop near the highway in Malibu Beach. A minute later, Casey drove by a Malibu beach mini mall. The Audi was parked next to a late-model Mercedes-

Benz. No one was in the Audi. Making a U-turn farther up the highway, Casey swerved into the crowded parking lot of a beachside restaurant across the street. Using binoculars, he focused across the highway at the mini-mall parking lot. He adjusted the focus until Vollero's Audi and the Mercedes-Benz next to it came into focus. Vollero, in the passenger seat of the Benz, was talking with a well-dressed man behind the steering wheel. Casey figured him to be about forty.

From his briefcase, Casey took out a camera and quickly attached the long-distance zoom lens. He focused on the Mercedes-Benz. Snapping a photograph, he checked the camera's digital index and saw a clear image of Vollero and the man sitting behind the steering wheel. Nineteen minutes later, Vollero climbed out of the Benz, got in the Audi, and sped south out of the lot and onto the Pacific Coast Highway.

Seconds later, the Benz exited the lot and drove north. Making a U-turn, Casey raced after it. Accelerating, he got close enough to read and copy the license plate number, after which he slowed, blended in with the traffic and began using the locator again to follow Vollero back to his Hollywood office. Casey parked two blocks away.

On his phone, he entered the Mercedes-Benz's license plate number into the DMV database. The name DESMOND ECKERSLEY flashed onto the screen along with a Malibu address. Copying the name onto the phone, he touched RETURN. The screen filled with a list of computer entries, including newspaper articles and photographs about Eckersley, a psychiatrist known for treating celebrity clients. He'd been interviewed frequently on radio and TV shows as an expert on the problems of motion picture celebrities and had once been named in a lawsuit filed against him by a former client, an actress. After a legal arbitration, Eckersley had been ordered to pay her a no-contest judgement protected by a secrecy clause.

Casey knew that without proper context, surveillance observations were often not what they seemed to be, that care needed to be taken to avoid false assumptions that might throw an investigation off track. A suspect observed watching a house might well be a potential real estate buyer rather than a burglar or voyeur. And a suspect carrying a folded newspaper from his home to an address a mile away and leaving the paper under the front door might not be a spy or a dope courier, but someone sharing a newspaper with a friend. Vollero, a private investigator, had legitimate reasons for meeting people in all walks of life. His meeting with Eckersley might have nothing to do with the Lanza murder. Or, Casey thought, Eckersley, a psychiatrist with celebrity clients meeting secretly with Vollero, might be a key member of a blackmail conspiracy.

—

Casey drove to the police headquarters. Only Sutherland was in the office. She stopped typing, turned her wheeled office chair toward him.

She said, "I'm ready to handle the next surveillance shift."

"No longer necessary."

"Why?"

"First, Vollero stopped by Gloria Channing's place."

"I wonder what that was about?"

"Your guess is as good as mine. Later, he drove to Malibu and met with a psychiatrist named Desmond Eckersley. They talked in Eckersley's car for about twenty minutes."

Sutherland said, "That sounds like a sex thing."

"They didn't do anything but talk."

"Maybe Vollero is having mental problems."

"The meeting was too short to be a counseling session," he said. "And what psychiatrist would leave his office to meet a patient in a beachside parking lot?"

"Maybe it's a special case."

"Like what?"

Sutherland shrugged. "I can't think of one."

"Neither can I."

Sutherland turned to her computer. "Desmond Eckersley." She tapped several keys, then stopped. "I thought the name sounded familiar. His telephone number is listed on Meredith Fox's cell phone bill."

"You're sure?"

"I scanned Fox's cell phone numbers and entered them into the Lanza murder book spreadsheet. My guess is that she was one of his patients."

Thinking out loud, Casey said, "A psychiatrist with celebrity clients would have access to a lot of valuable information that could be used for blackmail."

"And Vollero is known for sticking his nose into celebrity extortion cases."

"And a Hollywood publicity agent like Meredith Fox could be a valuable member of a shakedown crew."

"To hook Vollero," Sutherland said, "we need to tie him into a conspiracy with Lanza."

"One of the blackmail victims agreeing to testify against him would do the trick."

Sutherland nodded. "Like the platinum blonde pictured in the photographs from Lanza's car."

"Anthony Flair referred to her as Vivian."

"Legs, murder investigation or not, psychiatrists never reveal the names of their patients."

"One thing is for sure. To qualify as a blackmail victim, this Vivian, or whomever she is, must have a lot of money."

"So what?" she said.

"Rich people see psychiatrists. And a big-time celebrity shrink like Eckersley must have someone answering his office telephone, someone who handles billing his clients…"

After a discussion, Casey borrowed an untraceable cell phone from the narcotics squad and attached it to a digital recorder. He brought it to Sutherland's desk and handed it to her. Sutherland dialed Dr. Desmond Eckersley's office number. She spoke with Eckersley's assistant, a woman they later identified as Alice Graverton. The call was recorded and later transcribed as follows:

(Phone ringing)

Graverton: Offices of Dr. Desmond Eckersley.

Sutherland: Good morning. This is Rebecca Brown. To whom am I speaking?

Graverton: I'm Alice, Dr. Eckersley's office manager. How may I help you?

Sutherland: I'd like to make an appointment with Dr. Eckersley.

Graverton: May I ask who recommended you?

Sutherland: No one, actually. I saw Dr. Eckersley being interviewed on television and was very impressed.

Graverton: Are you aware Dr. Eckersley maintains a solely psychiatric practice?

Sutherland: Yes, I've been experiencing anxiety.

Graverton: Dr. Eckersley sees patients Monday through Friday except for every other Wednesday when he plays golf. He has no openings on his schedule until October.

Sutherland: That should be okay. I'll be in town then. My husband and I spend a lot of time in Aspen.

Graverton: How about... October 29 at 2:00 p.m.?

Sutherland: Very well. I'm writing that down. By the way, where is Dr. Eckersley's office?

Graverton: In Malibu.

Sutherland: Isn't that a residential area?

Graverton: He recently moved from his office in Beverly Hills and had an office built on his property.

Sutherland: I'll bet you love working in Malibu. It's such a beautiful area.

Graverton: Actually, Dr. Eckersley allows me to work from home.

Sutherland: How do you like remote working?

Graverton: It gives me more time to concentrate on work rather than fighting traffic to get to Malibu every day.

Sutherland: I'm a motion picture location manager and do a lot of traveling. I wish I could work from home.

Graverton: Sounds like you have interesting profession.

Sutherland: It's challenging. I get along well with movie directors and actors. That's what it's all about. The most difficult part is billing.

Graverton: Billing used to take me days, but computer software makes it easy.

Sutherland: I'll have to modernize. I'll call for an appointment after I confirm my schedule.

Graverton: I look forward to hearing from you, Miss Brown.

Sutherland: Call me Becky.

Graverton: Have a wonderful day, Becky.

Sutherland: Same to you, Alice. Bye now.

CHAPTER TWENTY-THREE

Casey and Sutherland sat in an air-conditioned Ford sedan parked on Beverly Boulevard across from the largest multiunit apartment complex in Los Angeles, the Wellington Quad: four twelve-story vertical rectangles with identical windows, balconies, and fountains at the entrance whose water incandesced green from 9:00 p.m. to 4:00 a.m. Alice Graverton's apartment was a two-bedroom in the east building. It was 11:46 a.m., and the third day of the surveillance. The temperature had already hit ninety-three degrees and the weather report said it would climb to over a hundred.

Construction of the Wellington complex had begun eight years earlier with laundered money from Chinese entrepreneurs and the help of a crooked Los Angeles city councilman whose conviction for bribery led to a court order shutting down the project. Two years later, after liens were paid and a New York conglomerate assumed control, construction began again—until it was hindered by the court filings of an environmental group. The conglomerate invited a novice developer who happened to be the governor's son-in-law to horn in on the deal. Shortly thereafter, the legal and political obstacles disappeared, and the project was completed. For all that, the Wellington Quad was a successful housing development with more than fifteen hundred apartments leased to permanent residents and several entrepreneurs who were allowed to buy at a discount and then rent apartments to tourists who came to LA to see the homes of the movie stars and the new statues at Grauman's Chinese Theater.

For the past two days, Casey and Sutherland had observed Alice Graverton leave the apartment building and walk to Goody's coffee shop at the end of the block, where she ate lunch alone before returning to her apartment. Her lunch lasted between fifty and sixty-three minutes from the time she walked out of the apartment house until she returned. The only ground-floor entrances to the Wellington were the lobby door and the driveway leading into the underground garage.

Sutherland said, "You're assuming Graverton has a list of Eckersley's clients in her apartment. For all we know, he might have someone else handling the medical billing."

"More than one person keeping his records?" he said. "I don't see a psychiatrist doing that."

"I don't like this."

"There's no other way to get ahead of these people."

Sutherland said, "It's not worth the risk."

"Who knows what anything is worth?"

"Legs, if we wait a few days, maybe there will be some better opportunity. We might have better luck some other time."

"You could say that about anything."

Casey didn't blame her for being concerned. Surreptitious entry was less risky during the day than at night, and the biggest problem would be the Wellington's lobby entrance. He felt a vague uneasiness, but he wasn't going to tell her.

"I don't like the whole idea, Legs. I say we forget this bullshit and walk. To hell with the risk taking."

"No one is gonna walk into headquarters and hand us the evidence. That's not in the cards."

He slipped rubber gloves and a small leather case containing locksmith's picks into an inside jacket pocket.

"What are you doing?"

"Going for it."

She cringed. "Let's watch the place for one more day."

"We're not going to be able make this case without something concrete to go on."

"I'm telling you I don't like it."

Alice Graverton exited the apartment house lobby door and walked toward the coffee shop.

"There she is," he said. "She's leaving early." He opened the car door.

Sutherland gritted her teeth. "Be careful."

Graverton walked toward the coffee shop. Casey got out of the car, crossed the street, and waited near a bus bench while keeping an eye on the apartment house lobby door. A few minutes later, a late-model Jaguar parked at the curbside loading zone near the entrance. A young woman got out on the passenger side. Opening the rear door, she lifted an infant out of a back-seat carrier, closed the door, and waved at the Jaguar's driver. He drove off. Carrying the infant, she walked to the lobby door and fumbled with her purse for a key to open the door. Casey seized the opportunity to politely assist her with the door.

She thanked him. He followed her inside the lobby and to the elevator landing, where others were waiting: a woman staring at a cell phone and a man holding a shopping bag. Seconds later, Casey heard a muffled bell. The elevator doors slid open. An elderly couple came out. Casey hung back a moment while the woman with the infant and the others got on. Stepping in, he became aware of piped-in Leon Bridges music. The doors closed. The cell phone lady tapped seven—Alice Graverton's floor; the grocery shopper six; the young mother eleven. Casey punched twelve and they rode up in silence. Quickly glancing at the interior of the elevator car, he saw no visible security camera lenses.

The man with the shopping bag got off, followed by the cell phone lady, and finally the mother and baby. Arriving on twelve, Casey stepped out and walked down the corridor. No security cameras were visible in the hallway, but every door had a peephole. Returning to the elevator, he pushed the DOWN button. The next car arrived empty. Riding back down, he quickly took the rubber gloves from his pocket, tugged them on, and then slipped his hands into his trouser pockets.

The seventh-floor corridor was empty, soundless. Walking to 717, Alice Graverton's apartment, he knocked and heard no sound inside. Waiting a few moments to make sure no one was inside, he glanced both ways in the corridor. Opening the lock pick case, he selected a tiny tension bar and a long pick. Inserting the bar and then the pick into the keyway, he probed for a tumbler. Feeling the pick catch, he turned the tension bar. Working with both hands, he heard a click. Slowly turning his wrists while nudging the door with a knee, he heard another but louder click. Removing the pick, he slid it back into the case and pushed open the door.

He stood silently for a moment before going inside. He closed the door behind him and walked through the apartment, making sure no one was there. Having assuaged his fear of someone inside shooting him with an AR-15, he moved to the kitchen and looked through some papers on the work counter; it was advertising mail addressed to Alice Graverton. He was in the right apartment. He returned to the front door and quietly locked it.

The living room furniture was brown leather and chrome: a sofa, lounge chair, and coffee table that didn't match. Graverton's Santa Monica City College graduation certificate hung on the wall. Accounting textbooks lined a two-tiered bookshelf. He glanced into a room with a queen-sized bed then checked the adjacent room, which was furnished with a desk and two cheap metal filing cabinets. Figuring it was Graverton's home office, he sat at the desk.

He touched the space bar key on the laptop computer. The screen came on. He studied the computer desktop for folders that might reflect medical billing or Desmond Eckersley. Seeing none, he keyed

ECKERSLEY into the search engine and touched RETURN. A list of files appeared in a dialog box. He tried opening one. It was locked. He tried the others. They were also encrypted. Angrily slamming his fist on the desk, he got up and opened the filing cabinets. Each of the four drawers held folders labeled with colored identification tabs. Working quickly, he checked them all. None of them had anything to do with medical billing.

Guessing the most important information would be in the cabinet, he began removing each file and thumbing through its contents. The files, marked "Insurance," "Household expenses," "Banking," and "Stocks and Bonds," were filled with receipts, copies of business correspondence, and other miscellanea related to Eckersley's personal finances. On the wall above the desk was a framed collection of photographs: Graverton and Eckersley in bathing suits on a beach that looked to Casey like Hawaii, another of them smiling up at a camera he guessed was attached to a selfie stick. In the background was the diving board of a swimming pool, and beyond, a white, sandy beach. The happy couple held tall cocktail glasses and looked red-faced and tipsy. Eckersley had wide shoulders and a slender waist. His left hand was cupping Alice Graverton's right breast. Other shots depicted them in a Polynesian-motif restaurant, in a bar with rattan furniture, and near a Hanama Bay road sign.

He began thumbing through neatly tagged file folders. The first drawer contained nothing but miscellaneous business correspondence. Shoving the last drawer closed, he returned to the laptop and studied the desktop again. He double-clicked on the calendar icon. It was Eckersley's monthly client schedule with names and times listed for each day. None of the appointments were more than an hour. He scanned backward. A few of the clients came to the office three and four times a week. Others were scheduled for one hour each week, usually at the same time each day.

Scanning for a whole year through lots of names he didn't recognize, he saw Meredith Fox's name as well as the names of dozens of well-known celebrities, including Solange Gazebo, the television talk show star whom Courtney Wellstone said Bobby Lanza had blackmailed after hiring a burglar to steal Gazebo's bestiality video.

He also found a client named Vivienne Kalen-Boudreaux. Double-checking the list to make sure there was no Vivian, he wondered if Kalen-Boudreaux might be the platinum-haired blackmail victim that Flair met at Wilfredo's. Casey opened the contacts icon on his phone and keyed her name and birthdate into the notes. He heard radio static in his earphone transmitter, then Sutherland's voice.

"That person left the restaurant and is walking toward that location with takeout food," she said in a nervous tone. "Get the hell out!"

Pressing the transmit button twice to acknowledge Sutherland's message, Casey glanced at his wristwatch. He'd been in the apartment twenty-two minutes. Quickly replacing documents in the file and making sure everything else in the office looked the way it did when he got there, he hurried to the front door. Hearing voices in the hallway, he used the peephole and saw nothing. He cautiously opened the door an inch, then checked the corridor. Two women and a man were talking near the elevator. The male was describing a minor traffic accident in a movie theater parking lot.

He closed the door again. He could exit the apartment and walk either to the elevator or to the stairwell. The people in the hallway, potential witnesses, might not notice him if he walked to the stairwell, but if the stairwell door were locked, he'd have to walk back to the elevator, surely drawing their attention.

His phone dinged. A text message from Sutherland read: *Entering lobby doors now.*

Feeling his heart rate increase, Casey cracked the door again. The man who'd been talking was alone, facing the elevator doors and holding a cell phone to his ear. The others were gone. The elevator chimed. Its doors opened. Exiting the apartment, Casey quietly closed the door. Dropping to one knee, he feigned tying a shoelace and waited for the elevator doors to close. After, he hurried to the elevator and tapped the call button.

A minute later, the doors opened.

Alice Graverton got off and walked by him carrying a food takeout bag. She didn't give him so much as a glance. Getting on the elevator, Casey pressed the CLOSE DOOR button. The car descended, then stopped. The doors opened to the ground-floor lobby. He got off, left the building by the main door, and walked to the corner where Sutherland was waiting in the sedan. He got in and pulled the door closed. The engine was running.

Sutherland stepped on the accelerator, and they sped west on Beverly Boulevard.

"Well?"

"The billing records were there. Eckersley's patients included Solange Gazebo and a lot of other celebrities: Meredith Fox, Graverton herself, and a Vivienne Kalen-Boudreaux, who—from the appointment schedule—looks like she spends a lot of time in his office."

He took out his cell phone, searched "image of Vivienne Kalen-Boudreaux" and pressed the return key. Eight photographs of women flashed onto the computer screen. One of them had platinum hair. He turned the cell phone screen toward Sutherland.

She glanced at it while driving. "That's her, Legs…the woman in the porno shots. The same flashy hairstyle. Without a doubt."

He spent a minute navigating from one website to another, then stopped.

"Vivienne Kalen-Boudreaux," he said, reading the internet information about her. "Graduate of the Lake Geneva International School for Girls in Switzerland…married three times…each marriage lasting about a year. Now married to movie producer Norman Molitor and has performed roles in two of his motion pictures. They live in a house he owns in Beverly Hills."

"A blackmail victim who's the wife of a big-time movie producer?" Sutherland said facetiously. "Getting her to tell us everything she knows should be no problem at all."

He smiled. "Maybe she'll be pro-police."

"I love your sense of humor."

CHAPTER TWENTY-FOUR

Dr. Eckersley leaned back in his comfortable black leather executive chair. Vivienne Kalen-Boudreaux had arrived for the therapy session with her hair pulled back and tied with a beige scarf and a pensive, faraway look of self-pity he interpreted as stemming from restrained anger.

"I went to a movie and got home around eleven thirty last night," she said. "Norman was still out with his friends. I took a shower and went to bed, but I couldn't sleep. I was jagged up." She crossed her legs. "I've been having bad dreams."

She looked generally frazzled. He opened the office liquor cabinet and mixed drinks. A few days earlier when he offered liquor she'd responded favorably. She'd told him that she considered him a friend. He hoped that today she might share something more useful than her standard complaints of anxiety and depression.

"Such as?"

"Drowning in a stormy, rolling sea. Being chased by a masked killer from room to room inside the tunnels of a dimly lit Egyptian pyramid. Being stuck in an underground pipe. Stranded at the end of a pier while struggling to fight off a rabid dog with my hands tied behind my back. That kind of thing."

He was familiar with her habit of dropping clues designed to elicit comments she could use to support her self-destructive and obsessive behavior. Her hidden agenda was tiresome though occasionally amusing. Vivienne Kalen-Boudreaux's life was about dancing on a tightrope in the presence of disinterested men, which included ex-husbands, psychiatrists, and anonymous one-night stand jerks she met at Wilfredo's. She was a scatterbrained, needy bitch who was good looking and knew it. What he found compelling about her was the challenge of a potential conquest. He was sure it was only a matter of time before he'd adroitly negotiate her into sex, either bent over his desk or on the office couch.

"What's going on?"

"Thad Cochran."

"What about him?"

"I've had him on my mind."

Her silent anger, the familiar precursor to whatever she was planning to share, always related to a man. In that way she was fully predictable. It wasn't the first time she'd mentioned Thad Cochran, her mother's boyfriend, who'd lived in the Hillcrest house with them when Vivienne was a child. Her mom, the movie actress Gloria Channing, met Cochran during the production of *San Quentin Sunrise*, directed by the son of some Italian director. Cochran, whom she'd described as ruggedly handsome, with dark hair and eyes, played the role of an inmate, and Channing played the long-suffering prison warden's wife who helped Cochran escape and then met him later in a motel in Modesto. Eckersley wasn't surprised that the director's thirst for hard-edged movie reality led the casting agent to select Cochran for the role in *San Quentin Sunrise*. In real-life, Cochran had served seven years in San Quentin for burglary. Vivienne also mentioned Cochran's disappointment when reviewers universally panned the movie and it was a box office flop.

"Thad moved into the Hillcrest house at a time when my mother was out of control because of her drinking," she said. "He became her unofficial business manager, alcoholism counselor, and all-around life coach. He called himself a *method actor*. I was eleven years old when he moved in. He was kind to me and told me how happy he was to be my stepfather." She sipped her drink. "Thad became my best pal."

Now Eckersley was interested. It was the first time she'd mentioned Thad Cochran as being anything other than another one of her mother's actor boyfriends.

"We played dominoes and Scrabble, and we watched TV together. He talked with me about movies and clothing, the things I was interested in. When I told him I was interested in ballet, he took Mom and me to a performance of *Swan Lake*. I used to think he knew everything. Over time, he became my companion, and I became more and more concerned about what he thought of me. We would swim in the pool while Mother was drinking her cognac and dozing off. Thad taught me how to barbecue steaks. Mother's drinking made her a nonfactor in my life. She was a zombie, walking around all day with a half-filled cocktail glass in her hand, talking about some movie she'd been in or how some director manhandled her or threw a tantrum. Whenever Thad left the house, I found myself missing him. After a while, I came to idolize him. In those days, if Thad Cochran had told me to jump out of an airplane without a parachute, nothing in the world could have stopped me."

Eckersley studied her face, the beguiling darkness under her eyes, her well-trimmed eyebrows, and luscious lips. Though her problems were a bore, he'd come to eagerly anticipate the sessions with her.

"I had no idea about Thad's criminal past," she said. "I'm not so sure I'd have believed it if Mother, or anyone else, had told me. I was at the age when I was looking for someone to explain the way things were in the world. The more my mother drank, the more I became Thad's special person. I grew away from Mother. The months between making movies, when she was home, she spent her mornings with her physical trainer and then the rest of the day sipping cognac and Coke, talking on the phone for hours while sitting by the swimming pool. Sometimes I would eavesdrop on her conversations. I would hear her tell the same story to four or five different people. It was always something about how she was a victim in some way or other. She thrived on attention.

"She used to invite her alcoholic friends over and they would stay at the pool laughing and drinking all day while Thad and I would be in the den building a birdhouse or playing Monopoly. I noticed when she and Thad stopped sleeping together. He moved from her bedroom into a guest bedroom. My mother is a selfish, one-way type…I alternated between worrying that Thad would leave altogether or turn to drinking with my mother all day and ignore me, and that he'd go away to make a movie on location and never return. I didn't want to be alone. Because there was no one else. Thad became like a father. The first time he told me he loved me, I spent a whole day writing a story about it. I began having romantic thoughts, imagining myself as much older. I watched *San Quentin Sunrise* again and again. I thought of him as the greatest motion picture actor in history. I imagined being his co-star in a romance movie. I wanted someone to be close to. Mother was unbelievably selfish. She was either hung over or schlepping around the house, half-drunk with a cocktail, snapping at everyone and everything. It was as if she was playing the role of the housewife prostitute in that movie she made in Bulgaria."

Finishing her drink, Vivienne got up from the chair, walked to the bar. Eckersley focused on her perfectly shaped breasts and buttocks as she made another cocktail and then moved close to the aquarium to stare at the fish.

She said, "One night after we'd been in the swimming pool and Mother had gone to bed after drinking all day, Thad and I we're watching TV in the den…he began massaging my shoulders. He told me I'd feel better if I relaxed. I had a feeling something was going to happen, but I didn't know what to do. He massaged one leg, then the other, then he touched me gently, as if it wasn't intentional. He asked me how I felt. He had sex on his mind, and so did I. The problem was, I wasn't sure what it was. I trusted him. I imagined being in *San Quentin Sunrise* with him, playing mother's role." Vivienne returned to the chair, sat.

How absurd, Eckersley mused, that Vivienne was paying *him* for the hour.

"He started slowly and took lots of time seducing me," she said. "Looking back, now I realize that as an out-of-work actor he had nothing else to do. Mother once told me Thad never got another role in a movie because he didn't like to audition—that his ego was too fragile for the acting business. Thad believed my mother would never ask him to leave. He enjoyed living like a king in Gloria Channing's Beverly Hills mansion…and I think one day he just asked himself, why not fuck Channing's daughter?"

Vivienne fidgeted, betraying her nervousness, her voice filled with emotion.

It wasn't the first child seduction story Eckersley had heard. She stopped speaking for a while. He remained silent, watching her drum her fingers. He was aroused.

"We were in each other's arms on the sofa when Mother walked through from the bedroom to the kitchen, made herself another drink, and then—without a word—walked back to her bedroom. She saw us but didn't say anything. Thad told me not to say anything to her, no matter what. I knew then that my mother didn't care about me, and that Thad would never hurt me. I knew he and I had done some sexual things, but I wasn't going to admit that to Mother. I decided it would remain my secret."

There was a long pause. Vivienne said nothing and only once sipped her drink. She was waiting for him to say something.

He said, "How did you feel?"

"What?"

"Did you feel guilty?"

"Yes…but a month or so later, when Thad and I were having sex two or three times a day, everything changed."

"What happened?"

"Mother confronted Thad."

"About the sex?"

She swallowed twice. "I still remember where I was standing when she said it. The three of us were in the kitchen. I can hear Thad's words. For me, it's a moment in time I'll never forget. I can picture it right now."

"What do you recall?"

"Thad blaming it all on me and reacting coldly rather than shocked when I started crying. I felt like it was my last day on Earth, that I was going to turn into ashes and be dead—the way it happened in zombie movies I'd seen."

"What were his words?"

"He told her that I'd come on to him, that I'd begged him for sex."

"He said that?"

"He told her that I'd told him all about having had sex with some older boys I met after school. Thad Cochran was able to make up that terrible lie and say it with a straight face, just like the way he said his lines in the prison movie. He was a professional actor, and I was twelve years old."

Eckersley guessed that she'd looked older than her years—that as a young girl, she was sexually appealing.

"How did that make you feel?"

"That's when my problems started."

He asked what problems.

"You're not the first psychiatrist I've visited. Like I've told you, some were good, some not. Some I trusted. Some I had trouble communicating with. But you're different, Dr. Eckersley. I trust you. And the sessions I've had with you have helped me more than anything. Your method of allowing me to work through my emotions and come up with needed answers has lowered my anxiety level. It's allowing me to challenge myself. I believe it's worked wonders for me."

He sensed that Vivienne had reached the discovery point, that place in therapy where she was touching on the simmering cauldron of resentment she'd been holding in her heart for many years. Now she was ready to pull back the curtain and peek inside.

"The problems you've mentioned—what frightens you the most about them?"

"I don't know."

"But you do. And you're ready to face it. You've developed the strength to do that."

She stared at the carpet for a while, then looked up and made eye contact. "I've never told anyone."

"Vivienne, you and I should trust one another while we are exploring your personality. We must remain as a team." Eckersley spoke softly, clearly, and confidently, massaging her psyche in the manner she expected of him.

"It involves something, a secret that I gave my word…I swore never to reveal to anyone."

"I'm here to help you," he said. "You can openly and honestly share it with me in confidence."

"I believe you, Doctor."

"And I appreciate your trust. No matter what, I would never do anything to harm you."

"I see you as a friend."

Maintaining eye contact, he said, "What you tell me will remain our secret forever."

He maintained a taciturn expression while cogitating how, after she shared her shitty little secret, he would easily be able to talk her into sex in the office. That she was so close to letting the cat out of the bag turned him on.

She said, "I remember everything as if it happened five minutes ago. Thad was arguing with Mother. He was screaming at her and had his fists doubled up, as if he might punch her. He was exerting control and at the same time humiliating me. It was as if I didn't matter to him. Thad, my trusted confidant, showed his true colors. I ran out of the kitchen to the bedroom and got Thad's gun out of the nightstand drawer. By the time I returned to the kitchen, he'd backed Mother up against the wall and was shouting at her. She was fearfully covering her face and sobbing as if she knew he was going to knock her down and then stomp on her. I moved close and put the gun to Thad's ear. When I pulled the trigger, Mother screamed like a banshee and dove under the kitchen table. She thought I was going to shoot her, too, but that thought had never crossed my mind. I was angry. Thad had been lying to me—about everything. I killed him because I knew in my heart that it was the correct and just thing to do."

His heart twinged; his stomach muscles tightened. He hoped she didn't notice his astonishment. He'd been right in guessing there had to be a seminal event in her life, the basis for the hidden, seething rage that kept her life off-balance. But he'd never expected to learn his client and victim—the sexy and attractive Vivienne Kalen-Boudreaux—had killed a man. He recalled her once mentioning that when she was in front of a camera, anger was the easiest emotion for her to communicate. Now he knew why.

"Loretta Molinari is the reason I'm not in prison right now. She was my mother's attorney."

"What did she do?"

"There was blood sprayed all over the kitchen when Mother called her sobbing hysterically. When Loretta walked into the house. Thad was lying there dead on the floor. Loretta knew exactly what to do. She altered the evidence to make it look like Thad committed suicide, then quickly made some calls. She told my mother and me exactly what to say to the police. She gave us lines and we memorized them before they arrived. I learned later that Loretta had connections with

Superior Court judges and with the Beverly Hills Police Department. And Loretta paid a connection in the coroner's office to rule Thad's death a suicide. Mother had to borrow money from a bank to pay Loretta's fee and the bribes."

"What about the press?"

"By the time the public knew about the Thad Cochran suicide, I was out of the country."

"How did that work?"

For a split second, he imagined being in a cage with a growling tiger.

"Loretta drove me to her home. A Superior Court judge, her former law partner, signed an order changing my name from Verna Channing to Vivienne Kalen-Boudreaux. Loretta got me a passport and flew with me to Switzerland and enrolled me in a private girls' school in Geneva. Mother visited me there a few months later. She stayed one day and was drunk the whole time, telling me that she was starting a movie and would be back soon. I wanted to go home but she convinced me that living there was the right thing to do. The next time I saw her was a year later. I remained out of the country for years. When I was fourteen, I realized that mother didn't miss me, that I meant nothing to her. I wrote and told her I never wanted to see her again. I came to hate her. When I was seventeen, I stopped blaming her for what happened. I'd come to view her as a disabled person. It wasn't her fault. The blame was on Thad. I see killing him as the best thing I've ever done in my entire life." Vivienne stopped talking for a while, then said, "Doctor, having told you, I feel like a thousand-pound burden has been lifted from my shoulders."

"Progress," Eckersley said, his voice cracking.

"You don't seem surprised."

He spoke impassively. "I don't make, uh…value judgements."

She stared at him for a full minute and her eyes looked like she was in a hypnotic trance. "I was concerned that sharing this with you might alter our relationship or become an obstacle between us."

"Not at all," he said.

He felt a sexual excitement at having captured her deepest secret, the one he knew would enable him and Vollero to extort more money from her. He owned her now. Dr. Desmond Eckersley would soon be placing an order for a shiny new Bentley Flying Spur with all the bells and whistles. He didn't doubt his ability to maintain control of her. But being a realist, he fully grasped that now nothing was more important than the murderer Vivienne Kalen-Boudreaux continuing to view him as her trustworthy confidante.

CHAPTER TWENTY-FIVE

In the office, while sipping their morning coffee, Casey and Sutherland discussed the priorities of the investigation and agreed that Sutherland would work on two reports that needed completion and Casey would interview Vivienne Kalen-Boudreaux. After obtaining her cell phone number from a telephone company source, he called it. She answered. Casey introduced himself and told her he needed to speak with her in person.

After a pause, Kalen-Boudreaux said, "About what?"

"A confidential police matter."

"That sounds mysterious."

"If you prefer, we can talk in my office."

"Call my attorney, Loretta Molinari."

"I can do that, but my questions to her may reveal facts you might not want to share."

"Now I'm curious."

"If we get together, of course you can stop the questioning at any time. I'm talking about nothing more than a few questions concerning an ongoing official investigation."

"How did you get this number?"

"I found it online."

Telling her he got it from a confidential source would do nothing but confuse her. Besides, private telephone numbers, like illegal narcotics, were available online.

She said, "I'll be home for the next two hours."

"I can be there in about fifteen minutes, if that's okay with you."

"I assume you have my Beverly Vista address?"

"Yes."

Kalen-Boudreaux gave him a code number that she said would unlock the front gate. He wrote it down.

"Thanks."

Casey left the office and drove to the Norman Molitor estate. Beverly Vista Drive was lined with mansions reflecting morning sun like glossy real estate advertisements. In the middle of the block, the house was built on a hill that had been landscaped like a multi-tier brush garden that got bigger as its rose. He stopped the sedan at the gated entrance. A camera mounted on a security stanchion move electronically to focus on his eyes. Reaching out the driver's window to a keypad, he tapped the code numbers Vivienne Kalen-Boudreaux gave him.

A male intercom voice said, "Detective Casey?"

"Yes."

"Vivienne Kalen-Boudreaux is expecting you. Please drive up to the courtyard."

The automatic gate opened slowly. Casey drove up an ascending driveway to a pristine cement courtyard in front of a mansion whose tall windows implied sweeping views of the distant coastline. He parked the sedan, turned off the engine, and got out. A middle-aged man came out of the house. He wore gray slacks and a blue sports jacket. They exchanged greetings. The butler asked to see his badge and police identification card.

The butler led him inside the house to a sterile-looking room with a high ceiling. On the facing wall hung five vertical six-by-three canvases splashed with blotches of green and black, contemporary art junk Casey assumed some clever gallery owner had unloaded for millions of dollars. They crossed the room and reached some sliding glass doors. Outside, Vivienne Kalen-Boudreaux was relaxing on a chaise lounge next to an enormous star-shaped swimming pool. The butler slid open the door and Casey walked out. Kalen-Boudreaux wore a black bikini bathing suit. From the looks of her hair and makeup, he guessed she hadn't been in the water.

Getting up from the recliner, she greeted him and said, "I imagined you as older."

"I feel older."

"Why?'

"I don't sleep well."

She smiled. "Let's sit at the bar."

He followed her to an outdoor cocktail bar with a black marble top, wondering how much more a star-shaped swimming pool cost than a standard rectangle.

She said, "A year ago, a homeless person came to the front gate and said he was looking for some basketball player. The police came and took him away. Would you like a drink?"

Yes, very much.

"No, thanks. It's a little early for me."

"Too bad." Using a silver scoop, she dumped ice cubes into a cocktail glass. "I used to drink Russian vodka but stopped ordering it after they invaded Ukraine. Now I have this thing for gin. What's this sensitive subject you want to discuss?"

"Is there somewhere we can talk without being overheard?"

She sipped gin. "I don't feel like going inside. Besides, no one can hear us out here."

He said, "Did you know Bobby Lanza?"

"You're referring to the murder victim, Gloria Channing's recently ex-husband?"

"Correct."

"Never met the man." She took another sip. "Why are you interviewing me about a murder victim?"

He considered asking her about Dr. Desmond Eckersley but decided to wait. He already knew she was his client. "Have you had dealings with anyone representing Lanza?"

"No."

He took the photographs from inside his jacket and put them on the bar.

She glanced at them. Surprisingly, she didn't blush.

"We found the photos in a car Bobby Lanza had been using."

"So what? What does this have to do with me?"

He'd expected her to express anger or shock, the way other blackmail victims responded. "It's you."

She sipped the drink. "You're mistaken."

He spoke softly. "I'm investigating a murder. And there is no doubt that you are the subject of the photographs. I didn't come here to either embarrass or confront you."

"It's not me."

"The photographs may well have been taken without your knowledge, but there's no question that it's you. And denying the obvious will do nothing but make you look bad in the report that I will have to write. I suggest you reconsider your position."

She put her drink down on the bar. "Detective Casey, it's no longer appropriate for me to answer any more of your questions."

He picked up the photos, slipped them back into his jacket. "You're not the first celebrity who's had to face an extortion problem. I understand that blackmail is difficult to deal with. But it isn't going to go away."

"I am unable to assist in your investigation."

"The Beverly Hills Police Department handles lots of extortion cases. We know victims would rather pay a blackmailer than risk revealing their secrets. Blackmailers get rich off that kind of fear."

"Thanks for the explanation," she said. "Sorry I can't help you."

"If you don't want to discuss the photographs, I'll have to show them to a lot of other people to further the investigation. Is that what you want?"

"Speaking hypothetically," she said, "if it *were* me in the photos, I'd have a lot to lose."

"To you, this may seem like an insolvable problem, but it's not. The law and the police department are on your side. And I'd rather not show the photographs to anyone else."

"I don't have anything to say."

The power elite didn't trust cops. Most feared them because they'd seen too many movies and made the mistake of believing they had anything to do with the real world.

"Sometimes when attorneys and private investigators try to buy their way out of this kind of difficulty, everything goes wrong."

She picked up the cocktail glass and turned from him to face the swimming pool. "You'd better go now."

"The longer you wait to fight back, the bigger the problem. Blackmailers never go away."

"I have nothing to say."

"I'm here today because three people involved with blackmail have been murdered. I give you my personal word that if you'll tell me what you know, I'll keep it from the media."

He'd made the same pitch to other blackmail victims. It seldom had any effect.

She said, "Where do blackmailers get their information—the secrets they use against people?"

"They actively investigate potential victims. They pay people to provide them with derogatory information they can use against them."

"Who are these blackmailers?"

"Criminal predators with access to the rich and famous. All celebrities get blackmailed at least once in their career. The only requirement for being a victim is to have the means to pay."

"The photographs you just showed me," she reluctantly asked, "what do you intend to do with them?"

"Keep them as evidence."

"What if I asked you to destroy them?"

"Destroying evidence is illegal."

"Are you trying to blackmail me into becoming a witness?"

"I'm trying to solve three murders. Of course, once the killers are prosecuted, I would immediately hand over the photographs. Then you could do whatever you want with them."

Her eyes flashed anger. "The last thing I will ever do is get involved with prosecutors, lawyers, and judges."

"Even if it is the best way to protect yourself?"

"The idea nauseates me."

"If you prefer, I'm willing to discuss all this with your attorney."

"Who are these blackmailers you're talking about?"

"I'm not allowed to share investigative information."

"Bullshit."

She was right. To solve a murder, he could do anything except falsify evidence.

He said, "Bobby Lanza may have been involved in the photos being taken."

"You think I killed Lanza? Is that it?"

"We don't know who killed him."

"Well, it wasn't me."

"The male in the photographs may well have been criminally involved in the extortion plot."

"How do you know that?" she asked.

"His face isn't in any of the photos. That may be a clue."

"It may also not be a clue."

He said, "I'm guessing that to solve your blackmail problem you may have already paid a monetary demand."

"I'm no pacifist. When it comes to people who harm me, I believe in playing catch up."

"At the moment, the information gathered during our investigation is closely held, but no one can predict what tomorrow may bring. Journalists get tipped and begin exaggerating facts, fanning the flames. This may be your last chance before the photographs suddenly take on a life of their own."

She turned to him with an angry expression. "You're very well-spoken, Detective. You're trying to frighten me."

"My message is that if you're in a jam, the police department stands ready to assist you in any way it can. The way for you to get control of the problem is to tell me what you know about this matter. And there is no better time to cooperate than right now. The blackmailers may be involved in the murders. You can secretly help me put them away."

"I need some time to think about it. If I decide it profitable for us to talk further, I'll get in touch."

He didn't want to press too far and alienate her. She was the witness he needed. She could break open the homicide cases. But if she notified her attorney, he wouldn't be able to come back again to try again to convince her.

He reluctantly took out a business card and handed it to her. "Thanks for your time."

"You're welcome."

Leaving her at the bar, he walked to the house. Inside, the butler slid open the glass door. Casey followed him across the living room to the front entrance. Driving away, he believed it doubtful the sexy Vivienne Kalen-Boudreaux would call him. She was no pushover.

CHAPTER TWENTY-SIX

At midday, Casey was driving an unmarked police sedan on a narrow hillside road in Malibu Canyon. A bank of slate gray clouds hugged the western sky. Sutherland was holding her phone to an ear and making notes.

"Appreciate it," she said. "Not to worry. I know…you too, and thanks again." She turned off the phone, dropped it into her purse.

Casey asked who it was.

"That was my courthouse pal. She checked the paperwork in the file about Desmond Eckersley's lawsuit. The plaintiff, an actress who played in the movie *Ghost Nun* claimed that during therapy in his office, she told him about her obsession with sadomasochism. Then, on more than one occasion, he invited her to his home, where he stripped her naked and spanked her with a leather belt before having sex with her. He told her it was a way to make her depression and feelings of guilt go away. After her lawyer threatened to go to trial, Eckersley agreed to pay a large monetary judgement that would be sealed for thirty years."

"*Ghost Nun*. Never heard of it."

She said, "I saw the movie. It was like a zombie flick, but more confusing. The actress used to be married to the guy who was the mechanic in all those motor oil commercials."

"The question is: what will Eckersley have to say?"

Sutherland said, "He'll smile and then tell us to go pound sand."

"I don't think so."

"Based on what?"

"His perception."

"What?"

"Like actors who go public with their political views, maybe he's come to believe his own advertising."

Casey said, "What are you talking about?"

"He's been getting rich by betraying his client's secrets, and he has never been tagged. And he'll have anticipated being asked about Meredith Fox. Being a shrink, he might believe that by allowing an interview he might learn the results of our investigation. Once he sees that isn't working, he'll stop talking."

"My sister was married to a psychiatrist. When watching football on TV, he would write down exactly how many kernels of popcorn he ate. Sometimes he would sleep all night in the bedroom closet. She was convinced that he became a psychiatrist to study his own diseased mind."

Casey spotted Eckersley's address on a mailbox atop a four-foot pole, swerved onto a gravel driveway, and drove up a slight grade to an acre-sized plateau centered by a sprawling, modern house and its three-car garage. A curved walkway connected it to a large bungalow he guessed was Eckersley's office. Both buildings had been professionally landscaped with identical assortments of plants and cacti to complement the terrain. Casey parked the sedan in front of the garage next to the black Mercedes-Benz sports car he'd seen parked in the Malibu beach mini mall. He turned off the engine. He and Sutherland got out of the car and walked to the bungalow. He knocked.

Eckersley came out of the main house. "May I help you?" he said, walking toward them.

Casey held out his badge. "Detectives Casey and Sutherland, Beverly Hills Police. We're here to speak with Dr. Eckersley."

"I'm Eckersley."

"Sorry to bother you, Doctor," Casey said. "We're here about your former client, Meredith Fox."

"Yes, of course. Unfortunately, I don't discuss my clients."

Casey said, "The district attorney can subpoena witnesses to appear before the county grand jury."

Eckersley said, "As a medical doctor, I can challenge that kind of subpoena."

"All we're asking is for a few minutes of your time," Casey said. "We promise not to ask you anything that would violate your medical oath."

Eckersley stared at them. "Come in."

Eckersley used a key to unlock the bungalow door. They went inside. The lights came on automatically. The furniture had been arranged with two separate seating areas: two chairs facing a large desk backdropped by a large aquarium filled with colorful tropical fish, and a chair and therapy couch ensemble. On the wall next to the aquarium hung a medical school diploma and three large oil paintings of Faberge eggs. Eckersley moved to his desk chair. Casey and Sutherland sat facing him across the desk.

Eckersley said, "How did you manage to find out Meredith was my client?"

"We have her financial information and contact lists," Casey said. "During the homicide investigation, we've learned a great deal about her personal life."

Casey hoped he wasn't laying on the know-it-all technique too thick. Eckersley had to know the press mentioning his name in the context of celebrity extortion would destroy his psychiatry business.

Sutherland said, "Did Meredith Fox ever mention to you that she was in danger?"

Eckersley raised his eyebrows in condescension said, "I thought she was killed in a carjacking."

"Who were her enemies?" Sutherland said.

"She…she didn't mention having any."

Sutherland said, "Why was she seeing a psychiatrist?"

"I thought you weren't going to ask those kinds of questions."

Casey said, "That was more of a general question, Doctor. We're hoping to develop a clue to her murder."

"Meredith is dead," Sutherland said, "and we're never going to tell anyone what you say, Doctor."

"Allow me to explain," Eckersley began. He spoke gracefully, as if delivering an introductory pitch to a prospective client. "My therapeutic approach to psychological problems is based on psychoanalysis that seeks to get to the bottom of internal conflicts resulting from childhood experiences. This is accomplished by exploring the patient's emotions and recollections. The exploration can be a long and arduous process. Of course, I always do my utmost to solve my client's problems quickly rather than drag things out. Unfortunately, that's not always within the realm of possibility. The process can take months or in some cases years."

"What would you say was Meredith's basic problem?" Sutherland said.

"Depression."

"How long had she been a patient?"

"I'd have to check my files for the exact dates."

Sutherland said, "Approximately."

Eckersley licked his lips. "Four years or so. She came here three times a week. Like with a lot of patients, I got the impression she derived a certain pleasure from exploring her psyche. Some patients make their relationship with a therapist a big part of their life. In a way, it fills a void for them. In layman's terms, Meredith Fox saw the dark side of everything: her friends, her relatives, and her romantic interests. She was a scornful, inveterate cynic—a clinical depressive who always pictured the glass of life as half empty."

Casey said, "We're open to any suggestions you might have as to who might have murdered her."

"It sounds to me like you're saying that Meredith wasn't some random victim of a robbery."

Casey said, "We're open to any clues or suggestions based on what you might know about her."

Eckersley smiled. "I wouldn't be able to even offer a guess. In a general sense, she hated everyone. She always believed her competitors in the publicity business were stealing clients from her. That might well be something for you to investigate."

Sutherland said, "Other than the depression, what would you say was her biggest difficulty?"

"Cocaine. It's no secret that she had an on-and-off addiction that almost destroyed her life. I finally talked her into a nine-month drug rehabilitation program. She cleaned up well and then returned to her publicity business. But while she was out of the business, she lost a lot of her customers. Hollywood is fickle. People are either 'in' or 'out.' She lost her home in the Hollywood hills to bankruptcy and moved into a Wilshire Boulevard penthouse condominium. She told me she was quickly regaining her stature in the publicity field, but whether that was true or not, I have no idea."

So far, Casey mused, he'd told them nothing they didn't already know. He decided to throw Eckersley a bone.

"Doctor," he said, "do you think it possible that she may have fallen back into her addiction and possibly been meeting with a narcotics buyer at the hotel garage where she was found?"

"That's certainly a distinct possibility. Meredith spent most of her adult life falling in and out of addiction. She had a basic addictive personality."

Casey said, "Was she involved in any business other than her publicity career?"

"If she was, she never mentioned anything to me about it. Have you learned anything along those lines?"

"Just asking," Casey said.

Sutherland said, "Who were her romantic interests?"

"More than once she claimed that her affairs were always for business reasons."

Sutherland asked, "How did you interpret what she meant by business reasons?"

"That she would without hesitation have sex with a prospective client to gather information on one of her rivals in the publicity field. She was mercenary, goal directed."

Casey said, "What about long-term relationships?"

"She was living with a man named Anthony Flair who manages the Greenroom on Sunset, which is where Meredith liked to meet clients for a drink. I imagine you've already spoken to him?"

Sutherland said, "What did Meredith tell you about this Mr. Flair?"

"I recall her saying something about him being a weightlifter and bodybuilder. I got the impression that he was a contestant in some Mr. Universe-type contest and that he was a would-be movie actor. Meredith told me he was kidding himself, that he didn't have the ability to memorize even a few simple lines. She said he was a loser and the closest he got to fame was a walk-on role in *Son of Spartacus*. Meredith was vain. For her, it was an ego boost to be escorted somewhere by a 'musclebound steroid freak,' as she often referred to him. Like a lot of women, she hated attending parties alone. She referred to Flair as a 'handsome dope' and an 'empty T-shirt.' She used him for her own selfish needs, as a crutch, a human conversation piece to dissect over dinner with her publicity clients." Smiling at Sutherland, Eckersley added, "She used to joke that unfortunately his weightlifting didn't do anything to increase the size of his penis."

"Could he have killed her?" Sutherland said.

"She never expressed any fear of him. In fact, she told me they got along rather well."

"Who referred Meredith to you?" Sutherland said.

"I don't remember. It was probably one of her colleagues in the publicity business."

Casey asked, "Do you have a lot of Hollywood clients?"

Eckersley sat back in his chair and stared at them as if they'd just walked into the room. "That depends on what you mean by *Hollywood*."

"Actors, directors, and others who happen to be involved in the entertainment industry."

"My clients are from many different backgrounds and occupations."

Sutherland said, "Are any of them celebrities?"

"That depends on how one defines the term celebrity."

"Did Meredith know any people who were both famous and wealthy?" Casey said.

"I'm sure she did. She was a well-known entertainment industry publicist."

Casey wasn't shocked at Eckersley's evasiveness. He knew offering names might lead to further questioning and lead to celebrities who could be questioned about whether they'd been blackmailed.

Casey said, "She must have mentioned the names of some of her clients."

Eckersley, sitting uncomfortably in the cozy office next to his Malibu home, no longer seemed to be enjoying the give and take of the interview. "If she did, I don't recall."

Sutherland said, "Did you and Meredith have a personal relationship outside of her therapy sessions?"

"What an unusual question."

Sutherland said, "For a police investigator trying to solve a cold-blooded murder, it's routine."

"Come to think of it, a couple of years ago Meredith invited me to lunch. She'd been hired to do publicity for some 'life-coaching company,' as she described it, and wanted to pick my brain about the topic of counseling skills."

Casey said, "Was this like a date?"

"Not in any way, shape, or form. It was what you'd call a business lunch."

"Did you ever have sex with her?" Sutherland said.

Eckersley smiled. "I hope that question doesn't imply that you consider me a suspect?"

Sutherland said, "Doctor, at this moment, unfortunately, we have no murder suspects."

Casey said, "Did Meredith ever mention Bobby Lanza?"

"I think she may have said she was having some problems with him," Eckersley said without hesitation. He seemed to be relieved. "As I recall, it was some misunderstanding about money she thought he owed her—something along those lines."

"Did she say anything else about him?"

"She told me Lanza was an underworld type and that he was involved with selling celebrity news to the press: rumors he picked up from Hollywood call girls, restaurant waiters, and hotel doormen, that kind of thing."

Casey nodded. Liars loved nothing more than assigning blame to the dead.

"Did Lanza ever threaten her?" Sutherland said.

"Now that you mention it, Meredith may have said something about having an argument with Lanza—a business dispute of some kind. At the time, I didn't make much of the comment. Is there some connection between her murder and Bobby Lanza's?"

"We're not ruling out anything," Casey said.

"Sounds like you have your work cut out for you."

"It's a challenge," Casey said. He slipped from his inside jacket pocket a copy of Vivienne Kalen-Boudreaux's driver's license and showed it to Eckersley. "Do you recognize this woman?"

Staring at it, Eckersley said, "She's no one I know."

"Are you sure about that?" Sutherland said.

"Who is she?"

"Her name came up during the homicide investigation," Casey said.

"What makes you think I know her?"

Casey said, "We've been busy trying to tie up some investigative loose ends."

"A lot of people have been interviewed," Sutherland said.

Glancing at his Patek Philippe, Eckersley said, "Sorry I wasn't able to solve your investigation."

Casey exchanged a glance with Sutherland, and they stood to leave.

"Thanks for your time," Casey said. "And sorry for barging in on you unannounced."

Eckersley walked with them to the door. "How confident are you that you'll be able to solve the murder?"

"In Beverly Hills," Casey said, "we solve all of them."

"I wasn't aware."

"We have very few homicides and plenty of time to spend on solving them. We keep plugging away until the facts finally fit together."

"I...wish you well."

Sutherland said, "Thanks, Doctor."

Departing the office, they walked to the car and got in. Casey drove along the gravel road and then off the property onto the winding asphalt leading back toward the coast.

Sutherland said, "He didn't blink an eye. Maybe we should have confronted him about Vivienne Kalen-Boudreaux."

"He'd say he has a lot of clients and that she skipped his mind, or that the photograph we showed him doesn't really resemble her, or that she was a fragile client and he didn't want to risk giving her name to the police. He knows admitting she is one of his clients would lead to nothing but more questions."

"You're right," Sutherland said. "The dude believes in himself. A real class-A Mr. Smooth. I can picture him ratting out every one of his clients."

"Eckersley has it all worked out. He rakes in the secrets and has Marty Vollero handling the shakedown business. And those who interfere get killed."

"Legs, making a case against these motherfuckers is going to be like pulling teeth."

"We can do it."

"What's next?"

"I'm going to stay on Vollero," he said. "If we're lucky, maybe he'll shake down some celebrity while I'm watching."

"By the way, when I was checking Gloria Channing's address in the radio call index, I saw a suicide listed there. It was twenty years ago, but she was living there at the time. It didn't list the victim's name."

"That was before I joined the department."

"I was working here but must have missed it."

Casey said, "Maybe it's a clerical mistake."

"I'll check further." She asked, "Do you think we're ever gonna be able to the solve these murders?"

"If we keep rocking the boat, eventually one of the players will make a mistake. Then we take them down."

"I like your attitude, Legs."

CHAPTER TWENTY-SEVEN

Sutherland drove from Beverly Hills to Tarzana thinking about Elaine Glatsch, who for years had served as personal secretary and assistant to Beverly Hills Chief of Police Donald Braun. Elaine retired from the department as an administrative specialist four years earlier after twenty-nine years of service. Sutherland always got along well with Elaine and figured she might be able to help her fill in the discrepancy in the department records regarding 13 Hillcrest Drive, Gloria Channing's address. After the passing of Chief Braun, it was acknowledged that Elaine was the one person who knew the most about what was happening during the time Braun headed the department.

Elaine lived in Tarzana, five miles from the intersection of the 101 and 405 freeways, in a small tract home that looked like a thousand others built in in the San Fernando Valley in the late 1940s when there were no freeways. The home had a tiny front yard covered with well-tended Bermuda grass and three healthy rosebushes under the front window.

Sutherland got in the driveway and rang the doorbell. Seconds later, Elaine greeted her, opened the screen door, and gave her a sincere hug before inviting her in. Elaine's age showed only in the few tiny wrinkles around her eyes and mouth. She looked older but she was still attractive. Sutherland would've recognized her anywhere. But for a few gray roots, her hair was the same: over the shoulder and light golden brown. Sutherland guessed Elaine spent a lot of time coloring it.

"You look great, Kristina," Elaine greeted her. "You always looked stylish and had great taste in clothes."

"My mother still tells me what to wear."

Elaine laughed. "How is she doing?"

"She walks a half hour every day and drinks one glass of wine with dinner. Other than having a knee replaced, she's eighty-seven and acts like she's forty."

"God bless her."

Elaine offered coffee, which Sutherland politely declined.

"Sit down and make yourself at home," Elaine said.

The living room was small but meticulously clean, with a large-screen TV on the wall and a matching sofa and lounge chair. The only kitsch was a framed black-and-white photograph of a young and handsome officer astride a motorcycle, former Chief of Police Donald Braun, who'd started his career as a motor officer. Sutherland had never seen the photo.

"Are you enjoying retirement?"

"Kristina, I'd be lying if I said I did. I thought it was going to be fun not having to make the drive to Beverly Hills every day, and it was for a while. Then I began to miss the gossip. I became a hospital volunteer. I put in my time every day, but because of all the sick people, I found myself getting depressed and gave it up. Now I read two romance novels a week and pick up my gossip from the members of the women's book club I belong to. The truth is nothing really replaces the day-to-day life of dealing with people and interesting matters, trying to do what's right and making important decisions. I guess what I'm saying is retirement isn't what it's cut out to be. So, what's this old information you're trying to find?"

Sutherland reached into her purse and took out a typed police radio call REQUEST FOR SERVICE log for a date many years earlier. Among a list of calls to Beverly Hills addresses was a call she'd highlighted in yellow that read: 13 HILLCREST DRIVE/CORONER/SUICIDE/BRAUN AT SCENE. Elaine looked at it. Her friendly expression disappeared. She handed it back.

"Gloria Channing still lives there," Sutherland said after waiting for Elaine to speak. "I'm investigating a double murder at the same address: Channing's housekeeper and her ex-husband, Bobby Lanza."

"I read about it."

"I couldn't find any of the usual files that would've been generated by a suicide there. The chief records clerk told me that if some incident had received special handling at Chief Braun's request, the reports might have been kept in the chiefs' office. She suggested that you might know about it."

Among Beverly Hills police officers, the term "special handling" was used to describe police incidents the chief of police chose to quash or adjust while assisting a victim or a perpetrator outside established procedures.

"Thirteen Hillcrest Drive," Elaine said. "I used to know all the movie star addresses."

"Do you remember anything about a suicide there?"

"That was a long time ago."

"Would you have known if Chief Braun gave...offered...special handling for a suicide?"

"Things were different in those days. In a lot of ways."

After a while, Sutherland said, "The investigation I'm working on involves three murders."

"What's the other one?"

"The publicity agent, Meredith Fox."

Elaine furrowed her brow. "Kristina, years ago, no matter what I'd have been asked about Don Braun, I wouldn't have said a word. Even to someone I trust like you."

"Casey and I are out of leads, and it looks like we might not be able to solve the case. Both of us are expecting to be replaced and then sent around the horn."

"Don Braun expected loyalty from the people he promoted. It was an unsaid thing with him. He trusted me, and I trusted him. In the old days, I kept my mouth shut and never thought twice about it. I was a team player."

Sutherland noticed that Elaine's eyes looked watery. She wondered whether Elaine knew about her affair with Braun.

"So was I," Sutherland said.

"But things change. Kristina, I need some coffee right now." Elaine stood and smiled. "And whether you like it or not, I'm going to pour a cup for you."

"Milk, please."

"You got it."

Elaine left the room and returned a few minutes later with coffee, milk and sugar, and raspberry cookies on a small silver tray with wooden handles. She put the tray on the table. For the next two hours, Elaine talked easily while Sutherland made careful notes.

—

At 6:00 p.m., Casey, alone in the detective squad room, dialed Vivienne Kalen-Boudreaux's private cell phone number. It rang five times. He left another message for her to call him. Resisting the urge to throw the phone receiver across the office and out the window, he set it in its cradle. Sutherland walked in the room, carrying her purse.

He said, "Kalen-Boudreaux isn't returning my calls."

"Maybe her lawyer told her to clam up."

"How did you do?"

"I have something." She motioned to him to follow her.

He got up, followed her into the conference room. She closed the door. They sat at the table. She took what looked like a copy of an official document from her purse and handed it to him. It was a Kern County, California, birth certificate dated twenty-nine years ago. The name on it was Verna Matasik. The mother's name was Carolyn Matasik. No father was listed. The mother's address was in Arvin, a town Casey knew was about a hundred miles north of Los Angeles off Highway 99, near the city of Bakersfield.

"What's this?"

"Proof that you were right when you said the people involved in this case were tied together."

"Lay it on me."

"When the baby listed on the birth certificate was two years old, her mother moved with her from Arvin to an apartment on Cherokee Street in Hollywood. Shortly thereafter, Mom, an aspiring actor, changed her name from Carolyn Matasik to Gloria Channing."

"Okay."

"After a couple of years, Channing got a role in a movie that did big at the box office. As a rising celebrity, Channing and her baby, Verna, moved from their Hollywood apartment to Hillcrest Drive in Beverly Hills. For the next few years, Channing made some successful romance movies. When the daughter was eleven, they were still living on Hillcrest Drive when Channing's boyfriend at the time, an actor named Thad Cochran, moved in with them."

"Never heard of him."

"I found an article about him in the newspaper archives. He played in a couple of prison movies. The final paragraph in the article mentions that Cochran committed suicide while living in Beverly Hills. I checked his name in the records bureau database. The Thad Cochran suicide is listed with a restricted file number. In that file is nothing but a short-form 181A signed by Chief of Police Donald Braun and a one-page coroner's report listing Cochran's death as suicide by gunshot."

"The address?"

"Thirteen Hillcrest Drive."

"Who was assigned the investigation?"

"There is nothing in the file indicating that any Beverly Hills detective was assigned to investigate. Chief Braun personally signed the paperwork."

She handed him a copy of a neatly typed Beverly Hills Police Department Report of Investigation form. The narrative section read:

After being notified of a possible suicide at 13 Hillcrest Drive, I responded to the location and met with one Gloria Channing, resident of the address, who stated substantially as follows: that her friend Thad Oliver Cochran, who was living with her at the location, was despondent over his career and had been drinking heavily and complaining of depressive thoughts when he committed suicide in her presence.

I observed Cochran's body on the kitchen floor in a supine position with what appeared to be an entry wound near his right ear. A Smith and Wesson .38-caliber blue-steel model six revolver was held tightly in his right hand, finger on trigger in what appeared to be a cadaveric spasm.

(See attached crime scene diagram and photographs.)

Reference is also made to the Los Angeles County Coroner's Report of Death number K364933 reflecting the pathologist's opinion that the cause of death was suicide.

See also the sworn statement of Gloria Channing, the sole witness who observed the incident.

"How did you put this together, Kristina?"

"Do you remember Chief Braun's admin assistant?"

"Elaine?"

"She just told me Chief Braun gave the Cochran suicide 'special handling.'"

"Interesting, but it doesn't help us solve our three homicides."

"There's more."

"Go on."

"Cochran was murdered. And Don Braun turned the murder into a suicide."

"Elaine said that?"

"Yes. She told me that if he were still alive, she'd have kept the secret and never said a word. But Braun personally approved and helped engineer the fix."

"Gloria Channing murdered Cochran?"

"She wasn't the shooter."

"Who?"

"The way it went down was that while movie tough-guy Thad Cochran was whooping up on Gloria Channing, her daughter shot him in the head."

"Why...why would Don Braun stick his neck out for Gloria Channing?"

"That's exactly what I asked Elaine. She told me he didn't do it for Channing, but for her lawyer, Loretta Molinari."

"Molinari was the connection to Braun?"

Casey and every other officer in the Beverly Hills Police Department knew that after his divorce, Chief of Police Don Braun dated lots of women, including a few movie starlets, a well-known opera singer, and Los Angeles's first female mayor. However, no one knew about Braun's close relationship with the well-known celebrity defense lawyer Loretta Molinari until Braun's memorial service, when she walked in and delivered the eulogy.

Sutherland said, "Loretta was living with Braun at the time of the Cochran murder. Not only was she Braun's girlfriend, but she was also the one who helped him keep his job when the city council tried to unseat him. Loretta saved Braun's career."

"I wasn't aware."

"Elaine knew all about it. She also told me Loretta Molinari served as Braun's secret bag woman. If a celebrity needed a police favor, they had to go through Loretta. Braun trusted her. Now you know why she specializes in defending movie celebrities."

"Why is Elaine saying all this?"

"She and Braun were lovers."

"Elaine?"

"Until the jealous Loretta Molinari insisted Braun kick her to the curb."

"I'll be damned."

"There's more. Elaine told me that after the Thad Cochran murder, to protect Channing's daughter and keep her hidden from the press, Molinari enrolled her in a boarding school in Switzerland. The cover story was that the daughter was overseas in a private girls' school when the suicide occurred. Before flying her to Zurich, Molinari got a Superior Court judge to approve and backdate a name change for her from Channing to Kalen-Boudreaux, the family name of someone connected to the school in Switzerland."

"Vivienne Kalen-Boudreaux."

"Vivienne grows up in the school," Sutherland said. "When she is nineteen years old, she leaves Switzerland, returns here, gets married and divorced a few times, and ends up marrying the movie producer Norman Molitor. Then Vivienne gets blackmailed, you and I are assigned to the Lanza case, and you find the porno photographs of Vivienne in Bobby Lanza's car."

Staring at Sutherland, an astonished Casey said, "Bobby Lanza… set a blackmail trap for his own stepdaughter."

"That's what it looks like," she said. "The bastard."

"Small town, Beverly Hills."

"One other thing. I just checked both Vivienne Kalen-Boudreaux's and Gloria Channing's recent telephone bills. There are no calls between them. None. They obviously don't get along."

He said, "We should send flowers to Elaine."

Sutherland glanced at her wristwatch. "As a matter of fact, I'm meeting her for an early dinner. She recommended Forte's in Reseda.

I told her I would meet her there in a few minutes and I don't want to be late."

She picked up her purse. "The brakes were squeaking on the pool car I was using today, so I dropped it at the shop. Can I take your Ford?"

He took out the car keys, handed them to her. "Good work, Kristina."

"Thanks."

"Tell Elaine I said hello."

"Will do."

Sutherland departed the office. Casey walked to the window and stared down at the parking lot as Sutherland exited the building, got in the car, and drove out onto the street. The information about Vivienne Kalen-Boudreaux was not only revealing but also bizarre. His mind focused on how to convince Kalen-Boudreaux to tell him what she knew. If Lanza set her up to be blackmailed, then it was likely Vollero made the pitch. And if Vollero collected hush money from her, he must have owed a portion of it to Lanza...

—

Kristina Sutherland drove north from Sunset Boulevard on Beverly Glen Boulevard, known as a secret shortcut through the Santa Monica Mountains to the San Fernando Valley by experienced LA drivers trying to avoid clogged freeways, but the easy access to both sides of LA made the hillside property near it prime real estate. Now the land adjacent to the once seldom-traveled road was in demand and property values were up. The area had grown into a maze of hillside houses and multiunit residential buildings, turning Beverly Glen into another one of LA's clogged traffic arteries. Traffic was moving along today, though. She was in luck.

As she followed the winding grade upward, her mind filled with thoughts about Don Braun, the way police departments work, and how no matter what happened, her own mother would have never sent her twelve-year-old daughter away from home to a school in Switzerland or anywhere else. Approaching the stop sign at Nicada Avenue, Sutherland applied the brakes. She glanced at white pickup truck in her rearview mirror. The driver and his passenger wore baseball hats. Accelerating north from Nicada, she quickly reached the highest elevation of the road, a curve overlooking Mulholland Canyon before the road took a downward path leading toward Ventura Boulevard at the southern edge of the San Fernando Valley.

The white pickup truck sped dangerously close to her rear bumper.

Assuming the driver was an idiot in a hurry, she slowed on the curve to allow him to pass. The driver raced into the oncoming traffic lane, swerved right, and crashed into her left front fender. The sedan crashed into a three-foot-high canyon guardrail, and then flipped clockwise over the cliff. Upside-down and falling while strapped into the driver's seat, Sutherland imagined the sedan somehow righting itself and landing safely back on the road, where she could then draw her gun and shoot the driver of the pickup truck. Slamming to the rocky canyon floor, the sedan ripped apart.

—

Casey was in the office when his cell phone rang. The screen indicated the caller was Beverly Hills Police Traffic Division Captain Lex Padua.

"Legs, Kristina Sutherland has been in a terrible traffic accident."

Casey felt like he'd been slugged in the gut.

"What happened?"

"She was on Beverly Glen near Nicada and crashed through the guardrail. The car ended up in the canyon. Paramedics just reached her. I just spoke with Dollinger. He's on his way to the scene."

"What's her condition?"

"All I know is that she's alive."

"I'm on my way."

With the sound of the phone disconnecting, Casey grabbed his jacket and hurried out the door and down the stairs. Ellen Brady was walking up.

"Legs, have you heard about the traffic accident?"

"It wasn't an accident."

"What?"

"Kristina came up with something on the Lanza murder—and she was driving my car. They might have thought it was me."

"What can I do to help?"

"Pick up her mother and bring her to the hospital. Make sure a uniformed officer is posted outside Kristina's hospital room."

"Got it."

Casey sped to Sunset and turned north on Beverly Glen. Near Nicada, the road was blocked by a police radio car. The traffic cop on duty recognized him and waved him through. Casey raced up the winding road to a fire engine and an ambulance. A police helicopter hovering above had lowered its stokes rescue basket into the canyon and was winching it slowly upward with Sutherland inside. Casey got out and ran to the shattered guardrail at the edge of the cliff. Sutherland was helmeted, bandaged, and strapped into the rescue basket.

He told the fire captain holding a two-way radio he was Sutherland's partner and asked about her condition.

"Both arms broken, a fractured leg, cuts. She's in shock."

The helicopter hovered while lowering the basket to three firefighters on the road. Quickly securing the basket to a wheeled gurney, they removed the winch line. The helicopter ascended as they carefully loaded Sutherland into the ambulance. Her head was bandaged, her eyes closed. Casey and a paramedic got in the ambulance with her. The paramedic pulled the rear door closed. The siren was turned on. The ambulance began to move.

"Kristina," Casey said, leaning close to her.

She opened her eyes.

He continued, "I know you're in pain, but I need to know what happened."

"White pickup truck ran me off the road. Two men, baseball hats, sunglasses. I couldn't see their faces. Am I gonna die?"

"No. You're gonna be okay."

"Pain..."

The paramedic inserted the needle of a syringe into her left forearm. She closed her eyes. The ambulance wound down toward Sunset Boulevard. Casey sensed the same guilt he'd felt after the jewelry store shoot-out that took the life of his partner. He knew logically he wasn't at fault, that criminals were the proximate cause of what happened, but he felt the same emotions, the nagging doubt. If he'd handled the investigation in a different way, would Sutherland be headed toward the hospital?

At Cedars-Sinai Medical Center, an enormous medical complex on Beverly Boulevard, an emergency team waiting at the ambulance entrance helped rush Sutherland into the emergency room. Casey found Dollinger at the nurses' station holding a cell phone to his ear. Quickly finishing his conversation, Dollinger led Casey down a corridor where they were alone.

"What happened?" Dollinger said.

"Kristina was making progress on the investigation," Casey said. "Whoever tried to kill her might have been after me."

"Vollero and his pals?" Dollinger said.

"Or Chief Slade."

"What do you mean by that?"

"A while back, she asked me to make a copy of the original Lanza murder book."

"Did she give you a reason?"

"She said she wasn't being properly briefed."

Dollinger's eyes flashed anger. "She told you that?"

"Yes."

"What did you say?"

"I told her she needed to talk to you."

"Why didn't you say something to me?"

"I don't know."

"What do you mean you don't know?"

"You didn't assign me to the investigation. She did."

"So what?"

"She's the chief of police, and I didn't want to end up back filing stolen car reports."

Dollinger nodded. "Between you and me," he whispered, "yesterday, sheriff's homicide requested to see your personnel file. I refused, so they went to Slade. She gave them access."

"Did you tell her Vollero is trying to frame me using my stolen wristwatch?"

"I told her everything, word for word. She allowed them to read the file anyway."

"She thinks I'm working for the other side?"

Dollinger blinked rapidly. "I don't know, Legs. And neither do you. But it's possible someone has sold her a bill of goods."

"Vollero is after me."

"And Kristina is in the hospital fighting for her life," Dollinger said. "I need some time to break this all down."

"Vollero is the key."

"Make yourself scarce. I'll call you the moment I come up with a strategy."

Casey returned to the department, walked upstairs to the detective office. He pulled open the top drawer of the filing cabinet where he kept the original Lanza homicide files and notes. It was empty. Someone had taken everything. He shoved the drawer closed. Vollero, Anthony Flair, Courtney Wellstone, Dr. Desmond Eckersley, Gloria Channing, and her daughter Vivienne Kalen-Boudreaux weren't cooperating. And Wanda Troxell was dead.

He'd seen investigations stalled by mistakes made early in the investigation, like choosing the wrong case theory, incorrectly targeting a suspect due to false information, or a mishap in the forensics lab. And he'd seen investigations sabotaged, like a bank robbery case that went offtrack because one of the detectives assigned to the case recognized the robber in the bank surveillance photo as his brother-in-law then did everything he could to close the case unsolved. Now, after all the investigative leads in the Fox, Lanza, and Hernandez murders had been followed, the cases remained unsolved.

Ordinarily, he mused, investigations were more of a challenge than a battle. In every city, twenty-four hours a day, someone was being chased by a cop. People were being shot while they slept, thrown through glass windows, crushed under the wheels of Land Rovers. Victims were tortured, strangled, and dragged by pickup trucks across gravel. Cities were filled with sobbing, fear, and anger. It was different in Beverly Hills. The crimes of the rich and famous were seldom violent. Quiet and sterile, Rodeo Drive remained undisturbed. The blackmail murders might as well have happened in Turkmenistan.

Other than Rosa Hernandez, an innocent, he didn't care for the victims. The attempt to murder Kristina Sutherland changed everything, though. Vollero and Eckersley had broken the rules. For Casey, the investigation was no longer about gathering evidence. It was about retribution. He knew it was time for him to make things happen, to do what was right. He walked downstairs to the Community Relations Office. The door was open. Ellen Brady was at her desk.

He said, "Dollinger told me to lay low."

"If you're in danger, you can move into my place for a while."

“Too risky for you.” She got up, closed the door, and wrapped her arms around him.

They kissed.

“I’ll call you later,” he said.

“Where are you going?”

“I’ll let you know.”

“Be careful.”

They kissed again, and he departed.

Ellen Brady sat at the desk for a moment, then got up. Walking to the window, she watched Casey cross the parking lot, get into an unmarked police car, and drive out of the lot. She took her phone from her purse and keyed a text message—*pizza*—to a phone number she knew by heart. Two minutes later, she received a text reply: *15 min.* She locked the office, departed the police building, and walked two blocks south to a three-story Beverly Hills public parking garage on Canon Drive, across from Trani’s restaurant.

Lingering at the driveway entrance for a minute, she checked to see if anyone was following her, then walked inside and took the stairs to the third parking level, where she waited near the elevator. Ten minutes later, a beige Cadillac exited the ramp to the third level, drove into an open space, and stopped. Brady walked to the Cadillac, opened the passenger door, and got in.

Chief of Police Donna Slade was behind the wheel.

CHAPTER TWENTY-EIGHT

On Beverly Vista Drive, Casey drove by the Norman Molitor estate. Vivienne Kalen-Boudreaux's silver Bentley was parked inside the massive wrought-iron gate next to her producer husband's black Lamborghini Jota. Parking nearby, he took out his cell phone and punched in Kalen-Boudreaux's cell phone number. She didn't pick up. Rather than leave another message, he disconnected the call. Kalen-Boudreaux had decided not to cooperate. He drove farther down the street and then tested the binoculars. He had a clear view of her front gate.

Without the testimony of Kalen-Boudreaux or some other victim proving Vollero and Eckersley were involved in a conspiracy, the district attorney would deem the evidence against them insufficient to prove motive. Casey wasn't going to be able to charge them with murder or anything else. Interviewing Kalen-Boudreaux hadn't succeeded in getting her to cooperate, but the information Sutherland had uncovered about Kalen-Boudreaux murdering Thad Cochran years earlier caused Casey to ponder other possibilities. Because important information gathered during an investigation always became less valuable when shared, he'd kept it to himself rather than brief Dollinger. Casey believed that with a little luck, he might be able to influence Kalen-Boudreaux. He was prepared to surveil Kalen-Boudreaux until he could confront her once more—alone.

Two hours and nineteen minutes later, the automatic gate at the Molitor estate began to open. Raising the binoculars to his eyes, he saw the silver Bentley exit the driveway and turn left. He focused on the windshield. Kalen-Boudreaux was driving. No one else was in the car.

Casey ducked down in the seat to avoid being seen. The Bentley drove by. He sat up and started the engine. Discreetly following the Bentley to Sunset Boulevard and then to Roxbury Drive, he saw Kalen-Boudreaux make a left turn and drive to Rodeo Drive. Near Wilshire Boulevard in downtown Beverly Hills, she swerved the Bentley into a diminutive parking lot between two businesses.

From a block away, Casey utilized the binoculars to continue the surveillance. Kalen-Boudreaux parked the Bentley in the corner of the lot, got out, and walked to a business establishment with a tinted bay window on which was painted in gold letters: Dirk Joseph Styling Salon. She went inside. Above the door, large three-dimensional gold letters spelled DIRK. A minute later, Casey drove into the lot.

Parking next to the Bentley, he turned off the engine and sat thinking about how to approach Kalen-Boudreaux. Anxiously musing about her attitude and personality and what she'd told him when he'd interviewed her at home, he got out of the sedan and paced about for a while without straying within view of the salon's bay window. He got back in the unmarked car and used his cell phone to call the hospital and check on Sutherland. Having learned that she was resting comfortably as the anesthesia was wearing off, he called Mark Fukunaga, who told him he and another officer were handling security at Sutherland's hospital room.

Casey decided to carry out his plan.

An hour later, Kalen-Boudreaux exited the salon and walked to her car. Her unusual hairdo had been freshly touched up by Dirk, a world-renowned hair stylist. Casey got out of the sedan. She saw him and stopped.

She said, "What are you doing here?"

"You didn't return my calls."

"I don't have anything further to say, Detective. I thought I'd made that clear."

"More witnesses have come forward."

"Is that supposed to be some clever new enticement to get me to talk to you?"

"I thought you'd be interested in a new development."

"Talk to my lawyer."

She walked to the Bentley. He stopped her from getting in.

"Your name was mentioned," he said. "More than once."

"Is harassing people what you do all day?"

He held out the booking photograph of Anthony Flair from his drunk in public arrest.

The color left her face.

"His name is Anthony Flair," he said.

"Please keep your voice down."

"I warned you about the investigation taking on a life of its own."

"If you think you can terrorize me into cooperating, you're mistaken. Is this the way you get your thrills?"

Casey whispered, "He said he met you at Wilfredo's. I thought you might be interested in what he had to say."

"Go ahead. I'm listening."

"He told me he's a shill for an extortion ring that targets celebrities."

"I don't have time to be bothered with this shit."

"You weren't the only victim. The same blackmailers are involved in at least three homicides."

"I'm not going to allow you to drag me into this low-life, vulgar nonsense."

"Anthony Flair told me that you and he went to a condominium in Brentwood."

"I don't give a fuck what anyone told you."

"If you don't cooperate, I'll be forced to ask other people the same questions. And I'll have to show them the color photographs I showed you."

She swallowed dryly. "How did you find me here?"

"What difference does that make?"

"I just asked you a question, you son of a bitch. And I expect an answer."

He didn't expect her to cry. He assumed that after what she'd been through since the age of twelve, her tears, if there ever were any, had all been shed.

"The next person on my interview list is your husband, Norman Molitor."

"What?"

"Without your answers to my questions, I'm left with interviewing him about everything."

She glared at him. "Why?"

"If you won't talk, maybe he will. It's a reasonable assumption. The investigation involves three unsolved murders."

"Norman will refer you to his attorney."

"Does that mean you've already told him about the man you met at Wilfredo's?"

"He'll tell you to go pound sand."

"So he's already seen the sex photographs?"

"You're trying to illegally coerce me to do something against my will. You're violating my constitutional rights."

"By asking a question?"

"I know what you're up to. It's no wonder that people hate the police. You're no different than—"

"The blackmailers?" he said. "Is that what you were going to say?"

"You're wasting your time if you think you can browbeat me into talking."

The first pitch hadn't worked. She was tougher than he thought. There was no reason to hold back any longer.

"Does your husband know about Thad Cochran?"

Her cheeks flushed with anger. Her expression changed to the wild-eyed look of someone ready to run, fight, or kill. He wondered if it was the look on her face when she murdered Cochran.

"Who?" she said coldly.

"An ex-convict who starred in a prison movie. Your mother's boyfriend…the man you murdered. Did you tell your husband you have a notch in your gun? Or, I should say, Thad's gun? You shot him with his own pistol. Does your husband know he's married to a killer? Have you told him that in the state of California there's no statute of limitations for felony murder?"

After a pause, she said. "What do you want?" Her voice dropped off.

Casey said, "To ensure no one can overhear us, I suggest we sit in my car."

"I prefer my car."

They got in the Bentley. She sat behind the steering wheel, he in the passenger seat. The dashboard and door side panels were leather, the knobs genuine pearl.

She cleared her throat. "Has…has…uh, some final prosecutorial decision been made?"

"I'm not sure what you mean."

"The Thad Cochran matter," she said staring through the windshield at the diminutive parking lot.

To Casey, the car, filled with tension, suddenly seemed stuffy and warm, as if permeated with invisible smoke.

"No."

"If you people are planning to dredge up the past and use it against me, I might just as well let the chips fall where they may."

"We'd much prefer to forget about Thad Cochran and let bygones be bygones—unless it becomes necessary to solve the Lanza murders."

"And I'm supposed to trust what you tell me?"

"You have no real choice."

"Oh, the police department authorizes you to go out on your own and dispense legal immunity?"

"The same people who blackmailed you just tried to kill my partner. She's in the hospital. Now, no one can stop me from solving this case. That goes for you, your husband, and all the clown cars full of lawyers you and he can bring. If you want to play tough, I'll put everything out to the media. Then the district attorney's office will be happy to have a nice big meeting with your lawyers. You'll be indicted for shooting Thad Cochran and the next day the world press will arrive with sound trucks to make a lot of money humiliating you."

As if reading his mind, she reached to the dashboard and turned on the air-conditioning. The whoosh of cool air coming from the vents cooled his face.

"I'm willing to assist, but not if it means that my life will be completely destroyed."

"All I want is the truth."

Vivienne Kalen-Boudreaux said in a nearly imperceptible tone, "Where do you want me to start?"

"With Marty Vollero."

"My husband, Norman, has a personal secret. Vollero asked for a meeting with him. Norman agreed. Vollero told him someone he called a 'media source' had learned the secret and was ready to reveal it. To resolve the matter, Norman paid Vollero a lot of money. A few weeks later, Vollero returned and said he needed more money to keep the secret hidden. Norman paid him again. That's when we realized Vollero wasn't some innocent private investigator acting as an intermediary: he was the blackmailer. Then Vollero blackmailed me over the man I met at Wilfredo's," she said. "There, is that want you wanted?"

"Who else knew the secrets?"

"I don't understand."

"I'm referring to those personal secrets that you and your husband paid Vollero to keep hidden."

"No one."

"In blackmail cases, the source of the secrets is frequently a close relative or confidante, someone a victim would never suspect: a trusted personal assistant, a security person, a business manager, a physical trainer, perhaps even a psychologist or psychiatrist. People who happen to know their clients' secrets by virtue of their close relationship with or access to them. Vollero had to learn the secrets from someone."

Her eyes closed for a few seconds, then opened. She said nothing.

"Have you or your husband shared any of your secrets with anyone like that?"

"No."

"It would be extremely unusual for Vollero to independently learn secrets about both you and your husband. Someone must have shared what they knew about you."

Casey drew from his jacket pocket the surveillance photograph he'd taken of Marty Vollero and Desmond Eckersley sitting in Eckersley's Mercedes-Benz, parked in a Malibu mini mall. He held it out for her to see.

She swallowed twice. "Vollero…"

"What about the other man?"

"I…I don't know him."

"He's Desmond Eckersley, a psychiatrist who treats a lot of celebrities."

"Never heard of him."

"He treats a lot of celebrities."

It didn't surprise Casey that she'd decided not to admit she was one of Eckersley's patients. Her whole life had been one big secret after the other. He assumed she wanted to think carefully about what secrets she'd shared with Eckersley and then decide what she might do about it.

She said, "I have a general question about people who may be blackmail victims."

"Okay."

"How...how do they escape their predicament?"

"Some cooperate with the police."

"Other than that."

"Some realize they are being bled dry and decide to take matters into their own hands."

"You mean...?"

"By striking back. For crooks, celebrity blackmail can be a dangerous game. Blackmailers must worry about their victims deciding to get even."

She looked him squarely in the eye. "Detective Casey, I've told you everything."

"Not enough to make a case against Marty Vollero."

"I've told you what I know."

"I need a statement from your husband."

"No way."

"You could tell him I questioned you about whether Vollero blackmailed him, that I told you I was aware he paid Vollero a lot of money."

"But that's not true."

"When I question him, I won't mention anything about you. I might be able to convince him the best way to keep his secret hidden is to help put Vollero in prison."

"I need some time to think about it."

To Casey, it sounded like she'd decided to discuss the matter with her attorney, Loretta Molinari.

She furrowed her brow. "Let me get this straight. What you and I discussed today will remain a secret?"

"Yes."

"What if Vollero goes to trial?"

"The chances of that are small."

"Who says?"

"All defense lawyers are aware that juries hate extortionists. In every blackmail prosecution I've been involved in, the defense lawyers convinced their clients to plead guilty rather than go to trial. No judge wants to air the victim's secrets in a public hearing."

She gritted her teeth. He hoped it wasn't because she questioned his presumption. He'd have a difficult time proving his premise. The truth was no one could predict with any degree of certainty what juries or judges would do during any criminal trial.

She spoke calmly and deliberately. "I need time to convince Norman that what you've suggested is the right thing to do."

"You have two days."

"That's not very long."

"Vollero and his pals are responsible for three murders. If I don't hear from you the day after tomorrow, you'll have lost the final opportunity for you and your husband to stay out of the headlines."

"I'm sorry I was rude to you earlier," she said. "You were just trying to do...the right thing."

"No problem."

"I'm late for an important meeting. Is there anything else?"

He shook his head.

She said, "I'll be calling you."

He met her eyes. "Whatever you do, don't tell Vollero we're on to him."

"You have my word."

He opened the door and got out of the car. Kalen-Boudreaux drove the Bentley out of the lot. Casey walked to the city car, unlocked it, and got in. Unbuttoning his shirt, he took off the miniature recorder/transmitter and microphone taped to his chest and flipped the PLAY switch. The conversation was loud and clear. If Vivienne

Kalen-Boudreaux and her husband decided not to cooperate, part of the recording would be enough to convince the district attorney's office to file an extortion case against Vollero and to force Kalen-Boudreaux to testify. Casey assumed her high-priced attorney would do everything possible to keep the recording out of court, but it wouldn't work. Casey was pleased with having made some progress. Now he, rather than Vollero or Eckersley, was the one pulling the strings.

CHAPTER TWENTY-NINE

At dusk, Donna Slade finished her daily workout regimen of running eight laps around the jogging track at Beverly Hills High School. It was a school holiday, and she was alone. For her, exercise was a way to take the edge off the usual daily stress, to help the mind sort conflicts and allow the proper pegs to drop neatly into the cribbage board game holes. Picking up a towel to dab perspiration from her face and neck, she saw Dollinger walking toward her from the school parking lot. He'd called a few minutes earlier and told her he had something to discuss with her in person. Detecting bitterness in his voice when she told him to meet her at the track, she assumed it was caused by his imbecilic belief that being born male endowed him with superior ability in police administration over all members of the opposite sex. To him, being forced to leave his office to meet with her was an imposition caused by an inferior.

"Have a good workout?" Dollinger asked.

"Just got in my last lap. That's what conditioning is always about, isn't it? Grinding out that final lap," she said. "What's up?"

"Casey is convinced Sutherland was run off the road by someone who is after him."

She spoke affably. "What do you think?"

"It's possible. She was driving the same department sedan he's been using."

Like all police bureaucrats, Dollinger was best understood in the context of self-protection. Everything he said was guarded, in anticipation of some prior decision being questioned, a mistake uncovered, a hidden agenda unveiled. She neither liked nor trusted him.

"Come on, Dollinger. Give me your take on the situation. Stick your neck out for once."

"Sutherland said someone in a pickup truck was passing her and swerved right...but that's not all."

"Am I supposed to guess what?"

"What I was going to say is that Casey's wristwatch was found on Wanda Troxell's corpse."

She dropped the towel onto the bench. "And what may I ask is the source of that nasty little morsel?"

"Sheriff's Detective Lenny Gomulka."

"Never heard of him."

"He's working the Troxell murder. He came into the office and asked to see me. He's a sergeant and he's been around for a while. I allowed him to question Casey."

"Was Casey fucking Wanda Troxell?"

"He says no."

She picked up the towel and draped it around her neck. "Do you believe him?"

"I have no evidence to the contrary."

"What a stupid remark. Do you believe Casey? You either do or you don't."

"Uh, I believe him. Casey said someone must have broken into his apartment and stole the wristwatch. I asked him whether after discovering the wristwatch was missing he made a burglary report. He said he didn't, that he thought he might have left the wristwatch in an athletic club locker."

"Just what we need," she said, "a nasty internal affairs investigation, a gigantic bag of worms on top of three unsolved homicides."

"There's something else," Dollinger said. "When I questioned Casey about the wristwatch, he told me you'd asked to see the original Lanza murder book, that you didn't think you were being properly briefed on the homicide investigations."

She watched his eyes widen as she moved close to him. "So what?"

"If there's a problem, I have a right to know."

"That's my decision. And if you disagree, or it doesn't fit the way you handle police business here in Beverly Hills, I could give a damn."

"I'm not a mind reader," he said.

"Did you expect me to just sit back and hope you'd eventually figure out what the fuck is going on with the three homicides? If so, you were mistaken. When blood is being spilled, that's not the way I roll. The murders are unsolved and you're responsible for the investigators. And, whether you like it or not, I'm in charge. I accept my responsibility. If you don't like it, put in your papers and I'll have one of the secretaries order a rum cake for your retirement party."

"I understand, Chief."

"Where's Casey?"

"Now?"

"That's what I'm asking."

"I don't know," Dollinger said.

"What's your current plan to solve the murders?"

"We have a number of ways to go…"

"Name one."

"We can concentrate on Vollero."

"Pick him up."

"Now?"

"Bring him in and sweat him," she said impatiently. "Then leak to the press that we are questioning him as a suspect in the Lanza murder."

"Are you sure you want to do this?"

"Do you anticipate some problem?"

"We don't have enough evidence to convince the district attorney to prosecute."

"But we have more than enough probable cause to arrest Vollero."

"Okay."

"You agree, right?"

"I'm just pointing out that the district attorney may not like the idea of—"

"Thanks for pointing that out. Now drag Vollero's ass in and let's see what he has to say. We know he's up to no good. If nothing else, at least the bad publicity will destroy his private-eye business. The next time he goes to a celebrity's house to shake them down, he'll be a disgraced private eye rather than a TV pretty boy."

Staring at Dollinger, she noticed fine beads of sweat across his brow. If it indicated she'd made an impression on him, she was pleased.

He said, "I'll have Casey do the honors."

After a pause, she said, "Has it occurred to you that Casey might be playing both sides?"

"Casey is no angel, but I've never heard anything about him being on the take."

"Supervisors are the last to know."

"True."

"If the FBI has Casey under surveillance," she said, "they obviously think he's up to something."

"They make mistakes…"

"People willing to commit murders to preserve a blackmail operation would love nothing more than to have a Beverly Hills cop on their payroll."

"If the FBI does arrest Casey," Dollinger said, "they'd be solving the homicides for us."

"I can see a dozen media stories accusing the department of being asleep at the switch."

He said, "We could counter with a press conference and say it was a joint investigation with the FBI. The Bureau would never deny that."

"Good suggestion. I wholeheartedly agree, but let's not get ahead of ourselves. Have Casey lean on Vollero. Record the interrogation and let's see how Vollero reacts."

"I'm on it, Chief."

Watching Dollinger walk back to his car, she decided to jog a few more laps before returning to the office.

—

Shortly after 9:00 p.m., Casey visited Sutherland at Cedars-Sinai. Despite the bandages and splints, she was doing well. Her mother and sister sat beside the bed, and for protection a uniformed Beverly Hills officer stood post outside the door of her room. Casey had spoken with the doctor earlier, who told him Sutherland would be fully recovered and back on the job in about sixteen weeks. His phone rang. The screen read: K. PAXINOU. Casey touched the ACCEPT icon.

"Hello, Mrs. Paxinou."

"Sorry to bother you, Mr. Casey, but I wanted to share some information about the vandalism at the apartment house."

"The security cameras?"

"Yes. My grandson has been repairing them. He just found a photograph of a man who had been recorded digitally shortly before the cameras stopped working. The image was recorded by the front door security camera."

"Does it show a face?"

"Yes, the man was carrying wire cutters."

"I need to see the photo as soon as possible."

"I'll tell my grandson."

"Have him text me the photograph."

"He'll send it right now."

"Thanks, Mrs. Paxinou."

The phone disconnected. Seconds later, Casey tapped on the cell phone TEXT icon. The message from apartment manager Paxinou was a color digital photograph of Anthony Flair holding wire cutters in his right hand. From the angle, Casey assumed his image had been captured by a camera outside the apartment building garage. Considering the circumstances, Flair, wearing a dark-colored business suit, white shirt, and necktie, looked foolish. Although he might try, it would be difficult to explain to a jury what he was doing carrying wire cutters seconds before the electrical connections to the cameras were severed. Flair must have stolen the Apple wristwatch and planted it on Wanda Troxell's corpse. After the drug arrest, Flair had promised to cooperate in exchange for getting released from the county jail. Now Casey would offer him another deal: tell him who killed Bobby Lanza and Rosa Hernandez or go to prison for burglary.

In the air-conditioning of his city sedan, he sat for a while thinking about where Anthony Flair fit in the homicide investigation before driving toward Sunset Boulevard. Arriving at the Greenroom a few minutes later, he saw Anthony Flair's car parked in the alley near the rear exit. In an open space adjacent to the alley, he turned off the engine and sat back to wait.

At 2:00 a.m., closing time, customers began exiting from both the front and back doors, walking to their cars, and departing. When the crowd had cleared, Casey got out of the sedan, walked to the Greenroom's back door, and went inside. Anthony Flair was behind the bar, chatting with two young women seated on barstools.

Flair smiled. "Is this a raid?"

Casey walked to the bar. "I'm here to talk."

"About what?"

Flair, looking disconcerted, turned to the women and cocked his head toward the door. They picked up purses, got up, and departed. He and Casey were alone.

Casey said, "Anyone else here?"

"No. I was just getting ready to lock up and go home."

"Who sent you to break into my apartment?"

"Whoever told you that is lying."

Casey took out his cell phone, held it out for Flair to see the security camera photograph taken at Casey's apartment house of Flair holding wire cutters.

"I was fixing my car."

"You and Vollero ran my partner off the road."

Casey heard footsteps and turned to see Vollero exiting the hallway, aiming a gun at him.

"Look who's here."

Vollero said, "Put your hands on your head."

Casey didn't comply. "Do you really think you can get away with shooting me here?"

"Coming here alone was a mistake."

Flair raised a Taser gun from behind the bar and fired. Electrode barbs pierced Casey's neck. Felled by a surge of electricity simultaneously jolting his tongue, teeth, and brain, he lay on the floor, temporarily immobilized. He saw Flair vault over the bar, aim the Taser at him again, and fire. Casey convulsed with the shock. Flair snatched Casey's gun from his cross-draw holster.

Vollero handcuffed him and then opened a small, hinged case. He took out a medical syringe. Casey struggled, but Vollero shoved the needle into Casey's neck. He felt heat, and then, as if time itself no longer existed, the sensations of being dragged, wrapped in something that smelled like beer-soaked carpet, lifted, carried, then dropped hard. His head bounced. Alone in the darkness of a carpeted automobile trunk and still unable to move, he felt a whoosh of air as the trunk was slammed shut.

Losing consciousness, he tried to shout but no sound came out. He heard a car engine. His eyelids became heavy, then involuntarily closed. He imagined the canyon in Afghanistan and smelled the dust, then he heard the deafening fusillade inside the jewelry store, a siren, distant radio static, emergency calls, and a paramedic describing bullet wounds. Then he was enveloped in a cold, blue cloud that suddenly turned black.

CHAPTER THIRTY

Vivienne Kalen-Boudreaux said, "I want to know what you really think of me."

Sitting back in the chair with her arms crossed, she wore a cerise puff-sleeved minidress that contrasted nicely with her tanned legs and gold earrings and matched the elegant olive-leaf-pattern cuff bracelet on her left wrist, as if she'd come from a private cocktail party held in the back room at Nicky's on the Sunset Strip. He could tell from the moment she'd walked into the office that she needed an ego massage. Rather than stall and allow her to continue yakking about herself for the remainder of the therapy session, he decided to assume his sagacity mask.

"To your husband and the members of the corporate boards he put you on," Eckersley said, "you appear to be a model executive, a well-reasoned professional woman, an accomplished, powerful personage. Because of your beauty, women aspire to be you. You're one of a kind. Being a natural-born leader and a beautiful lone wolf, you have few female friends."

Her lips forming her petulant Mona Lisa smile. "Desmond, you know nothing about me."

It was the first time she'd used his first name. He was surprised at the remark but wasn't going to let it bother him. He was babysitter, and the same general patter had worked well on many of his other wealthy female neurotic clients.

"Your attractiveness hides deep-seated feelings of low self-worth. You consider your husband a fool for marrying you. You trust your own sexual needs. You've had sex with women as well as men, but neither gender, in any sense, has managed to conquer you."

The truth was Vivienne Kalen-Boudreaux was an enigma to him, as were all women. Understanding the opposite sex wasn't taught in medical school or anywhere else. Not that by performing his well-honed therapy guru act he couldn't manipulate and control them. Hell, he'd had sex with several of his female patients but that didn't mean he understood them. No one ever claimed Sigmund Freud understood the opposite sex. Worse, the inability to comprehend them meant it was impossible to predict their behavior. An image flashed through his mind of being outside the office and looking in the window at Desmond Eckersley sitting behind his desk narrating meaningless cookie-cutter nonsense to a nude Vivienne Kalen-Boudreaux, who listened to him with a spellbound expression—an image that might have come from an imaginary textbook.

She licked her lips. "Some of what you said may be true."

What she was thinking didn't matter. He liked her flat stomach, her breasts, her round, shapely buttocks. And while in the therapy room, she was completely his.

"Such as?"

"You tell me, Desmond."

"Juvenile consensual sex with an adult causes more guilt than rape," he said, thinking back to his bullet list of advice to victims of sexual abuse. "You were an abused child. Children feel shamed, sinful. They get confused about their thinking, their emotions. The trauma of sexual abuse caused by Thad Cochran sabotaged your brain's erotic responses. Your sexual feelings were turned on solely because he touched you in a certain way, not from some great transgression. You didn't cause this to be brought on yourself. He impaired you. You did nothing iniquitous. Eventually, victims manage to relegate their confusing emotions to that great steel vault of guilt buried in their unconscious mind. Then one day they realize that they must confront anything and everything inside it."

"How bewildering."

Eckersley's first sexual experience was when he was nine years old and a cadet in a military school. A sixteen-year-old fellow cadet raped him. Now, bolstered by a medical school diploma, he was administering snake oil to immature men and gabby, damaged women he both coveted and disdained: clients bound together by extraordinary conceit and self-admiration that kept them following anyone's advice.

"Part of your confusion is that you don't hate Thad Cochran for what he did."

"The hell I don't."

"Cochran was your ally, the only one who understood you. The rest of the world was ignoring you. If he were still alive, you would be fully passionate with him again."

Vivienne Kalen-Boudreaux stared blankly at him for a full minute and then said, "I sometimes imagine Thad being alive and unable to control himself with me."

"People who don't have love survive by making their imaginings correspond with their own unique experiences," he said, recalling a magazine article he'd recently skimmed. "But surely you regret having, uh…that incident with the gun?"

"No."

"Surely you wish that it would have never happened, that you could erase what you did?"

"Not at all."

"I'm referring to shooting Thad Cochran."

"I know what you're talking about. What I'm telling you is that if Thad walked in here right now, I'd gladly kill him again."

"You don't mean that."

"But I do, Desmond."

"Others failed you during your upbringing, and you didn't choose to react in that way."

"It was different with Thad."

"In what way?"

"He used me."

"Others haven't done that?"

"I trusted him. Then he treated me like I was nothing but a plaything. For that, he deserved to be punished."

Her grim and determined expression made him recall the stories he'd heard in medical school about dangerous patients stalking their psychiatrists. For the first time, he imagined Vivienne Kalen-Boudreaux as a stalker, watching someone from afar and then sparking a confrontation to carry out a threat. It did not deter his intention of talking her into having sex on the office couch, however. Having shared with him her secret of secrets, she was now his property. He owned her ass and he intended to manipulate her into a quick fuck in the office. To please him, she would writhe and squeal, and then to satisfy him fully, use her limited acting ability to fake an orgasm.

She said, "Detective Casey came to see me again."

Aware of a steady warm breeze coming in through the office window, he nodded. He waited a few anxious minutes for her to continue. She didn't. He realized that she was waiting for him to react.

"What did he want?"

She avoided his eyes. He interpreted it as an indication she was both agitated and angry.

"He showed me a police booking photograph of the man I met at Wilfredo's."

Eckersley felt his guts quiver. He'd believed he was above the fray, in the clear, and that Detective Casey nosing around wasn't a cause for worry. Not only had Eckersley never killed anyone, but he'd also never so much as spoken with Meredith Fox's stupid boyfriend, Anthony

Flair, and he remained scrupulously cautious in his dealings with the sociopathic private investigator Marty Vollero, whom he believed would never cooperate with the police under any circumstances. For the first time, Eckersley sensed that his own thinking may have been flawed by greed, a weakness he'd discovered during his personal psychoanalysis, a training element required of all physicians aspiring to become psychiatrists.

"Anything else?"

"Casey told me the man in the photos was Anthony Flair...and that he belonged to a group of blackmailers suspected of being involved with some murders."

"Then what did you say?"

"That I didn't know who he was talking about."

"What was Casey's reaction?"

"He threatened to go to my husband and tell him I murdered Thad Cochran."

Eckersley felt a heavy pulsing behind his eyes. He swallowed. His throat was dry. "He said that?"

"Yes. He's a well-spoken police goon with ice in his veins."

Eckersley needed time to think. "Hearing him say that, how did it make you feel?"

"Feel? How do you feel, Desmond?"

He wiped perspiration from his upper lip. "Why the sudden unfriendliness?"

"I love how your questions always begin with basic interrogatives. Why the anger? Why this? How so? Who said? Did it ever occur to you that the answer to such questions is always '*Because*'?"

"Not always..."

"Fuck the *who* and *why*," she said. "When people get blackmailed, it's because someone opened their big mouth. Are you aware of that, Desmond? Don't you know that the bottom line of blackmail and extortion is always a rat, someone who learned something and then began telling it to others who had no business knowing?"

He saw anger and resentment in her eyes and in the way she pursed her lips.

"I understand your concern. Being interviewed by the police is enough to cause anyone anxiety."

"Do you know Marty Vollero?"

His mind fast pedaling for a plausible answer, he said, "May I suggest that the proper method in this kind of therapy is for the therapist to ask the questions?"

"Fuck the method."

"Very well," he said, maintaining eye contact. "No. I don't know this Mr. Vollero."

"Detective Casey showed me another photograph."

"Of whom?" he said.

"Vollero. He was sitting in your Mercedes-Benz."

"Someone was in my car?"

"Yes. While you were behind the steering wheel. The photo was of you and Vollero having a conversation in the front seat of your car."

Eckersley recalled being fourteen in Queens, walking home from Brandon High School, carrying his books, when he slipped crossing the street and landed solidly on his back with such force the air was knocked from his lungs. Gasping and unable to catch his breath for a minute, he scrambled to his feet, fearing he would die before he began to breathe again.

"I see."

She spoke in a caustic tone. "As your client, should I believe that is really all you have to say to me, *Desmond*?"

Smirking condescendingly, he said, "Police detectives have been known to doctor photographs."

"That sounds to me like the kind of answer liars give when being questioned."

She was right. He couldn't just sit there mute; he had to respond in some way or other, and he regretted his words the moment they left his lips. He sounded foolish.

"Maybe I was near him at some time or another."

"You just said you'd never met him."

The lie wasn't plausible. He'd made a big mistake.

"Not that I recall."

She said, "Casey pointed out to me that most psychiatrists know their clients' deepest secrets."

Eckersley had answered too many of her questions. She was gaining on him, leaving little room for him to maneuver. By sitting back and letting her run her mouth, he'd lost control.

"Vivienne, when I became a physician, I took a sacred oath to protect my clients. Because I trust you—because we trust one another—I'm going to violate my scruples just this once and resolve your doubt by telling you something I shouldn't. There is a reason that I skirted telling you everything. It's that, at one time, Vollero was someone I treated."

"Really, now."

"He called me with a problem and begged me to meet with him. He insisted on not coming to my office and meeting in my car because he feared that if anyone learned that he was consulting a psychiatrist it would harm his public image as a hotshot Hollywood private detective. That meeting in the car was the first and last time I ever spoke with him. His problem related to, uh…a member of his family who was suffering from…dementia."

"When Vollero confronted my husband with a blackmail demand, you advised me to convince him to pay. I followed your advice, Desmond. Later, when Vollero blackmailed me, you gave me the same advice. You play your part so well. I didn't realize it at the time, but you are a clever, accomplished liar."

Glancing at the clock, he said, "I'm afraid your hour is up."

"I'm not leaving."

"My other patients—"

"Today is Friday. I'm the last patient you see."

"Uh, yes, of course."

She smiled without taking her eyes off his. "Desmond, I feel like a cocktail, a nice Hendrick's gin fizz."

"Sure."

She smiled. "It's attitude adjustment time."

His prediction: that after a drink or two, she'd return the next day for her scheduled appointment and spend the hour chattering her usual narcissistic meanderings and never mention Vollero again. He knew her emotional strength wasn't up to abandoning her *listener*, the daddy figure she believed was guiding her safely along the river of life's dark and swampy banks. He was sure of it.

CHAPTER THIRTY-ONE

Casey dreamed of swimming across Lake Tahoe, where as a child he'd fished for trout with his mother and sister. He imagined the trees on the shoreline as blood red; the doctor's office where Mom took him when he broke his arm after falling off a bicycle; a dirt road in Afghanistan that led into a valley where the enemy fired at him from the natural camouflage of shrubland and fir trees; being strapped to a gurney inside an ambulance speeding from the jewelry store shoot-out while a paramedic shouted over into a phone describing his sucking chest wound and falling blood pressure.

Fearing he was dead, Casey slowly regained consciousness. Struggling to open his eyes, he wondered if his eyelids were paralyzed. His entire body felt like it was weighted down with a heavy blanket. Blinking rapidly, his eyes focused. He was strapped to a sturdy wooden chair, gray duct tape wrapping his legs, torso, and arms. The chair was facing a dresser mirror. He was in a bedroom. The door was open to a hallway. He tried to concentrate on his reflection in the mirror. His neck and back ached. He heard the distant sound of a television in another part of the house and the occasional footsteps made by someone moving about on a hardwood floor.

He concentrated on moving the fingers of his right hand, then his toes. He was exhausted. While Casey was temporarily disabled by the Taser, Vollero had used a medical syringe to inject something into his neck. Casey wondered if the drug had damaged his reasoning. Silently assessing his condition, he strained to move his left leg, then the right. The tape was tight, but it hadn't cut off circulation. He made a fist with each hand, then relaxed. Everything was working. The events at the Greenroom didn't come back to him in order. He wondered where he was, how much time had passed, whether Vollero had discovered the GPS locator hidden on his car, and when they would begin interrogating him about the evidence he'd gathered about the murders and the blackmail ring. It was clear to him that after the questioning they would kill him.

He tried to focus. Straining to stretch the tape binding him, he began bending and twisting while ensuring he was not tipping over the chair and alerting whoever was in the house. After what he guessed was about two hours, he'd loosened the tape enough to slightly wriggle his legs. He felt less groggy, but thirsty. No longer confident he could budge the tape enough to manage an escape, he wondered how they'd kill him and where they would dispose of his body, a concern he never had in the Army. If he'd have gone down fighting, there would have been a record. The Army handled such matters. Now he was alone. Vollero, an ex-cop, knew not to leave any clues. It was conceivable Vollero could get away with murdering him, disposing of the body, and then driving back to his Hollywood office, where he would continue smoking cigarettes and flicking ashes into his marble ashtray.

He heard the footsteps of more than one person coming down the hallway in his direction. To stall the inevitable, he feigned unconsciousness by closing his eyes and dropping his head. The footsteps entered the bedroom. Someone poked him.

"Wake up," Vollero said.

Someone poked him again.

"Maybe he's dead."

"He's breathing."

Casey recognized the second voice as Anthony Flair's.

Vollero said, "Wake up, Casey."

Casey continued to feign unconsciousness. Someone slapped his face, but he didn't dare move. His life depended on making them think he was still not in a condition amenable to questioning. Stalling provided more time for him to loosen the bindings.

"Maybe there was too much juice in the needle," Flair said.

Casey heard Vollero thumbing a cigarette lighter. Detecting cigarette smoke, Casey felt a burning cigarette touch his left earlobe. Stifling the urge to shout and pull away, Casey only moved his head slightly without opening his eyes, as if struggling to regain consciousness while still under the influence of the drug.

Vollero said, "Are you awake?"

Remaining still, Casey bore the excruciating pain. He smelled singed flesh.

The torture stopped.

"What now," Flair said.

"I'll put in a call."

Casey heard them leave the room, close the door, and walk down the hallway. Hearing their muffled voices in the other room, he ignored the pain of the cigarette burn and continued squirming in the chair, concentrating on freeing his arms. Struggling for what he guessed was at least two more hours, he stopped now and then to take deep breaths, then began again. After a while, he managed to loosen the tape around his right forearm. A half hour later, he managed to free the arm. Twisting violently, he used it to loosen the tape from the left arm and raise his torso. His legs were still strapped to the chair. Stretching his arms out, he gauged how far he could reach. His throat was dry. He needed water. Fearing someone might return to the room before he was free, he quickly replaced the tape on his arms, to make it look like he was still restrained, then continued to struggle.

Hearing a car outside, he stopped to listen. A car door opened and closed. Seconds later, he heard voices mixed with the TV sounds in the house, then shortly thereafter footsteps in the hallway. The bedroom door opened. Dr. Desmond Eckersley walked into the room, followed by Vollero and Flair. Vollero had a .45 automatic tucked into his waistband. Eckersley wore a sports coat and slacks.

Feigning drowsiness, Casey said, "Thirsty."

Eckersley said, "I thought you said he was unconscious."

"He was," Vollero said.

Eckersley took out a medical stethoscope. Inserting the tips of the earpieces into his ears, he moved close and pressed the chest piece to Casey's heart. After a few seconds, Eckersley lifted the chest piece and shoved the stethoscope into a jacket pocket.

"He's okay," Eckersley said.

"Water," Casey said.

The three men left the room and closed the door. Alone in the bedroom, Casey heard them walking down the hallway, then distant muffled voices followed by a car engine starting and then driving away from the house. Casey deduced that they'd made their plan. He guessed Eckersley, called in for a medical opinion, was leaving to return to his patients to gather blackmail secrets. Casey prayed Flair didn't accompany Vollero back to the room to begin the interrogation. Every cop in the world knew the odds of surviving a fight with two opponents was a hundred to one. His attention focused on the sounds in the hallway as he continued to struggle with the tape on his legs. A minute later, the footsteps returned. Quickly adjusting the tape on his arms, he sat back. The bedroom door opened. Vollero came in.

"You're in luck," Vollero said. "I convinced Eckersley that I could talk you into a deal."

"For what?"

"The results of your investigation, everything. Like me, he's interested in everything—all the homicide evidence you've gathered."

"Before you kill me?"

"Both he and I prefer to avoid that."

"Sure."

"No one knows where you are right now. If you tell us everything we want to know, I'll take you back to your car. If anyone in the department asks where you were, you say you were at your apartment, that you took a sick day. Both Eckersley and I prefer to avoid being suspects in the murder of a cop. Not that there would be any evidence. But I know the kind of heat we'd have to take."

"What's my end?"

Without hesitation, Vollero said, "Four hundred thousand dollars cash."

"You could have made the offer without knocking me out."

"Not at the Greenroom. This is the way it panned out. The offer is on the table. Take it and have a happy life, or pull the plug. It's strictly your decision."

Vollero's offer was evidence of the strange conceit that makes crooks believe that the impossible is within their grasp, that they are clever and everyone else is stupid.

"Make it five," Casey said.

"Four hundred thousand. That's the final offer."

"How do I know you're not going to ice me two seconds after I tell you what you want to know?"

"Because after your divorce you were left broke. I know you can use the money."

Casey recognized stalling any further was risky. If Flair came back in the room, it was over. Casey had to somehow take out Vollero without alerting Flair.

"What are you going to do?" Vollero said.

"I'll take the deal."

"Start talking."

"Flair ratted you out."

"Casey, as you sit here tied to a chair, do you think you're smarter than me?"

"Flair signed a sworn statement against you. He agreed to testify against you in court."

"Bullshit."

"I have a copy of his confession. Flair's signature is on it. No one in the department has seen it except Sutherland."

Vollero had a questioning look. "Where is it?"

Cocking his head down and left, Casey said, "Inside jacket pocket. I haven't shown it to anyone."

Before reaching into the pocket, Vollero cautiously moved closer and began to check Casey's bindings. Lunging up and forward with arms outstretched, Casey clutched Vollero's neck. Squeezing with both hands, he yanked him close and pressed his thumbs into Vollero's Adam's apple. Eyes wide, Vollero kicked, flailed, grabbed Casey's forearms, and tried to shout. Nothing but guttural sounds came out.

Vollero fumbled to reach the gun in his waistband. Casey continued to apply maximum pressure. Panicking, Vollero desperately dug his fingernails into Casey's forearms and began to throw his head back in powerful, convulsive efforts. Vollero's face grew pink, then red. Twisting mightily, Casey maintained the chokehold. After another minute, Vollero's lips turned bluish, his eyes rolled upward, then closed. He lost consciousness and slumped.

Casey, his legs still strapped to the chair, used all his remaining strength to slip his right forearm around Vollero's neck and then arch back, applying the bar-arm chokehold. He held it for what he guessed was another five energy-draining minutes, until he was sure Vollero was dead. Slowly releasing his grip, he lowered him to the carpet. Reaching down, he snatched the .45-caliber automatic from Vollero's waistband and waited for the sound of someone walking in the hallway. Hearing nothing, he held the gun in his right hand and used his left to rip away the remaining duct tape from his legs.

Free, he took deep breaths and tried to concentrate. The bedroom seemed airless, fetid. His head and shoulders ached from the struggle. In his drug fog, everything had a slight bluish tint, as if he were wearing eyeglasses with tinted lenses. Assuming it was a residual effect of the knock-out drug, he hoped it was temporary. Gun in hand, he got to his feet. Slightly dizzy, he quickly searched Vollero's pockets and found no cell phone. He scanned the room. There was no telephone, only an expandable cord plugged into a phone jack in the wall under a dresser table.

He stretched his calf muscles, then moved silently to the window and tugged back the curtain. In the fading twilight, he saw a yard and a barn structure that he guessed might be a garage. A weathervane on the peak of its roof was moving with the breeze. Beyond the barn were heavily wooded rolling hills and in the distance was a rustic countryside of scattered dwellings. He recognized no landmarks.

Gun in hand, he moved to the bedroom door and peeked into the hall. He heard nothing. Looking for Flair, he crept silently by the open doors of two other bedrooms to a spacious living room adjoining an open kitchen area. The furniture looked new. Folk art, including a large oil painting of a farmhouse, hung on the living room walls. He moved to a large bay window and looked out at a front porch. To the right, a dirt road wound away from the house into the woods. The place looked like a pseudo-prosaic farmhouse designed for urban dreamers seeking a weekend hideaway. He guessed it was about 8:00 p.m. Looking for a telephone, he found two wired jacks—one in the kitchen and one in the living room. Neither was attached to a telephone. He returned to the two bedrooms he'd passed by in the hall. In the first, he found no phone and the closet and drawers empty. Checking the second bedroom, he found no phone. There was men's clothing in the drawers. He opened the closet. Men's clothing items were on hangers. Two leather briefcases were on the top shelf. He took them down, opened one. It was filled with hundred-dollar bills banded in three-inch stacks. He assumed Vollero had been collecting so much cash he didn't have time to launder it all into a secret offshore bank account. The second briefcase was also filled with cash. He put them back in the closet.

He walked to the kitchen sink, took a glass from the cupboard, and drank water. He felt his circulation increase. Cautiously exiting the front door with gun in hand, he walked to the barn and peeked through a space between the doors. A shaft of gray moonlight coming in through a windowpane illuminated a portion of a large camouflage tarp covering the shape of an automobile. Slipping inside, he lifted the tarp and found a white Ford pickup truck with damage to the right front fender, probably the truck that ran Kristina Sutherland off the road. He opened the driver's door. The interior light came on. There were no car keys, cell phones, or handheld radios. He exited the barn.

Walking back toward the house, he heard something he thought was a tree branch cracking. Stopping to listen, he heard the breeze blowing through the trees and something else: the faint sound of rock music. He wondered if he was imagining it. He walked across the narrow dirt road, toward where he thought it was coming from. He entered the tree line. Cherry trees. The music grew slightly louder. He cocked the .45.

CHAPTER THIRTY-TWO

Moving cautiously from tree to tree, he still heard the music mixed with a faint intermittent crunch sound. Casey stopped for a moment to listen. Unable to decipher the other sound, he continued moving. The music got louder. He advanced slower, using one tree at a time for cover. When he was close to the sound, he hid behind a tree, then peeked out and saw a bare-chested Anthony Flair standing in a rectangular ditch between two trees. The excavation was about two feet deep, three feet wide, and six feet long. The sound Casey had heard earlier was Flair spading dirt. The rock music was coming from a portable radio on the ground a few feet away. Casey assumed Vollero had chosen the spot and assigned Flair the task of digging Casey's grave where it would never be found, in the middle of a cluster of trees where a natural carpet of leaves would quickly cover any traces of digging.

Studying the scene as if preparing to write an investigation report, he observed that Flair had a cell phone attached to his belt. The plaid shirt Flair had been wearing inside the house earlier lay on the ground next to the shallow trench. The radio was on it. After a minute, Flair stopped digging. Dropping the shovel, he got out of the trench and moved a few feet to the shirt and radio. Casey saw the butt of a blued steel revolver protruding from Flair's right rear pocket. Reaching down to the shirt, Flair took from the pocket what looked like a marijuana cigarette and a book of matches. Lighting the dope, he took a big puff and then exhaled loudly before changing the portable radio to a different station. He slipped the matches into a trouser pocket, hung the cigarette on his lower lip, and stepped down into the trench to resume digging.

Dry-mouthed, slightly dizzy, and pleased that he'd taken the time to reconnoiter the terrain, Casey began moving closer to the grave. He raised the .45 in the two-handed combat stance. A woman's voice came from the radio—an advertising narrative about laundry soap.

Casey walked from behind a tree into the open and aimed the gun at Flair.

"Put your hands on your head," Casey said.

Flair startled, dropped the shovel, and raised his hands. "No... please...don't shoot."

"Is the grave for me?"

"The digging was Vollero's idea."

"Now you can use it for him."

"He's dead?"

"I strangled him to death."

"I want to cooperate."

"Who killed Meredith Fox?"

"Vollero talked Lanza into shooting her in the hotel garage and making it look like a robbery. Vollero gave him the gun to use, a .22," he said. "Lanza gave it back to him after the job."

"Who killed Lanza?"

"Vollero. He told me that when the housekeeper showed up for work, he had to shoot her too."

"Where did Vollero get the blackmail secrets?"

"Dr. Eckersley, who has an office in Malibu. He and Vollero had a fifty-fifty deal on the profits from every blackmail caper. I have some names of the celebrities Vollero blackmailed. One of them is Norman Molitor, the big movie producer. I can tell you everything you need to know."

"Where do you fit in?"

"Vollero forced me to help. He threatened to kill me and said that because of his law enforcement connections he could get away with it and no one would ever find out. I'm willing to testify to everything."

"Who killed Wanda Troxell?"

"Vollero. He owed her some money and told her she could pick up the money in Palmdale. She asked me to drive her there. I would've never agreed if I had known Vollero would kill her. And I never made any money on the shakedowns. I'm willing to testify in open court. To everything, including Vollero running your partner off the road. I did everything I could to stop him. So help me God."

"Do you have a cell phone?"

"In my shirt."

"What's your code to unlock it?"

"I keep it unlocked."

"Do you have any weapons?"

"No."

For some ungodly reason, for a split-second Casey considered wisecracking about cops being good observers.

"We're going to the house now, Anthony. I'll be right behind you. Start walking."

"May I put my shirt on?" Flair said.

Tightening his grip on the automatic, he calmly said, "Go ahead."

Hands raised, Flair got out of the shallow trench and slowly walked backward toward the shirt. Without turning around, he slowly reached down with his left hand and picked it up. Lowering his right hand into a sleeve, he shrugged on the shirt, and reached deftly to his rear trouser pocket, drawing his revolver.

Casey pulled the trigger three times. The fire flashes from the .45 illuminated Flair being blown down by the slugs into the pile of the freshly dug dirt and sliding headfirst into the partially dug grave. While the gunfire was still echoing through the trees, Casey knelt, took the revolver, and then verified Flair was dead. Searching Flair's pockets, he found his cell phone. He opened it and checked Google Maps to learn the address. The radio commercial ended. The rock music resumed. Casey began to dial the Beverly Hills police emergency number, then stopped. He needed to know more.

He followed the dirt road from the house out of the woods, about two hundred yards to a metal mail receptacle attached to a five-foot wooden post at the edge of the property, a paved street cutting through farmland. He reached inside the mailbox and took out advertising postcards and flyers addressed to Vollero, each with the same address in Beaumont, a rural town Casey recalled passing on Highway 10 while driving the ninety-mile trip from Beverly Hills to Palm Springs. Shoving the mail back inside, he steadied himself by holding onto the box. Dehydrated and feeling a residual effect of being drugged, he was tired and slightly confused. He keyed Dollinger's private number into Flair's phone.

It rang four times.

—

Dollinger returned to Beverly Hills police headquarters after finishing a mile and a half jog. After showering in the police locker room, he toweled off and put on a fresh white dress shirt and the business suit he'd worn to work. Cool and relaxed, he left the building and crossed the parking lot to his car. Driving on Sunset Boulevard to the Bel Air sign, he followed the winding Bellagio Road north to the hilly and elegant Bel Air Country Club, an enormous manicured green space looking down on the UCLA campus and Beverly Hills.

Leaving his car with a valet parking attendant, he moved confidently to the club entrance and went inside. In a bar adjacent to the dining room, only a few tables were occupied. The bartender greeted him warmly. Dollinger ordered a tomato juice. After filling an icy cocktail glass, the bartender set a napkin in front of him on the bar, then the glass. Dollinger glanced at the antique clock above the liquor bottles. He resented those who made a point of being late to satisfy their own ego, but it was nothing new. His host was a control freak with a God complex, and Dollinger knew not to mention the tardiness to his host even in jest. Dollinger's long career in Beverly Hills had instilled in him a keen sense of protocol.

His cell phone vibrated. Though aware cell phone use in the bar and restaurant was contrary to Bel Air Country Club social regulations, he snatched the phone from his belt loop holster to see who it was. The name on the screen was Anthony Flair. For a moment, he considered not answering, then decided it was riskier to not take the call.

Pressing the green icon, Dollinger said hello. "Captain Dollinger speaking."

"This is Casey."

Dollinger recognized the voice. "The phone screen says a different name."

"Flair was one of the people who abducted me."

"What?"

"He and Vollero Tasered and drugged me. But I managed to escape."

"Where are you?"

"Beaumont, west of Palm Springs."

"Are you injured?"

"No. But they gave me the needle and I'm fuzzy."

"Give me an address."

"9661 Highland Farm Lane. There's a house and a barn. It looks like a cherry farm. Vollero gets mail here."

"Remain there. I'm on my way with the troops."

"Roger that."

Dollinger turned off the phone and glanced at his wristwatch. He figured the trip would take him about ninety minutes. Desmond Eckersley walked in the front door and joined him at the bar.

"I'm starving," Eckersley said. "Shall we sit down?"

Dollinger whispered, "Casey is on the street."

"What?"

"He just called me…from Flair's phone."

Eckersley's eyes widened. "You have to fix this."

"Like I don't know that?"

—

Casey resisted the urge to stop and rest on the walk from the mailbox to the farmhouse. Though two suspects were down and the facts gathered from Anthony Flair generally fit the big questions concerning the three murders, Casey knew there was no reason to believe he was no longer in jeopardy. Eckersley was still on the street. And Casey thought it likely others might be involved in the blackmail scheme and all it created.

He went inside the house, filled a glass at the sink, and drank more water. Concentrating on the entire investigation, beginning with the Meredith Fox murder, he knew the big picture of the investigations had been skewed. Nothing had gone right. He exited the house and crossed the road into the cover of the woods, where he could wait for Dollinger to arrive with a team of detectives while maintaining the element of surprise in case someone else arrived. Alone in the darkness, he watched the road leading from the mailbox to the house. Noises made by a breeze swaying tree branches mixed with the distant sound of Flair's radio still playing rock music. The only light outside the house was a solitary bulb illuminating the front door. He relived following Halloran in Topanga Canyon, finding Vollero in the bar, and Chief of Police Donna Slade coming to his apartment. He sat on the ground. Resting his back against a tree, he stared at the road and went over the facts again. Feeling jumpy and ill at ease, he wondered if it had something to do with the drugs they'd injected into him or if the investigation itself had been somehow internally tainted. It wasn't like strange things didn't happen in every big investigation. Officers took sides, argued over informers, and now and then someone cut corners for a department friend or ally.

An hour and twenty minutes later, about how long he guessed it should have taken Dollinger to drive from Beverly Hills, he heard a car approaching on the dirt road. Seeing the headlights, he got up and hid behind a tree. The car drove into the illumination of the light outside the house. It looked like Dollinger's car. Dollinger opened the door and got out. He was alone. Casey drew his gun.

"Casey?" Dollinger shouted.

Casey came from behind the tree and walked toward him, aiming the gun.

Dollinger said, "What are you doing?"

"Where is everyone?"

"What?"

"You said you were bringing troops with you."

"I...I decided to find out exactly what had happened here before making phone calls."

"I briefed you," Casey said. "I told you what happened to me."

"Put the gun down."

"Put your hands up."

Dollinger complied. "Put the gun away, for God's sake. Have you lost your mind?" Casey moved closer, took Dollinger's revolver, shoved it in his own waistband. "What the hell happened here? I'm giving you a direct order to put the gun down. What the hell is wrong?"

"That's what I intend to find out."

Casey saw headlights on the road. "Who's that?"

An expression of fear crossed Dollinger's face. "How would I know?" The headlights went off. Casey grabbed Dollinger by the collar, pulled him away from the road and behind a tree. "What are you doing?"

"You said you didn't tell anyone," Casey said.

"That's the truth."

In the darkness Casey saw the moonlit silhouette of the car approaching the house on the dirt road. It was a black Cadillac. Casey touched the tip of the gun barrel to Dollinger's back.

"Talk and you're dead," Casey whispered.

The Cadillac stopped in front of the house. The driver's door opened. Donna Slade got out with her purse. She wasn't wearing a gun. He stepped from behind the tree, holding Dollinger in front of him as a shield.

"Toss your purse back into the car!" Casey said.

Slade stared at them. "What's wrong?"

"Do it now."

She complied, then slowly raised her hands. "What's going on here, Legs?"

Casey said, "Both of you know exactly what happened to me."

"She's the one who demanded to see your murder book," Dollinger said. "That was so she could alter it."

Slade said, "It was a loyalty test."

Dollinger said, "She helped Vollero frame you for Wanda Troxell's murder."

"That's a lie," Slade said.

"Ellen Brady helped her," Dollinger said.

Casey stared at Slade. "Ellen is working for you?"

"Yes. I've suspected Dollinger since the day I took command of the department."

"She's lying," Dollinger said. "She used Brady just like she used you. Blackmail money is funding her campaign for sheriff."

Slade said, "You lying son of a bitch."

"I thought I was your right-hand man," Dollinger said. "That's what you told everyone."

She said, "You're going to prison, Dollinger."

Desperately lunging toward Casey, Dollinger grabbed the gun with both hands and frantically tried to pull it away. Casey struggled to maintain control of it. Dollinger kneed him. They both slammed to the dirt, fighting for the weapon.

"Legs!" Slade shouted.

As Casey struggled, Dollinger slipped his finger into the trigger guard. The gun fired. Casey's upper left arm felt as if he'd been slammed with a jackhammer. Wounded, he held onto the gun with his right hand. Dollinger headbutted him and used both his hands to pry the gun away. Four rapid gunshots thundered in the darkness from the open passenger window of Slade's Cadillac.

The slugs struck Dollinger in the face and chest, knocking him down into the dirt a few feet from Casey.

The Cadillac door opened. Ellen Brady got out, aiming her gun at Dollinger. Moving to him, she reached down, took the gun from his hand, and gave it to Slade.

Kneeling next to Casey, Brady carefully examined his wound. "It's a through and through and didn't hit bone," she said. "You'll be okay."

Donna Slade hurried to the Cadillac, opened her purse, and used her phone to call an ambulance. She opened the trunk, took out an emergency first aid kit, and brought it to Brady. Casey flinched at the pain as Brady applied pressure to the wound. Suddenly, the night was still. The distant sound of the radio had stopped. He thought he heard a truck passing by the farm on the nearby road.

Slade said to him, "I was counting on you to shake things up."

"You almost got me killed."

"It's called police work."

CHAPTER THIRTY-THREE

At 2:41 p.m., in the emergency room at the nearby Loma Linda Veterans Hospital, Casey had been given X-rays, administered injections, and undergone surgery to clean his bullet wound. Fully conscious but feeling the effect of the pain drugs, he was talking by speakerphone to Chief Slade, who'd chosen to remain in Beaumont to coordinate with the local authorities. Brady stood next to the hospital bed, making notes as Casey explained to Slade and a Riverside County sheriffs' detective on the phone with her how he'd ended up in Beaumont and what had occurred there. He also told her about the cash he found in the closet.

Casey said, "I can write one search warrant affidavit for the farmhouse, Eckersley's home, and his office."

"That can wait, Legs."

"No way. Eckersley will find out what happened and destroy evidence."

"When will you be released from the hospital?"

"I'm not staying here."

"Are you up to handling a search warrant affidavit?"

"Brady will assist," he said. "In the meantime, we need to stake out Eckersley's Malibu property."

"Who do you trust?"

"Fukunaga. I'll call him."

Slade said, "When you complete the search warrant affidavit, head west. I'll find a judge who will sign the warrant."

"Will do."

Casey called Fukunaga and sent him to Malibu to keep the Eckersley property under surveillance pending arrival of the search warrant. A VA nurse gave Casey permission to sit and use a desk in a vacant X-ray room. Brady sat with him and opened her iPad keyboard and typed while Casey dictated a fact narrative for the search warrant for Eckersley's office and home. She interrupted him now and then to clarify addresses and names. Two hours later, the draft of the search warrant was completed. Casey read it. Agreeing with Brady that it was sufficient, they departed the hospital.

While Brady was driving on Interstate 10, Casey leaned back in the passenger seat and closed his eyes. Over the course of the day, the pain of the bandaged wound had dulled and become barely tolerable with the help of drugs.

"What are you thinking about, Legs?"

"Getting through this search warrant so I can double up on the pain pills."

His mind was also on how, from the first moment they met, Brady must have been reporting everything Casey said to her directly to the chief.

Brady said, "I wonder how long Vollero had been using Dollinger as his pipeline."

"How did the chief find out about him?"

"Slade said the word came to her indirectly from the FBI."

"What does that mean?"

"I asked Slade the same question. She told me she got a call from her father, who is a retired FBI agent. He'd gotten a call from the Los Angeles FBI agent in charge, who asked him to deliver a message about Dollinger. Apparently because FBI headquarters was known to leak, the Los Angeles FBI field office didn't trust following their usual procedure of requesting headquarters for permission to share information with a local police department."

"How…how did Slade get you involved?"

"I met her at a narcotics enforcement conference about two years ago. I'd just finished two years of working undercover in a multistate heroin ring. A few months ago, I resigned from Phoenix PD and planned to enter the USC nursing program in the fall. I got a call from her. She asked me to help her with an internal investigation. I agreed because I had some free time before I started school. That's still my goal."

"Congratulations."

She said, "I know you have a right to hate me."

His cell phone rang. It was Chief Slade. He touched the ACCEPT button.

"Casey."

"Where are you?" Slade said.

"Leaving the hospital."

"I've recruited one of my college sorority sisters, an LA Superior Court judge, to review your affidavit and authorize the search warrant. I just sent you a text message on how to reach her."

"Got it, Chief."

"Don't get your hopes up for prosecuting the psychiatrist."

"Eckersley is the Mr. Big," he said. "Without him ratting out his clients, there'd be no blackmail or murders over the payoff loot. And Sutherland wouldn't be in the hospital."

She said, "I don't see him keeping any relevant evidence in his office or home."

"We still have him for conspiracy. I can testify to his coming to the Beaumont house when I was being held there."

"Eckersley will say Dollinger forced him, that he was working to help a former law enforcement officer. In a trial, he might be able to create a reasonable doubt."

"No jury will believe him."

Slade said, "That doesn't alter the fact that the district attorney, who'll make the final decision, is a world-class bleeding heart and a wimp. Eckersley getting off easy will be an injustice, but that's nothing new these days. Call me after you serve the warrant."

"Sure."

"Good luck."

She disconnected the call.

Ellen said, "How do you feel?"

"Angry."

Arriving back in Los Angeles at the Century Plaza Hotel where the judge and her husband were attending a Shriner's Hospital fundraising meeting, Brady parked the city car in a space adjacent to the main driveway reserved for emergency vehicles. They got out and walked inside to the dining room. Casey and the judge left the banquet hall and sat at a table in a secluded corner of the hotel lobby. Whispering to shield their conversation from hotel guests, Casey brought her up to speed on the homicide cases and his abduction. While reading the search warrant affidavit, she took notes and asked a lot of pointed questions. More than once she had him repeat what he said about Desmond Eckersley coming to Beaumont to examine him while he was bound with duct tape. After more than an hour, satisfied with his answers to all her questions, she signed the search warrant.

It was dusk when he and Brady left the hotel, followed by two uniformed officers in a black and white. Brady drove Casey south from Century City to the Interstate 10 freeway and then to the Pacific Coast Highway and north toward Malibu. He'd lost track of time since being abducted, and the pain-relieving effect of the pills had diminished. His shoulder ached. She turned east into the hills and the burnt orange twilight behind them reflected harshly off the rearview mirror.

He said, "If we don't find any evidence, I can see Eckersley giving us a smug, condescending smile."

"Years ago, that kind of thing would have caused me to stay up all night," Brady said. "Not now."

"But," he said, "fortune doesn't smile on crooks any more than it does on people on the square. There's as much chance that Eckersley's luck will run out."

She furrowed her brow. "What about you and me, Legs?" she asked. "Are we out of luck?"

"Who knows," he said without taking his eyes off the road ahead.

Near Eckersley's office, Casey reached Fukunaga via radio and told him their location. Minutes later, Brady pulled up next to Fukunaga's car, parked at the beginning of the gravel road leading onto the Eckersley property.

Fukunaga got out and came to the passenger window. "I prowled both the home and the office structure. The light is on in the office. There are three cars parked there, Eckersley's Mercedes-Benz, a silver Bentley that registers to a Vivienne Kalen-Boudreaux, and a new Lincoln Town Car with no license plate."

"You and your partner cover the back," Casey said. "We'll go to the front door. Keep your radios on."

Fukunaga got back in his car and followed them up the gravel road. The lights were still on in Eckersley's office. They got out of the car. Fukunaga and his partner hurried toward the rear of the property.

Walking with Brady toward Eckersley's office, Casey glanced inside the Mercedes-Benz and the Lincoln. There was nothing on the seats in either car. Thick hardcover books and yellow writing tablets were strewn across the back seat of the Lincoln. Casey pressed the doorbell and heard it ring inside. He tried the door handle. Locked.

He knocked loudly. Brady drew her gun.

"Police officers with a warrant to search!" he said. "Open the door!"

Hearing footsteps inside, Casey drew his gun. A tall, statuesque woman with gray hair opened the door.

"I'm Attorney Loretta Molinari," she said. "I was just going to call you."

Casey and Brady walked by her with their guns drawn. The office was well lit. The corpse of Dr. Desmond Eckersley was on the bloodstained carpet behind his desk. He had at least five bullet wounds. On the other side of the room, Vivienne Kalen-Boudreaux was sitting on a sofa, staring at the corpse. Her arms were crossed and she wore a tight-fitting black T-shirt, designer jeans, and heels.

Molinari said, "I was called here by my client Vivienne Kalen-Boudreaux. During a scheduled therapy session, Dr. Eckersley attempted to rape and strangle her. In fear of her life, she was forced to defend herself by shooting him with a revolver for which she has a legal permit to carry issued by the Los Angeles County sheriff. Although she is strictly a victim and has no criminal culpability whatsoever, I've advised her not to make any statements at this time. You may direct any questions you have to me."

Feeling throbbing pain from the shoulder wound, Casey looked into Ellen Brady's eyes. They holstered their guns.

END

ABOUT THE AUTHOR

Gerald Petievich is a former US Secret Service Agent. Mr. Petievich numbers among his novels *To Live and Die in LA*, *Boiling Point* (published as *Money Men*), and *The Sentinel*, all of which were made into major motion pictures. His other novels include *Earth Angels*, *Shakedown*, *To Die in Beverly Hills*, *One-Shot Deal*, *Paramour*, and *The Quality of the Informant.*

To learn more about Gerald Petievich go to www.petievich.com.